SAND

Also by Hugh Howey

Wool
Shift
Dust

SAND

HUGH HOWEY

arrow books

Published by Arrow 2014

2 4 6 8 10 9 7 5 3 1

First published in Great Britain in 2014 by Century

Arrow Books
Random House, 20 Vauxhall Bridge Road,
London SW1V 2SA

A Penguin Random House Company

www.randomhouse.co.uk

Addresses for companies within The Random House Group Limited can be found at:
www.randomhouse.co.uk

The Random House Group Limited Reg. No. 954009

A CIP catalogue record for this book
is available from the British Library

ISBN 9780099595151

Typeset in Adobe Caslon by Palimpsest Book Production Ltd, Falkirk, Stirlingshire
Printed and bound by CPI Group (UK) Ltd, Croydon, CR0 4YY

To the stricken

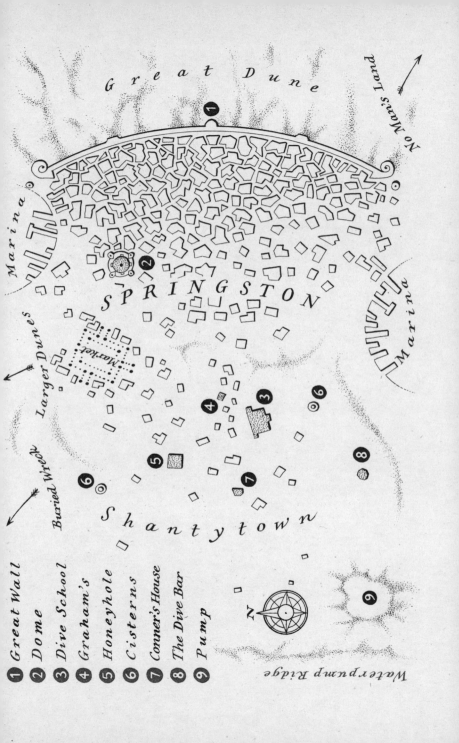

Great Dune

No Man's Land

Marina

2 SPRINGSTON

Larger Dunes

Market

Buried Wreck

3

⑥ 6

4

⑤ 5

7

8
⑧

S h a n t y t o w n

Marina

Marina

N

9

Waterpump Ridge

1 Great Wall
2 Dome
3 Dive School
4 Graham's
5 Honeyhole
6 Cisterns
7 Conner's House
8 The Dive Bar
9 Pump

PART 1 – THE BELT OF THE BURIED GODS

The Valley of Dunes

PALMER

Starlight guided them through the valley of dunes and into the northern wastes. A dozen men walked single file, kers tied around their necks and pulled up over their noses and mouths, leather creaking and scabbards clacking. The route was circuitous, but a direct line meant summiting the crumbling sand and braving the howling winds at its peaks. There was the long way and there was the hard way, and the brigands of the northern wastes rarely chose the hard way.

Palmer kept his thoughts to himself while the others swapped lewd jokes and fictitious tales of several kinds of scored booty. His friend Hap walked further ahead, trying to ingratiate himself with the older men. It was more than a little unwise to be wandering the wastes with a band of brigands, but Palmer was a sand diver. He lived for that razor-thin line between insanity and good sense. And besides, these braggarts with their beards and foul odours were offering a month's pay for two days of work. A hike into the wastes and a quick dive were nothing before a pile of coin.

The noisy column of men snaked around a steep dune, out of the lee and into the wind. Palmer adjusted his flapping ker. He tucked the edge of the cloth underneath his goggles to keep it in place. Sand peppered the right side of his face, telling him they were heading north. He could know without glancing up at the stars, know without seeing the high peaks to the west. The winds might abate or swell in fury, but their direction was as steady as the course of the sun. East to west, with the sand that rode along lodging in Palmer's hair, filling his ears, stacking up in curving patterns of creeping dunes, and burying the world in a thousand metres of hellish grit.

As the piratical laughter from the column died down, Palmer could hear the other voices of the desert chorus. There was the moaning of the winds, and a shushing sound as waves of airborne sand crashed into dunes and raked across the men like gritpaper. Sand on sand made a noise like a hissing rattler ready to strike. Even as he thought this, a wrinkle in the dune beside him turned out to be more than a wrinkle. The serpent slithered and disappeared into its hole, as afraid of Palmer as he was of it.

There were more sounds. There was the clinking of the heavy gear on his back: the dive bottles and dive suit, the visor and fins, his regulator and beacons, all the tools of his trade. There was the call of coyotes singing to the west, their piercing wails uniquely able to travel into the wind to warn neighbouring packs to stay away. They were calling out that men were coming.

And beyond these myriad voices was the heartbeat of the desert sands, the thrumming that never ceased and could be felt day and night in a man's bones, day and night from womb to grave. It was the deep rumble that emanated from No Man's Land far to the east, that rolling thunder or those rebel bombs or the farting gods – whichever of the many flavours of bullshit one believed.

Palmer homed in on those distant grumbling sounds and thought of his father. His opinion of his dad shifted like the dunes. He sometimes counted him a coward for leaving in the night. He sometimes reckoned him a bold son of a bitch for setting off into No Man's Land. There was something to be said for anyone who would venture into a place from where no soul had ever returned. Something less polite could be said about an asshole who could walk out on his wife and four kids to do so.

There was a break in the steep dune to the west, an opening in the sand that revealed a wide patch of star-studded sky. Palmer scanned the heavens, eager to dwell on something besides his father. The ridgeline of the impassable Stone Mountains could be seen even in the moon's absence. Their jagged and daunting edge was marked by a black void where constellations suddenly ended.

Someone grabbed Palmer's elbow. He turned to find that Hap had fallen back to join him. His friend's face was underlit by the dive light dangling from his neck, set to dim.

'You aiming for the strong and silent type?' Hap hissed, his voice muffled by ker and wind.

Palmer hitched his heavy dive pack up his shoulders, could feel the sweat trapped between his shirt and the canvas sack. 'I'm not aiming for anything,' he said. 'Just lost in thought.'

'All right. Well, feel free to cut up with the others, huh? I don't want them thinking you're some kinda psycho or nuthin'.'

Palmer laughed. He glanced over his shoulder to see how far behind the next guy was and which way the wind was carrying their words. 'Really?' he asked. 'Because that'd be kinda boss, dontcha think?'

Hap seemed to mull this over. He grunted. Was probably upset he hadn't come up with it first.

'You're sure we're gonna get paid for this dive?' Palmer asked, keeping his voice down. He fought the urge to dig after the sand in his ear, knowing it would just make it worse. 'I don't wanna get stiffed like last time.'

'Fuck no, these guys have a certain code.' Hap slapped him on the back of the neck, sand and sweat mixing to mud. 'Relax, Your Highness. We're gonna get paid. A quick dive, some sand in our lungs, and we'll be sipping iced drinks at the Honey Hole by Sunday. Hell, I might even get a lap dance from your mom.'

'Fuck off,' Palmer said, knocking his friend's arm away.

Hap laughed. He slapped Palmer again and slowed his pace to share another joke about Palmer's mom with the others. Palmer had heard it before. It got less funny and grew more barbed every time. He walked alone in silence, thoughts flitting to his wreck of a family, the sweat on the back of his neck cooling in the breeze as it gathered sand, that iced drink at the Honey Hole not sounding all that bad, to be honest.

2

The Belt of the Gods

A camp had been made in the lee of a large dune, tents huddled together and flapping in the swirling wind. The marching men arrived to find a tall fire burning, its beating glow rising over the dunes and guiding their way in a dance of shadows. Other men emerged from the tents, and there were manly reunions of slapped backs and shoulders held, sand flying off with each violent embrace. The men stroked their long beards and swapped gossip and jokes as though they'd been apart for some time. Packs were dropped to the ground, canteens topped from a barrel. The two young divers were told to wait by the fire as some of the others ambled towards a large tent nestling between steep dunes.

Palmer was thankful for the chance to sit. He shrugged off his dive pack and arranged it carefully by the fire. Folding his aching legs beneath him, he sat and leaned against the pack and enjoyed the flickering warmth of the burning logs.

Hap settled down by the fire with two of the men he'd been chatting with during the hike. Palmer listened to them argue and laugh while he gazed into the fire, watching the logs burn. He thought of his home in Springston, where it would be a crime to fell a tree and light it on fire, where coals of hardened shit warmed and stunk up homes, where piped gas would burn one day but then silently snuff out a family in their sleep the next. In the wastes, such things didn't matter. The scattered groves were there to be razed. The occasional animal to be eaten. Bubbling springs lapped up until they were dry.

Palmer wiggled closer to the flames and held out his palms. The sweat from the hike, the breeze, the thoughts of home had turned him cold. He smiled at an eruption of voices that bravely leapt through the tall flames. He laughed when the others laughed. And when his twisting stomach made noises, he lied and said it was because he was hungry. The truth was that he had a very bad feeling about this job.

To start with, he didn't know any of these men. And his sister had warned him of the savages he *did* know, much less those strange to him. Hap had vouched for the group, whatever that was worth. Palmer turned and watched his friend share a joke in the firelight, his face an orange glow, his arms a blur of enthusiasm. Best friends since dive school. Palmer figured they would go deeper for each other than anyone else across the sands. That made the vouch count for something.

Beyond Hap, parked between two steep dunes, Palmer saw two sarfers with their sails furled and masts lowered. The wind-powered craft rocked on their sleek runners, the twin hulls cobbled together from scraps of tin raised from the depths. A knotted net of ropes spanned the bows of each craft – what his father called the trampoline – and Palmer thought of days spent riding with his dad east of the wall, whooping as one hull lifted from the sand in a fierce gust, a glimpse of his father's grin behind his flapping ker as if all was completely under control. Palmer missed that sensation of speed. Life had become a slow crawl across the sand. He wondered if after this job, maybe these guys would give him and Hap a ride back into town. Anything to avoid the night hikes and the bivouacking in the lee of blistering dunes.

A few of the men who had hiked with them from Springston dropped down and joined the loose circle around the fire. Many of them were old, in their late forties probably, more than twice Palmer's age and about as long as anyone was meant to last. They had the leather-dark skin of nomads, of desert wanderers, of gypsies. Men who slept beneath the stars and toiled under the sun. Palmer promised himself he would never look like that. He would make his fortune young, stumble on that one cherry find, and he and Hap would move back to town as heroes and live in the shade. A dune of credits would absolve old sins. They would open a dive shop, make a living selling and repairing gear, equipping the unlucky saps who risked their lives beneath the sand. They would see steady coin from the fools chasing piles of it. Chasing piles just as he and Hap were right then.

A bottle was passed around. Palmer raised it to his lips and pretended to drink. He shook his head and wiped his mouth as he leaned to the side to pass the bottle to Hap. Laughter was thrown into the fire, sending sparks up towards the glittering heavens.

'You two.'

A heavy hand landed on Palmer's shoulder. He turned to see Moguhn, the black brigand who had led their march through the dunes. Moguhn gazed down at him and Hap, his silhouette blotting out the stars.

'Brock will see you now,' he said. The brigand turned and slid into the darkness beyond the fire.

Hap smiled, took another swig and passed the bottle to the bearded man at his side. Standing, he smiled at Palmer, an odd smile, cheeks full, then turned and spat into the flames, sending the fire and laughter higher. He slapped Palmer on the shoulder and hurried after Moguhn.

Palmer grabbed his gear before following along, not trusting anyone to watch after it. When he caught up, Hap grabbed him by the elbow and pulled him aside. Together they followed Moguhn down the packed sand path between the firepit and the cluster of tents.

'Play it cool,' Hap hissed. 'This is our ticket to the big time.'

Palmer didn't say anything. All he wanted was a score that could retire him, not to prove himself to this band and join them. He licked his lips, which still burned from the alcohol, and cursed himself for not drinking more when he was younger. He had a lot of catching up to do. He thought of his little brothers and how he'd tell them, when he saw them again, not to make the same mistakes he had. Learn to dive. Learn to drink. Don't burn time learning wasteful stuff. Be more like their sister and less like him. That's what he would say.

Moguhn was nearly invisible in the starlight, but came into relief against tents that glowed from the throb of flickering lamps. Someone threw a flap open, which let out the light like an explosion of insects. The thousands of stars overhead dimmed, leaving the warrior god alone to shine bright. It was Colorado, the great sword-wielding constellation of summer, his belt a perfect line of three stars aimed down the path as if to guide their way.

Palmer looked from that swathe of jewels to the dense band of frost fire that bloomed back into existence as the tent was closed. This band of countless stars stretched from one dune straight over the sky to the far horizon. It was impossible to see the frost fire in town, not with all the gas fires burning at night. But here was the mark of the wastes, the stamp overhead that told a boy he was very far from home, that let him know he was in the middle of the wastes and the wilds. And not just the wilds of sand and dune but the wilds of life, those years in a man's twenties when he shrugs off the shelter of youth and before he has bothered to erect his own. The tent-less years. The bright and blinding years in which men wander as the planets do.

A bright gash of light flicked across those fixed beacons, a shooting star, and Palmer wondered if maybe he was more akin to this. Perhaps him and Hap both. They were going places, and in a hurry. A flash and then gone, off to some-where new.

Stumbling a little, he nearly tripped over his own boots from looking up like that. Ahead of him, Hap ducked into the largest of the tents behind Moguhn. The canvas rustled like the sound of boots in coarse sand, the wind yelped as it leapt from one dune to the next, and the stars overhead were swallowed by the light.

3

The Map

The men inside the tent turned their heads as Hap and Palmer slipped inside the flap. The wind scratched the walls like playful fingernails, the breeze asking to be let in. It was warm from the bodies and smelled like a bar after a work shift: sweat and rough brew and clothes worn for months.

A dune of a man waved the two boys over. Palmer figured him for Brock, the leader of this band who now claimed the northern wastes, an imposing figure who had appeared seemingly out of nowhere as most brigand leaders do. Building bombs one year, serving someone else, until a string of deaths promotes a man to the top.

Palmer's sister had warned him to steer clear of men like this. Vic claimed all men were a pack of liars but that those capable of leading – the men who could fool other men – were the worst kind. Instead of obeying his sister, Palmer steered towards the man. He set his gear down near a stack of crates and a barrel of water or grog. There were eight or nine men standing around a flimsy table set in the middle of the tent. A lamp had been hung from the centre support; it swayed with the push and pull of the wind on the tent frame. Thick arms plastered with tattoos were planted around the table like the trunks of small trees. The tattoos were decorated with raised scars made by rubbing grit into open wounds.

'Make room,' Brock said, his accent thick and difficult to place, perhaps a lilt of the gypsies south of Low-Pub or the old gardeners from the oasis to the west. He waved his hand between two of the men as though shooing flies from a plate of food, and with minimal grumbling, the two bearded men pressed to the side. Hap took a place at the waist-high table and Palmer joined him.

'You've heard of Danvar,' Brock said, forgoing introductions and formalities. It seemed like a question, but it was not spoken like one. It was an assumption, a declaration. Palmer glanced around the table to see quite a few men watching him, some rubbing their long and knotted beards. Here, the mention of legends did not elicit an eruption of laughter. Here, grown men looked at hairless youths as if sizing them up for dinner. But none of these men had the face-tats of the cannibals of the far north, so Palmer assumed he and Hap were being sized up for this job, being measured for their worthiness and not for some stew.

'Everyone's heard of Danvar,' Hap whispered, and Palmer noted the awe in his friend's voice. 'Will this lead us there?'

Palmer turned and surveyed his friend, then followed Hap's gaze down to the table. The four corners of a large piece of parchment were pinned down by meaty fists, sweating mugs and a smoking ashtray. Palmer touched the edge of the parchment closest to him and saw that the mottled brown material was thicker than normal parchment. It looked like the stretched and tanned hide of a coyote, and felt brittle to the touch, as though it were very old.

One of the men laughed at Hap's question. 'You already *are* here,' he roared.

An exhalation of smoke drifted across the old drawing

like a sandstorm seen from up high. One of Brock's sausage fingers traced the very constellation Palmer had been staring at dizzily just moments before.

'The belt of the great warrior, Colorado.' The men around the table stopped their chattering and drinking. Their boss was speaking. His finger found a star every boy knew. 'Low-Pub,' he said, his voice as rough as the sand-studded wind. But that wasn't the name of the star, as Palmer could tell him. Low-Pub was a lawless town to the south of Springston, an upstart town recently in conflict with its neighbour, as the two wrestled over wells of water and oil. Palmer watched as Brock traced a line up the belt, his fingertip like a sarfer sailing the winds between the two towns and across all that contested land. It was a drawn-out gesture, as though he was trying to show them some hidden meaning.

'Springston,' he announced, pausing at the middle star. Palmer's thought was: *Home*. His gaze drifted over the rest of the map, this maze of lines and familiar clusters of stars, of arrows and hatch marks, of meticulous writing built up over the years in various fades of ink, countless voices marked down, arguing in the margins.

The fat finger resumed its passage due north – if those stars really might be taken to represent Low-Pub and Springston.

'Danvar,' Brock announced, thumping the table with his finger. He indicated the third star in the belt of great Colorado. The map seemed to suggest that the buried world of the gods was laid out in accordance with their heavenly stars. As if man were trapped between mirrored worlds above and below. The tent swayed as Palmer considered this.

'You've found it?' Hap asked.

'Aye,' someone said, and the drinking and smoking

resumed. The curled hide of the map threatened to roll shut with the rise of a mug.

'We have a good guess,' Brock said in that strange accent of his. 'You boys will tell us for sure.'

'Danvar is said to be a mile down,' Palmer muttered. When the table fell silent, he glanced up. 'Nobody's ever dived half of that.'

'Nobody?' someone asked. 'Not even your sister?'

Laughter tumbled out of beards. Palmer had been waiting for her to come up.

'It's no mile down,' Brock told them, waving his thick hand. 'Forget the legends. Danvar is here. More plunder than in all of Springston. Here lies the ancient metropolis. The three buried towns of this land are laid out according to the stars of Colorado's belt.' He narrowed his eyes at Hap and then at Palmer. 'We just need you boys to confirm it. We need a real map, not this skin.'

'How deep are we talking?' Hap asked.

Palmer turned to his friend. He had assumed this had already been discussed. He wondered if the wage he'd been promised had been arrived at, or if his friend had just been blowing smoke. They weren't here for a big scavenge; they were here to dive for ghosts, to dig for legends.

'Eight hundred metres.'

The answer quietened all but the moaning wind.

Palmer shook his head. 'I think you vastly overestimate what a diver can—'

'We dug the first two hundred metres,' Brock said. He tapped the map again. 'And it says here on this map that the tallest structures rise up another two hundred fifty.'

'That leaves . . .' Hap hesitated, waiting no doubt for someone else to do the maths.

The swinging lamp seemed to dim, and the edges of the

map went out of focus as Palmer arrived at the answer. 'Three hundred fifty metres,' he said, feeling dizzy. He'd been down to two fifty a few times on twin bottles. He knew people who'd gone down to three. His sister, a few others, could do four – some claimed five. Hap hadn't warned him that they were diving so deep, nor that they were helping more gold-diggers waste their time looking for Danvar. Palmer had feared for a moment there that they were working for rebels, but this was worse. This was a delusion of wealth rather than power.

'Three fifty is no problem,' Hap said. He spread his hands out on the map and leaned over the table, looking like he was studying the notes. Palmer reckoned his friend was feeling dizzy as well. It would be a record for them both.

'I just wanna know it's here,' Brock said, thumping the map. 'We need exact coordinates before we dig any more. The damn hole we have here is a bitch to maintain.'

There were grumbles of agreement from the men that Palmer figured were doing the actual digging. One of them smiled at Palmer. 'Your mom would know something about maintaining holes,' he said, and the grumbles turned into laughter.

Palmer felt his face burn. 'When do we go?' he shouted over this sudden eruption.

And the laughter died down. His friend Hap turned from the dizzying map, his eyes wide and full of fear, Palmer saw. Full of fear and with a hint of an apology for bringing them this far north for such madness, a glimmer in those eyes of all the bad that was soon to come.

4

The Dig

Palmer lay awake in a crowded tent that night and listened to the snores and coughs of strangers. The wind howled late and brought in the whisper of sand, then abated. The gradual glow of morning was welcome, the tent moving from dark to grey to cream, and when he could no longer lie still and hold his bladder, Palmer squeezed out from between Hap and the canvas wall, collected his bag and boots and slipped outside.

The air was still crisp from a cloudless night, the sand having shucked off the heat soaked up the day before. Only a few stars clung to the darkness in the west. Venus stood alone above the opposite dunes. The sun was up somewhere, but it wouldn't show itself above the local dunes for another hour.

Before it could beat down between the high sands, Palmer hoped to be diving. He relished the coolness of the deep earth, even the pockets of moist sand that made for difficult flow. Sitting down, he upturned his boots and clopped the heels together, little pyramids of scoop[1] spilling out. Slapping the bottoms of his socks, he pulled the boots back on and laced them up securely, doubling the knot. He was eager to attach his fins and get going.

[1] Sand that collects in boots.

He checked his dive pack and went over his gear. One of the prospectors emerged from the tent, cleared his throat, then spat in the sand near enough to Palmer for it to register but far enough away that he couldn't be certain if it had been directed at him. After some consideration, and while the man urinated on the wall of a dune, Palmer decided the range of questionable intent was between four and five feet. It felt scientific.

A wiry man with charcoal skin emerged from Brock's tent: Moguhn, who looked less fearsome in the wan daylight. He had to be Brock's second in command, judging by the way the two men had conferred the night before. Moguhn lifted his eyebrows at Palmer, as if to ask whether the young man was up to the day's challenge. Palmer dipped his chin in both greeting and reply. He felt great. He was ready for a deep dive. He checked the two large air bottles strapped to the back of his dive pack and took a series of deep and rapid breaths, prepping his lungs. There was no pressure to get all the way down to the depths Brock was asking. His dive visor could see through a couple of hundred metres of sand. All he had to do was go as deep as he could, maybe clip three hundred for the first time, record whatever they could see and then come back up. They couldn't ask more of him than that.

Hap emerged from the tent next and shielded his eyes against the coming dawn. He looked less prepared for a deep dive, and Palmer thought of the people he'd known who had gone down into the sand never to be seen again. Could they feel it in the morning when they woke up? Did their bones know that someone would die that day? Did they ignore that feeling and go anyway? He thought of Roman, a classmate from dive school, who had gone down to look for water outside of Springston, never to be found and never to return. Maybe Roman had known that he shouldn't go, had felt it right at the last moment, but had committed anyway, and shaken off the nag tugging at his soul. Palmer thought maybe that's what he and Hap were doing at that very moment. Moving forward, despite their doubts and trepidations.

Neither of them spoke as they checked their gear. Palmer produced a few strips of snake jerky from his pack and Hap accepted one. They chewed on the spicy meat and took rationed sips from their canteens. When Moguhn said it was time to go, they repacked their dive bags and shrugged on the heavy packs.

These men claimed to have dug down two hundred metres to give them a much-needed boost. Palmer had seen efforts such as these, and every diver knew to choose a site as deep as possible between slow-marching dunes – but two hundred metres? That was deeper than the well in Springston his kid brother hauled buckets out of every day. It was hard to move that much sand and not have it blow back in. Sand flowed too much for digging holes. The wind had many more hands than those who pawed at the earth. The desert buried even those things built *atop* the sand, much less those made below. And here he and Hap were banking on pirates to keep the roof clear for them.

If his sister were there, she would slap him silly and drag him over hot dunes by his ankles for getting into this mess. She would kill him for getting involved with brigands at all. That, coming from someone who dated their kind. But then, his sister was full of hypocrisy. Always telling him to question authority, as long as it wasn't hers.

'That all your stuff?' Moguhn asked, watching them. He kept his black hands tucked into the sleeves of his white garb, which he wore loose like a woman's dress. Stark and brilliantly bright, it flowed around his ankles and danced like the heat. Palmer thought he looked like the night shrouded in day.

'This is it,' Hap said, smiling. 'Never seen a sand diver before?'

'I've seen plenty,' Moguhn said. He turned to go and waved for the boys to follow. 'The last two who tried this had three bottles apiece. That's all.'

Palmer wasn't sure he'd heard correctly. 'The last two who tried this?' he asked. But Moguhn was sliding past the tents and between the dunes, and he and Hap with their heavy packs had to work to catch up.

'What did he say?' Palmer asked Hap.

'Focus on the dive,' Hap said grimly.

The day was young and the desert air still cool, but the back of his friend's neck shone with perspiration. Palmer shrugged his pack higher and marched through the soft sand, watching it stir into a low cloud as the first morning breeze whispered through the dunes.

Once they were past the gathering of tents, Palmer thought he heard the throaty rattle of a motor in the distance. It sounded like a generator. The dunes opened up and the ground began to slope down, the piles of sand giving way to a wide vista of open sky. Before them loomed a pit greater than the waterwell back in Shantytown. It was a mountain in reverse, a great upside-down pyramid of missing earth, and in the distance, a plume of sand jetted out from a pipe and billowed westward with the prevailing winds.

There were men down the slope, already working. Had to be a hundred metres down to the bottom. It was only half of what they'd been promised, but the scale of the job out here in the middle of the wastes was a sight to behold. Here were pirates with ambition, who could organise themselves for longer than a week at a time. The great bulk of the man responsible, Brock, was visible down at the bottom of the pit. Palmer followed Moguhn and Hap down the slope, plumes of avalanche rushing before them, which the men at the bottom looked at with worry as it tumbled their way.

As Palmer reached the bottom, the sound of the blatting generator faded. He pulled his boots out of the loose and shifting sand, had to do so over and over, and saw that the others were standing on a sheet of metal. The platform was difficult to see, as it was dusted from the sand kicked loose by the traffic. Palmer didn't understand how the pit existed at all, what was causing the plume he had seen, how this was being maintained. Hap must've been similarly confused, because he asked Brock how this was possible.

'This ain't the half of it,' Brock said. He motioned to two of his men, who bent and swept sand from around their feet. Palmer was told to step back as someone lifted a handle. There was a squeal from rusted and sand-soaked hinges as a hatch was lifted. Someone aimed a light down the hatch, and Palmer saw where the other hundred metres lay.

A cylindrical shaft bored straight down through the packed earth. One of the men uncoiled a pair of ropes and began to flake them onto the sand. Palmer peered into the fathomless black hole beneath them, that great and shadowy depth, and felt his knees grow weak.

'We ain't got all day,' Brock said, waving his hand.

One of his men came forward and pulled the ker down from his mouth. He helped Hap out of his backpack and started to assist with his gear, but Hap waved the old man off. Palmer shrugged his own pack off but kept an eye on the man. His beard had grown long, wispy and grey, but Palmer thought he recognised him to be Yegery, an old tinkerer his sister knew.

'You used to have that dive shop in Low-Pub,' Palmer said. 'My sister took me there once. Yegery, right?'

The man studied him for a moment before nodding.

When he moved to help Palmer unpack his gear, Palmer didn't stop him. He couldn't believe Yegery was this far north, way out in the wastes. He forgot the dive for a moment and watched Yegery's old and expert hands handle his dive rig, checking wires and valves, inspecting the air bottles that Palmer had roughened with gritpaper to add the appearance of more dives to his credit.

He and Hap stripped down to their unders and worked their way into their dive suits, keeping the wires that ran the length of the arms and legs from tangling. Palmer's sister had told him once that Yegery knew more about diving than any ten men put together. And here he was, licking his old fingers and pinching the battery terminals on Palmer's visor before switching the headset on and off again. Palmer glanced up at Brock and marvelled at what these brigands had brought together. He had underestimated them, thought them to be disorganised and wishful treasure-seekers. He hoped they weren't the only ones that day who might more than live up to expectations.

'The hatch keeps the sand out of the hole,' Yegery said, 'so we'll have to close it behind you.' He looked from Hap to Palmer, made sure both of them were listening. 'Watch your air. We had a ping from something hard about three hundred or so down, small but steady.'

'You can probe that deep?' Hap asked. He and Palmer were nearly suited up.

Yegery nodded. 'I've got two hundred of my dive suits wired up here. That's what's holding the shaft wall together and softening the sand outside it so we can pump it out. We've got a few more days of fuel left in the genny, but you'll be back by then, or dead.'

The old tinkerer didn't smile, and Palmer realised it wasn't a joke. He pulled his visor on but kept the curved screen high up on his forehead so he could see. He hung his dive light around his neck before attaching his fins to his boots. He would leave the gear bag and his clothes behind, but he strapped his canteen tight to his body so it wouldn't drag – he didn't trust these men not to piss in it while he was gone.

'The other two divers,' he asked Yegery. 'What happened to them?'

The old dive master chewed on the grit in his mouth, the grit that was in all of their mouths, that was forever in everyone's mouths. 'Worry on your own dive,' he advised the two boys.

5

The Dive

T he ropes pinched Palmer's armpits as he was lowered down the narrow shaft. He descended in jerks and stops, could feel the work of the men above handling the rope with their gloved hands. The dive light illuminated the smooth walls of the shaft as he spun lazily this way and that. Hap drifted a few metres below him on his own line.

'It's fucking quiet,' Hap said.

Palmer added to the silence. He reached out and touched the wall of this unnatural shaft and felt with his fingers the unmistakable packed grit of stonesand.[2] This shaft had been made. A chill spread across his flesh. He remembered Yegery saying something about two hundred suits. 'They created this,' he whispered.

He and Hap inched downward, spinning as they went.

'They're using vibes to hold this together. And to loosen the sand before they pump it.' Palmer remembered the soft and slushy feel of the sand as they had worked their way down the crater.

'The bottom's coming up,' Hap announced. 'I can see the sand down there.'

---

[2] Sand held rigid by a dive suit.

Palmer imagined the generator shutting off, or someone killing the power that held back this wall of sand, and all of it collapsing inward in an instant. It became difficult to breathe, thinking about the press of earth. He nearly turned his dive suit on, just in case.

'I'm down,' Hap said from beneath him. 'Watch your fins.'

Palmer felt Hap's hand on his ankle, steering him so he wouldn't land on top of his partner's head. The shaft was tight with the two of them on the ground. They worked the knots around their chests loose and tugged twice on the ropes like Brock had said. 'I'll take lead,' Hap offered. He pulled his regulator from his chest, checked the line, then reached over his shoulder to spin the air valve. He made sure it was locked before biting down on his regulator.

Palmer was busy doing the same. He placed his regulator between his teeth and nodded. Somehow an odd calmness overcame him as he pulled that first deep breath from his bottle. Soon he would be beneath the sand, the only place he had ever felt at peace, and all of this craziness around him would be forgotten. It would be just him and the depths, the calm cool sand, and the chance, however crazy, of discovering Danvar deep beneath their fins.

Hap powered on his suit by slapping the large button on his chest. Standing this close, Palmer could feel the vibrations in the air. They both set their homing beacons on the sand and turned them on. Palmer reached to his own chest and turned on his suit, then folded the leather flap over the switch so the journey through the sand couldn't accidentally shut it off and trap him.

Hap pulled his visor down over his eyes, smiled and waved one last time. And then the sand loosened around his feet and seemed to suck him downward – and Hap disappeared.

Palmer turned off his dive light to save the juice. He pulled his visor down and switched the unit on. The world went black, then gelled into a purplish blotch of shifting shapes. The air screwed with the sandsight, making it impossible to see. With the visor's headband pressed to his temples, Palmer thought about what he wanted the sand to do, and it obeyed. The suit around him vibrated outward, sending subsonic waves trembling through molecules and atoms, and sand began to *move*. It began to act like water. It flowed around him, and down Palmer went.

Once the sand enveloped him, Palmer felt the exhilaration a dune-hawk must feel in flight, a sense of weightlessness and liberation, the power to glide in any direction he liked. He directed his thoughts like his sister had taught him so many years ago, loosening sand below and pressing with a hardening of sand from above, keeping a pocket loose around his chest so he could breathe, diverting the weight of the earth around him to hold back the pressure, and taking calm sips from his regulator to conserve his air.

The wavering purple splotches were replaced with a rainbow of colours, the cool purples and blues of anything far away, bright orange and red for anything hard or close by. Glancing up, the shaft above him glowed bright yellow. It glowed like only the sand hardened by a suit could glow. It was so bright that the white pulsing of the transponders above was difficult to spot, but one beacon was as good as any other. He looked down and found Hap, a spot of orange with green edges. His new visor worked great, had a much better seal to keep the sand out and far better fidelity than his last set. He could clearly make out Hap's arms and legs where once he would've seen a single blotch. Diving down after his friend, he spoke in his throat to let Hap know he had a visual on him.

I hear you, Hap responded. The sound came from behind and below Palmer's ears, vibrating in his jawbone. The two of them dived straight down, letting the sand flow around them. The pushback on the suits grew, making the flow more strenuous the deeper they went, making it more difficult to breathe. Palmer calmed himself by thinking of this as a quick down-and-up. No need to scavenge. Just one of those braggart dives where you go hard and fast as deep as you can, take a glance, come back up. A dive like his sister warned him about. But this wasn't for ego; this was for coin. This was a job, not him proving something.

You picking anything up? Hap asked.

Not yet. Palmer watched the depth gauge in his visor. The distance was fed from the transponder left behind. Fifty metres. A hundred metres. It grew more and more difficult to breathe, and it required more concentration to move the sand. The further down they went, the more packed and heavy the column of sand above them. This was where many divers panicked and 'coffined', or let the sand freeze stiff. His sister had pulled him out of a coffin twice while training him on some of her old gear. When the desert wraps its great arms around your chest and decides you won't breathe any more, that's when you feel how small you are, just a grain of sand crushed among infinite grains of sand.

Palmer kept his mind clear as they drifted through one fifty. He hit two hundred metres. This was about as deep as he liked to go. He calmed his mind, ignored the bit of sand getting past his visor and into his ears, the sand at the corner of his mouth as it filled that gap between lips and regulator, the sand crunching between his teeth, and just concentrated on the flow. The batteries on his suit were strong; he'd doubled them up a few dives ago. His gear and his mind were good. He felt that serenity that would hit him when he was able to hold his breath for minutes at a time, that complete feeling of peace, the sand cool on his scalp and neck, the world drifting further and further away.

Two hundred and fifty metres. Palmer felt a surge of pride. He couldn't wait to tell Vic—

Shit. Shit. Shit.

The words rattled through his teeth – Hap must be shouting in his throat. Palmer looked down at his friend, and then he saw it too. A bright patch. Something hard. Something *huge*.

Where's the ground? Palmer asked.

No fucking clue. What is that?

Looks like a cube. Maybe a house? Quicksand got it?

Quick don't go this deep. Fuck, it goes down and down.

Palmer could see that now. The square of bright red glowed into orange as they got closer, and he could see how the hard edges of the structure faded through to greens and blues as it went down. It was a square shaft of some sort, buried beneath the sand, sitting vertical and massive and deep.

Getting hard to breathe, Hap said.

Palmer felt it as well. He thought it was this strange object in his sandsight making it difficult to breathe, but he could feel how much more packed the sand was, how much harder to make it flow. He could still sink, but rising up would be a test. He could feel the weight of all that sand above him.

We turn back? Palmer asked. His goggles said two fifty. It was another fifty or so down to the structure. With the two hundred metres they'd cheated from the dig, they were technically at four fifty right then. *Damn.* He had never dreamed of diving so deep. Only two fifty of it was him, he reminded himself. But still, his sister had told him he wasn't ready to go even that far. He had argued with her, but now he saw she was right. Goddamn, was she ever wrong about anything?

Gotta see what it is, Hap said. *Then we go back.*

The ground must be a mile deep. Don't see an end.

I see something. More of these.

Palmer wished he had Hap's visor. His own was digging into his face, pushing on his forehead and cheekbones as though it might smash right through his skull. He worked his jaw to lessen the pain, strained downward, and then he saw something too. Bright blues down there, more square shafts, and another to the side a little deeper, just a purple outline. And was that the ground down there? Maybe another three hundred metres down?

I'm getting a sample, Hap said. His words came in loud. The sand was dense, the visor bands transmitting the words from throat to jawbone louder than usual. Palmer remembered Vic telling him about this. He tried to remember what else he'd heard about the deep sand. He was sucking so hard to get a breath now that it felt like his tank was empty, but the gauge was still in the green. It was just the tightness around his chest, which was growing unbearable. It felt like a rib might snap. He'd seen divers taped up before. Seen them come up with blood trailing from their noses and ears. He concentrated. Told the sand to flow. He followed Hap, when his every impulse was to get out of there, to turn and find his beacon, to push the sand up as hard and as fast as he could, pile of coin be damned.

Hap reached the structure. The walls appeared perfectly smooth. A building. Palmer could see it now – an impossibly tall building with small details on the roof, some so hard and bright that they must be solid metal. A fortune in metal. Machines and gizmos. Something that looked like ducting, like the building used to *breathe*. This was not built by man, not by any man Palmer knew. This was Danvar of legends. Danvar of old. The mile-deep city, found by a bunch of smelly pirates, Palmer thought. And discovered by *him*.

6

Danvar

Hap reached the building before Palmer. It was a sandscraper that put all the sandscrapers of Springston to shame, could swallow all of them at once the way a snake could eat a fistful of worms. The top was studded with goodies, bright blooming flashes of metal untouched by scavengers: threads of pipe and wire and who knew what else. Palmer could feel his skin crawl, even with the sand pressing him so tight.

I'm taking a sample, Hap said.

Normally they would grab something which had fallen loose, an artefact or scrap of metal, and rise up with it. Palmer pushed deeper and watched Hap scan the vast landscape of the building's roof. The adrenalin and the sight of such riches made it a little easier to move the sand – the sudden rush of willpower and desire helped as well – but breathing had become an effort.

Nothing loose, Hap complained, exploring the roof. The top of the building had to be as large as four blocks of Springston.

I'll break something free, Palmer said. He was now as low as Hap. Lower. His competitive spirit had driven him down past the edge of the building, dipping well past three hundred metres. The concept of breaking a personal record was lost in the rush of such a monumental discovery. He worried no one would believe them, but of course their visors would record everything. They would store the entire dive, would map the shapes beneath them, those great pillars reaching up like the fingers of a deity long buried.

And now the palm of this great god, the ground between the scrapers, was dimly visible. It was studded with bright metal boulders that Palmer recognised as cars, all perfectly preserved, judging by the signal bounce. But it was hard to read the colours this deep. He was in unfamiliar territory. As if to highlight this, the air indicator in his visor changed from green to yellow. One of his tanks had gone dry, a dull click as a valve switched over. Not a problem. They weren't going any deeper. This was halfway. And he would use less air going up. Fuck, they were going to get out of here. They were going to do this. Just needed to look for something to break loose, a souvenir.

He probed for any sand that might be inside the building, sand he could grab and flow towards himself in order to breach the scraper and grab some small artefact. The flat wall before him had the signal bounce and the wavering shimmer of colours that screamed 'glass'. *Hollow*, he told Hap. *I'm ramming it.*

Palmer formed a sandram with his mind, pictured a hardening of the sand in front of him and a loosening of the sand around that. His left hand twisted and turned inward the way it did when he concentrated, and he could feel himself sweating inside his suit despite the coolness of the deep sand. The ram was there. He made himself *know* the ram was there. And then he threw it forward, flowing the sand around it, losing control of the sand around his body for a moment, feeling it tighten everywhere at once like a coffin, his throat held fast by two great palms on his neck, chest wrapped with a wet and shrinking blanket, arms and legs tingling as the blood was cut off, and then the ram hit the building and dissipated and Palmer had the sand flowing around him once again.

He took a deep breath. Another. It felt like pulling air through a narrow straw. But the flashes of light in his vision stopped their blinking. Palmer sank a little, but finally he righted himself. The view before him had changed. There was sand inside the building now. He had shattered the glass. A wavering patch of purple told him that there was air in there. A hollow. Artefacts.

I'm going in, he told Hap.

I'm going in, he told himself.

And then the sandscraper swallowed him.

7

A Burial

For as long as Palmer could remember, he'd dreamed of being a diver, dreamed of entering the sand – but he had since learned that it was the *exiting* that took practice. A diver quickly learns a dozen flashy ways to get into a dune, each more spectacular than the last, from falling face first into the sand and having it softly claim him, to jumping backward with his arms over his head and disappearing with the slightest of splashes, to having the sand grab his boots and spin him wildly on the way down. Gravity and the welcoming embrace of flowing sand made many a glorious entry possible.

Exiting required finesse. Palmer had seen many a diver come sputtering out of a dune, sand in their mouth and gasping for air, clamouring with their arms as they lost concentration and got stuck up to their hips. He had seen many more come flying out with such velocity that they broke an arm or smashed their nose as they came spinning back to earth. Boys at school tried flipping out of dunes with disastrous and often hilarious results. Palmer, on the other hand, tried always to aim for a calm and unspectacular arrival, just like his sister. She told him the calm looked braver than the boast. Look like a pro. Pretend that one of those ruined sandscraper lifts still worked and was depositing him on the topmost floor. That's what he aimed for. But that was not how he arrived just now.

This exit was more like being belched out from the sand's unhappy maw. He was spat sideways through the small avalanche that had slid inside the building and was ejected into the open air.

Palmer landed with a thud and a crunch, first on his shoulder, then sprawling painfully to his back, his tanks jolting his spine. The swimming purples vanished as his visor was knocked from his eyes. There was sand in his mouth, his regulator half out, his lungs emptied by the impact.

Palmer removed the mouthpiece and coughed and spat until he could breathe again.

Breathe again.

The air was foul and musty. It smelled like dirty laundry and rotting wood. But Palmer sat in the utter and complete dark of eyelids squeezed tight on moonless nights, and he took another cautious sip. *There's air in here*, he told Hap, speaking with throat whispers, but of course his friend couldn't hear him. His visor band had been knocked askew, and anyway he was no longer buried in sand, had no way of projecting his voice.

Shouting wouldn't do, either. Palmer fumbled for his dive light and flicked it on. A world of the gods unfolded dimly before him. He turned away from the avalanche of sand, which seemed to writhe and creep ever inward as the deep dunes snuck inside to seek solace from their own crushing weight.

The objects in the room were recognisable. Artefacts just like those found beneath Springston and Low-Pub. Chairs, dozens of them, black plastic arms with cracked and rotting fabric seats and backs, all identical. A table larger than any he had ever seen, big as an apartment. Palmer tugged off his fins and set them aside. He lowered his air tanks to the floor and killed the valve, made sure he saved his oxygen. Powering down his suit and visor, he relished the chance to gather himself, to give his diaphragm a rest from the struggle of breathing against the press of sand, a chance for his ribs to feel whole again.

On a side table, his expert salvaging eyes spotted a brewing machine. The pipes were rusted and the rubber appeared brittle, but it would fetch fifty coin at market. Double that, if his brother Rob could get it working first. The brewer was still plugged into the wall as if someone expected to use it still. The fit and finish of everything in the room felt eerily advanced and ancient at the same time. It was a feeling Palmer got from all the relics and spoils of a dive, but here the feeling overwhelmed, here it hit him on an inconceivable scale—

There was a crash and the hiss of advancing sand behind him. Palmer startled, expecting the drift to crush the rest of the weakened glass and consume him with his visor up on his head and his suit powered down. Instead, there was a thump and a grunt as Hap tumbled into the room.

'Fuck—' Hap groaned, and Palmer hurried to help him up. Sand slid around their feet as it found its equilibrium. It was wet and packed enough that it wasn't free to flow inside and fill the room. Not immediately, anyway. Palmer had swum through enough smaller buildings in shallower sand and had seen what sand would do if given the time.

'There's air,' Palmer told Hap. 'A bit foul. You can take your visor off.'

Hap stumbled around in his fins for a moment as he regained his balance. He was breathing heavily. Wheezing and gasping. Palmer gave him a chance to catch his breath.

Once he got his goggles off, Hap blinked and scanned

the room. He rubbed the sand out of the corners of his eyes. His gaze seemed to flit across all the coin stacked here and there in the shape of ancient things. And then he found his friend's face, and the two of them beamed at one another.

'Danvar,' Hap said, wheezing. 'Can you fucking believe it?'

'Did you see the other buildings?' Palmer asked. He was out of breath as well. 'And I spotted the ground another three hundred metres or so further down.'

Hap nodded. 'I saw. I couldn't have gone another metre, though. Fuck, that was tight.' He held his goggles to his face for a moment, checking his readouts most likely, and frowned. Hap shrugged his tanks off.

'Don't forget to kill your valve,' Palmer said.

'Right.' Hap reached to spin the knob. There was sand stuck to his face and neck where he'd been sweating. Palmer watched his friend shake a veritable dune out of his hair. 'What now?' he asked. 'Do we poke around? You got dibs on the brewer?'

'Yeah, I already spotted the brewer. I say we check a few doors, catch our breath, and then get the fuck out of here. If we stay longer than two bottles should last, our friends up top might think we only made it as far as the *last* assholes, and then they'll close that tunnel on our asses. I don't think I have enough air to get all the way back to the surface without that shaft.'

'Yeah . . .' Hap appeared distracted. He popped off his fins, shook the scoop out of them and dragged his gear away from the drift invading through the busted window. 'Good move popping through the glass like that,' he said. 'I just saw you disappear, but I couldn't see inside.'

'Thanks. And this is good, catching our breath. It would've been tight getting back up. We can get our strength.'

'Amen. Hey, did you happen to spot the other divers on the way down?'

Palmer shook his head. 'No, did you?'

'Naw. I was hoping they'd stand out.'

Palmer agreed. There was almost nothing more valuable to salvage than another diver. It wasn't just their gear – which could run a pretty coin – it was getting cut in on any bounties they had or wills they'd left. Every diver was afraid to some degree of being buried without a tombstone, and so the bone-bounties, as they were called, made every diver a comrade of the dead.

'Let's try those doors,' Hap said, pointing at the double set at the far end of the room.

Palmer agreed. He got there first and ran his hands across the smooth wood. 'Fuck me, I'd love to get these out of here.'

'You get those out of here and you could fuck someone prettier than me.'

Palmer laughed. He gripped the handle and the metal knob turned, but the door was stuck. The two of them tugged, grunting. Hap braced his foot on the other door, and when it finally gave way, both of them fell tumbling back into the table and chairs.

Hap laughed, catching his breath. The door creaked on its hinges. And there was some other sound, a popping like a dripping faucet, like a great beam settling under some weight. Palmer watched the ceiling closely. It sounded like the scraper was adjusting itself, like its belly was grumbling around these new morsels in its gut.

'We shouldn't stay long,' Palmer said.

Hap studied him a long while. Palmer could sense that his friend was just as afraid as he was. 'We won't,' he agreed. 'Why don't you go first. I'll save my dive light in case yours burns out.'

Palmer nodded. Sound thinking. He stepped through the door and into the hallway. Across from him, there was a glass partition with another door set in it, a spiderweb of cracks decorating the glass, the effect of the building settling or being crushed by the sand. There appeared to be a lift lobby on the other side of the partition. Palmer had been in a few lifts in smaller buildings, found them a good way to get up and down if a building was full of sand. The hallway he stood in extended off in both directions, was studded with doors. To his right, there was a high desk like some kind of reception area, but everything was so damn nice. He coughed into his fist. Hopefully the air here wasn't—

Behind him, the door slammed. Palmer whirled in panic, thinking the drift must've flowed into the room and pinned the door shut, burying their gear. But he was alone in the hallway. Hap was gone.

Palmer tried the door. The handle turned, but the door wouldn't push open. He could hear the rattle on the other side as something was pressed against the door.

'Hap? What the fuck?'

'I'm sorry, Palmer. I'll come back for you.'

Palmer slapped the door. 'Stop fucking around, man.'

'I'll come back. I'm sorry, man.'

Palmer realised Hap was serious. Lowering his shoulder, he slammed against the door, could feel it budge a little. Hap must've shoved a chair under the knob. 'Open the goddamn door!' he yelled.

'Listen,' Hap said. His voice was distant. He was across the room. 'I burned my air getting down here. One of us needs to go up and tell the others what we found. I'll get more bottles and come back, I swear. But it's gotta be me.'

'I'll go!' Palmer shouted. 'That's my air, man. I can make it back up!'

'I'll be back,' Hap called out. Palmer could hear a faint hiss as valves were opened and a regulator was tested. *His* valves. *His* regulator.

'You motherfucker!' Palmer shouted. He tried the adjacent door but it wouldn't budge. He went back to ramming himself against the first door. He jerked the handle towards him as tight as he could, then threw his shoulder into the wood, thought he felt the chair budge a little. Again and again. The door opened a crack. And then a gap. Enough to get his arm through. He reached inside and felt the rim of the chair, held it while he pulled the door shut tight against his arm, and the chair popped off the knob and went tumbling. Palmer shoved his way inside, banging his elbows on the two doors, swimming between those priceless walls of wood, tripping over the upturned chair, to see Hap still on the floor, tugging on a flipper.

Hap scrambled to his feet as Palmer raced around the table and past the long row of chairs. His friend lowered his visor down over his wide eyes, had a grimace of determination on his face as he staggered towards the slope of sand, running awkwardly in his fins, one of them flapping with its buckles loose.

Palmer ran and dived after Hap, who jumped head first into the sand. The drift gave way, absorbing him, but Palmer caught one of his fins. The sand was hard and unyielding; it knocked Palmer's breath out of him as he crashed into it. He looked down at his hands, at the flipper that had come loose. His friend was gone. And he had taken Palmer's air with him.

8

What Pirates Do

HAP

Hap kicked his way out of the building and into a wall of sand. So thick. He hadn't been prepared, felt like he was moving through mush.[3] He concentrated on the flow, tried to breathe, realised he had a fin missing. Goddamn. He was going to die out here. Die right on top of fucking Danvar.

He coaxed a sip of air out of Palmer's regulator. There was sand in his mouth. Hadn't had time to clear it off. Fuck, the look on Palmer's face. But what choice did he have? Stay down there and wait for Palmer to come back for him? Fuck no. Fuck that.

He loosened the sand above him and kicked off the hard pack below. It was almost impossible to move his arms. He let the sandflow do most of the work, tried to remember all the older divers who laughed at noobs for using fins in the first place. It wasn't kicking, it was thinking that moved a man. That's what they said. He'd never believed them. He tried to now. He tried to breathe. So damn hard to breathe. Like a tourniquet across his chest,

[3] Wet sand.

as if his ribs were knitted together, as if the whole world were sitting on top of him.

Up. He made the mistake of looking down, could feel the pull of gravity, the sucking of those purples and blues, that hard earth far below, fading now, becoming invisible, just a handful of buildings until there was only one, and then he kept his visor pointed up, looking for the blinking transponders, watching the gauge drop back to under three hundred metres. Two fifty. Hell yeah, a breath. He sucked on the tanks, was damn glad for Palmer's lungs for once, wasn't jealous in the slightest, and as he rose up and up he felt that distance between him and his friend grow, that crushing depth, and some part of him knew, some dark sliver, that there was no going back. He had discovered Danvar. Him. It would be for some other asshole to risk his neck exploring it, pulling up all those artefacts. Hell, he hadn't even grabbed that brewer. Hadn't been any time. Breathing deeply now, sucking the tank down from yellow to red, he got under a hundred metres and no longer cared how much air was in the tank. He could get there. He could make it. The transponders above were blindingly bright. The orange-and-yellow glow of the shaft walls could be seen. Hap kicked straight for the white beacons and the soft bottom of the shaft, his legs sore, his ribs bruised from the effort, a joy in his throat—

Hap!

He heard the faint murmur in his jawbone. Palmer. Probably had his head in the sand, his visor on, holding his breath and yelling after him. Hap didn't answer, didn't raise the voice that happened in a man's throat when he whispered in his mouth, when he thought aloud. He kept those thoughts to himself.

Hap, you fucker, get back here! Hap—!

Hap didn't hear the rest. His head broke through the bottom of that well. He lifted himself up clumsily, dragging his legs out of sand softened by the vibrations of his suit, until he was sputtering and balled up in the open air once more.

He spat out his regulator. The tanks were almost empty. Hap moved the visor up to his forehead and took a few deep breaths in the pitch black. He fought the temptation to whoop for joy, to whoop for surviving. The others would be waiting up on that metal hatch and might hear him. *Act cool. Act like you've done this before.* A fucking hero, that's what he was. A legend. He'd never pay for a drink in any dive bar for the rest of his life. He flashed forward to himself in old age, in his forties, weathered and grey, sitting in the Honey Hole with two girls on his lap, telling people about the day he discovered Danvar. Palmer would have some heroic role to play. He'd see to that. He'd have the bartender buy him another round so he could toast Palmer's name. And the girls . . .

With his dive light on and his suit powered down, he fumbled for one of the dangling ropes, knotted it securely under his arms, gave it three sharp tugs. Oh, the girls. He thought of the girls as the slack went out of the rope. Almost too late, he remembered the beacons, which weren't cheap, and reached for his. The rope caught and started lifting him. Hap yelled for them to wait and scrambled after Palmer's beacon, which was worth a good twenty coin. He got his fingers on it as the rope began to haul him up, clutched the small device in his palm. While they hauled him through the shaft, he kept his one flipper on the wall to keep him from bouncing around and tucked the two transponders into the hip pocket on his suit. Fuck. He'd made it.

The disc of light above grew larger and brighter as Hap was pulled skyward. He could see the sun shining down from directly overhead, so it must already be noon. Damn. Had they been down there that long? Someone above him barked orders to the men handling the rope. He could hear men grunting as they took up the line hand over hand, lifting him in swaying jerks. When he got to the lip, Hap helped, grabbing the hot edge of the metal platform, feeling the burn through his gloves as he pulled himself up on weary arms, kicking with his feet.

Two of the pirates grabbed him by his dive suit and tanks and hauled him out.

'Where's your friend?' someone asked, peering over the lip.

'Didn't make it,' Hap said. He tried to take deep breaths. The old man who had checked over Palmer's gear searched Hap's face for a beat, and then waved his arms towards the high dune where the generator could be heard and a plume of sand filled the sky. But Brock pushed the old man's arms down and glared up in the same direction, waving some command off. Soon everyone was looking at Hap. The dive master studied the deep shaft as if hoping Palmer would appear.

'How far'd you get?' Moguhn asked, his dark eyes flashing. 'What'd you see?'

Hap realised he was still out of breath from the excitement, the adrenalin. 'Danvar,' he wheezed, beaming with triumph. 'Sandscrapers like nobody's ever seen.' He looked to Brock, whose eyes shone bright. 'Sandscrapers everywhere, hundreds of metres tall, like twenty or thirty Springstons put together. Artefacts all over the place—'

'You were down a long time on two tanks,' the dive master said. 'We'd almost given you up.'

'We found a pocket of air in one of the tallest scrapers, so we looked around a bit.' He tried to make it sound matter-of-course. 'We wanted to get you your money's worth.' Hap beamed up at Brock. All of this would go in his stories, all would be embellished over the years.

'Did you record it all?' Brock asked in that deep and guttural accent of his. 'Did you get a map of the area? Precise coordinates? Everything has to be precise.'

'It's all stored in my visor.' Hap tapped the band pushed up on his head.

'Let's have it,' Brock said, holding out his hand. Two of the other men were behind Hap, holding that large metal hatch open. Hap was about to say that he'd want to see the coin first when he felt his visor tugged off his head and handed over. It took him a pause to realise that Brock's command hadn't been directed at him at all.

'Thank you,' Brock said. He smiled at Hap. 'And now, I trust you can keep a secret.'

Hap was about to answer, to tell him that he damn sure could, but he quickly realised that this wasn't directed at him either. This flash of understanding came right before Moguhn shoved him in the chest and Hap felt himself go backwards. He windmilled his arms, stirring the air, a grunt and a helpless squeak escaping his lungs, his heels rocking back dangerously, before he tumbled into the dark.

He hit the hard wall of that deep shaft and spun down, the air whistling past his ears, his stomach up in his throat and choking off his screams. He fell swiftly. Felt a dangling rope, and the wild swinging of his arms caught a wrap. A wrap on his wrist, catching tight, and then the sting, the burn, as it caught his weight and he slid down and down, the rope whistling as it rubbed his flesh, biting, on fire, cutting through his skin and sinking to the bone, tumbling and tumbling until he hit the ground in an explosion of agony.

His leg, his back, the tanks, and then his head, so fast it was almost at once. He couldn't feel his body. *He couldn't feel his body.* His arm was in the air, hung up in the rope. By his dive light, he could see the rope buried deep in his flesh, squeezing bone, blood racing down to his elbow.

Hap tried to move, but he couldn't. Turning his head, he saw his boot near his shoulder. His boot was near his shoulder. And Hap realised, numbly and sickeningly, that his foot was still in it.

Oh fuck, oh fuck. His body was ruined. His mind was still aware, could see what had happened to him, and he knew it wasn't something he would ever recover from. He was an unnatural heap, but still alive.

Far above, shadows bent over the small disc of light. Hap tried to scream up at them, yell for help, yell a curse on them for all their days, but all that leaked out of him was a whimper, a rattle. One of the shadows moved, an arm waving, and some receding part of Hap's mind thought they were waving down at him. But they were waving beyond the rise of that great crater at whoever was holding the walls of that shaft open – because the power was killed, a connection severed, and those walls collapsed suddenly and all at once. And Hap's mouth, locked open in quiet agony, filled with sand. And the earth sat upon his broken chest.

Part 2 – A Visitor

9

The Brief Hiss of Life

CONNER

'You're letting the sand in,' Conner warned as Rob returned from his piss.

His little brother fell into the tent and onto his ass, remembered to knock his boots together before swinging his feet inside, then wrestled with the canvas flap. 'If we aimed the door to the west, the wind wouldn't get in,' Rob complained.

'We always do it this way. Just don't dally when you go in and out.'

Rob sulked while Conner readied the lantern. Outside, the world pulsed red from the dying fire. The wind rocked the tent and sand hissed against the canvas. 'Did you go?' Conner asked.

'Yeah.'

'Will you need to go again?'

'Not until morning.'

'Good. Let's begin.'

Rob situated himself on the other side of the tent. Conner adjusted the wick. He pinched the top to feel that it was wet with oil, held his flint and striker above it and scraped them together until the fuel caught. He turned off his dive light and the tent was filled with the more primitive and inconsistent glow of a beating flame. It was the light of childhood and nostalgia. The ephemeral light. That which does not last.

Both boys stared at the living flame for a long while, drawn back in time to simpler days, family days, when the concern for light meant another jar of rendered fat and not some rechargeable battery.

'This was Dad's lantern,' Conner said. 'He left it for us the night he departed so that we could find our way home.'

This was how Conner began the yearly ritual. It was how he always began it. His older brother Palmer had said these lines before him and their sister Vic, the eldest, had spoken them before that.

Conner looked up from the lantern, breaking the spell, and realised suddenly that Rob would never have a reason to speak these words. There would be no one to listen. No one to care. Rob coughed into his small fist, almost as if to say: *Let's get on with it.*

'Dad left us . . . twelve years ago today. We will never know why. All that remains is our memory of him, and that is what we honour. This tent . . . our father's tent . . . was the last place we saw him. It was less crowded in the morning when we woke. You were sleeping in Mother's womb. Palmer used to say that I kicked him all night and stole the blankets. Vic says she awoke as Father made ready to go, saw him in the moonlight when he flapped the tent, and that his face told her everything. In the morning, we all knew. I was six. Palmer was a little older than you are now. Mother was young and beautiful. And breaking down the tent that morning was the first thing we ever did without him.'

Conner fumbled with the canteen. His hands were shaking. His convictions too. He poured water from the vessel into the lid, rationing as was proper. He handed the cap across to his brother, who drank it down in a gulp. Conner poured a cap for himself. 'The last night we were together, Father shared his canteen, and he told us stories. Mom was given two caps that night, one for you.' Conner tipped the water into his mouth and swallowed. He poured another.

'The first time Father brought Palmer and Vic here, it was before I was born. He and Mother spoke of their parents, their past, the need to remember. After he left us, we made a vow to come back once a year so that we wouldn't forget.'

Conner caught Rob looking to the side where Palmer would normally be sat. Gone, just like Vic. So much for promises. Conner dipped a finger into the cap and held it over the open flame, ashamed of his plans, of growing up to be like his dad. 'This is the hiss of life,' he said. The flame ducked and sputtered as the water hit, and then it leapt back up. 'Our lives are the sweat on the desert floor. We go to the sky, over the jagged ridge, and we fall in the heavens where it rains and floods.'

He passed the cap to Rob, who repeated the ritual and the old saying that went with it. They were, the pair of them, religious for one day of the year. There was no pastor to finish the cap, so Conner told Rob to drink it. And he did. The cap went back on the canteen.

Rob studied the flame for a long while. His eyes shone in the beating light. And then he looked up at Conner. 'Tell me about Father,' he said.

In that instant, Conner was peering at his old self. He was young again, and his older brother was telling him stories of Father back when he'd been Lord of Springston, before the land was corrupt, before the wall took its lean, before Low-Pub took its independence, back when their dad had walked the streets and clasped hands and clapped backs and privately wept while his hair fell out, back before the office of Lordship and the suffering of his people had driven him to No Man's Land with all the others who left and never returned.

Across the recovered lamp-flame sat a younger Conner, eyes aglow. He could see himself huddled there beside his older brother while Vic told them both about Father when he'd been younger still, the great sand diver who'd shunned tanks of air for the sickness they caused, who had been able to go down for ten minutes at a time and bring back wonders from impossible depths, who'd saved the waterpump of Low-Pub and discovered the hills that became the western gardens. Father when he'd been young and reckless and bold.

But Conner remembered a different man. His last memory of their dad was of a man grey and weathered, like a piece of wood exposed to the wind and sun. He remembered his father that night in the tent, kissing them all on their foreheads, whispering that he loved them and to be safe. He remembered that terrible year as they had been forced to leave the great wall and had begun a slow drift westward, with the wind, through the best and then the worst parts of Springston and out to Shantytown. He remembered thinking they would never use the family tent again.

And yet they had. Every year since, while the family dwindled and promises were unkept. There had been that first fatherless year when their mother had come along and had helped them figure out how to erect the tent, the last year she would ever come. That night, she had told them of their father when he was a boy, the oldest stories of him any of them had heard, how he had forever been in trouble, wrangling goats and taming snakes, and burying sarfers in the dunes, mast first.

Conner had woken early that year before the sun was up, had found his mother gone, had thought she'd left them like their father had, but there she had been outside in the starlight, rocking and weeping beyond the tent, her feet dangling in the Bull's gash, clutching baby Rob to her chest and moaning in time to the drums of the east.

Conner remembered all of this, but these were not the stories he told. 'This is what I remember of our father,' he said. And he whispered memories of memories, only the best ones, because after that night they would be for his brother to recall and no one else.

10

Sissyfoot

The day before

The monster squealed and bucked its head beneath the canvas shroud. With a hideous screech, muffled by the tattered burlap, it bent its long neck down, driving its steel beak deep into the sand. It did this over and over, like a thirst-mad hummingbird probing the same dry desert flower for what little nectar it held.

Conner watched these gyrations while his buckets were filled with sand. The wind lifted a loose corner of the protective shroud and he caught a glimpse of the mighty waterpump beneath, the heavy plated head with its rusty rivets rising and falling, the grease-streaked piston pushing in and out, water flowing through pipes like coins pouring into pockets.

'Whatcha waitin' on, boy? You're topped and ready. Get to it!'

Conner turned his gaze to Foreman Bligh, who leaned on his shovel and slid the long splinter between his lips from one corner of his mouth to the other. Conner knew better than to say anything and get another mandatory load. Besides, this was his fortieth haul of the day, enough to fulfil his after-school requirement, and quite possibly the last bucket he would haul for the rest of his life.

'Sir, yessir,' he barked, and Foreman Bligh showed him the gaps between his teeth. Conner stooped to collect his buckets. The fine sand was piled up in flowing and shifting cones, precious veils of it cascading over the sides. Balancing his haulpole across his shoulders – the two buckets swaying from notches at either end – he forced his sore legs to straighten, turned to face the outhaul tunnel and staggered up the long sloping walk out of there. It was programmes like these new work requirements that made him itch to leave, even if he never came back. It was programmes like these that made him feel less than sorry for the Lords when rebel bombs clapped over in Springston and someone was violently voted from office.

Above him – further up the gentle slope of sand that rose on all sides from Shantytown's lone waterpump – he could see tomorrow's work blowing over the lip and drifting down on the winds. What he carried up in his buckets was replenished by the minute, the grains rolling over each other like marbles, all seeming to seek the pump like thirsty little brigands rushing down for a sip.

Conner passed several other sissyfoots on his way up the ramp. Empty buckets swung on the ends of their haulpoles and sweaty grime coated them just as it did Conner. A girl from his class, Gloralai, smiled as she passed with her buckets. Conner returned the smile and nodded, but too late realised she was laughing at something Ryder had said. The older boy followed, his haulpole and buckets balanced on one of his broad shoulders. He laughed and flirted and acted as if it were a day at the Dome, but still took the time to bump Conner's bucket as he passed, spilling a handful of sand from one and sending the imbalanced haulpole teetering.

Conner shifted the pole and recovered. He watched the

precious sand from his bucket drift back down to where it came from. Probably not enough to keep him from his quota. And not worth telling Ryder to fuck off. It was Friday, the day before his camping trip, and none of this bullshit mattered.

He continued his climb up the string of wood planks that zigzagged up the slope of shifting sand. A couple of young pluckers from the lower grades stomped up and down on either side of the planks, pulling them out of the sand by their ropes when no one was on them, to prevent them from getting buried. The after-school programme was meant to provide a respite for the two shifts of full-time pluckers and sissyfoots who worked mornings and nights. The wind and sand never took a day off – and so neither did anyone else. They all toiled in that pit, working to keep the well from being buried, when everyone up and down the slope knew it would happen eventually.

But not today, they told themselves as they hauled their sand and shook their planks. *Not today*, they said. And the pump beneath the shroud bowed its head in agreement.

Conner neared the outhaul tunnel of corrugated tin and steel trusses that burrowed through the bowl's lip and out to the other side. It was a public works project from a decade before, a visible admission that the sand would one day win, that they could only dig so much, that the way out was too steep. Laughter echoed inside the tunnel as several of Conner's peers returned for another load. Most of them worked slowly, shuffling their feet until dusk. Conner preferred to grind it out and get it over with.

He entered the cool shade of the tunnel and passed his friends without a word. He chewed on the grit in his mouth, the sand that had frustrated him when he was younger, that he'd wasted time scraping his tongue after and wasted precious fluids spitting from his mouth, but that he'd finally learned to grind to nothing between his teeth and swallow down. It was the sand that was trying to bury his town, the sand that wanted to work its way into pistons and gears until things fell apart, the sand that paid for his day's water if he lugged enough of it out of the pit and into the dunes where tomorrow it would blow west. It would blow west while new sand flew in from the east to take its place. One grain for every grain. An even trade.

Out of the tunnel, Conner entered the weigh station and bent his knees until his haulpole caught in the crook of the scales. The assayer flicked weights down a long rod. 'Don't lean on the pole,' he ordered.

'I'm not,' Conner protested, showing his hands.

The assayer frowned and made a note in his ledger. 'That's your quota.' He sounded almost disappointed. Conner nearly sagged in relief. He lifted the pole again, was glad to be done for the day, and hiked off towards the edge of the steep rise known as Waterpump Ridge. It was a new dune they were building here, a man-made dune downwind of the pump, which itself stood on the leeward side of Springston's Shantytown. Conner reached the lip, dumped his sand, and watched plumes of his hard work spiral towards the distant mountains beyond the dunes. *Go*, he urged the sand. *Go and never come back.*

As he watched his last load swirl on the wind, he considered what sand and man had in common. Both were forever disappearing over the horizon. Sand to the west and man to the east. More and more of the latter in recent years. Entire families. He'd seen them from the ridge heading off towards No Man's Land with their belongings piled up on their backs, fleeing the bombs and the violence, the wars between neighbours, the uncertainty. It was the uncertainty that drove men away. Conner knew that now. He used to see the beyond as some great unknown, but the fickle tortures of life among the dunes were worse. What could be certain was that elsewhere was *different*. This was a fact. A compelling one. It drew souls to the east as fast as Springston could birth them.

A gust of wind whipped his hair into a frenzy and tugged at his ker. Conner turned away from the view and saw Gloralai heading up with her own sagging haulpole. He gave her a hand dumping the buckets.

'Thanks,' she said, wiping her forehead. 'You done for the day?'

He nodded. 'You?'

Gloralai laughed. Her hair hung down over her freckled face in sweaty clumps. She untied what was left of her ponytail, gathered the loose strands off her face, and began to tie it back up. 'I probably got two more hauls. Depending how much I spill. Don't know how you haul as fast as you do.'

'It's 'cause I don't want to be here.' He hoped the *here* didn't sound as general as he meant it. It was more than school or the pump-pit. It was all of Shantytown. He picked up his pole and adjusted one of the buckets in its notch so it wouldn't slide out. 'C'mon. We'll haul one load each, and you can be done for the day.'

Gloralai smiled and finished knotting her hair. She was seventeen, a year younger than Conner, bronze-skinned and pretty with dark freckles across her nose. Conner didn't want to admit it, even to himself, but part of him didn't want to leave the pump right then. And hauling one more load didn't feel like hell when it wasn't mandatory, when he could *choose*.

Over Gloralai's shoulder, he spotted Ryder trudging up the slope. The boy seemed to catch this moment between his two classmates. He turned his haulpole sideways, the buckets heavy and swaying dangerously, and Conner had to dodge out of the way. He danced down the loose sand and nearly lost his footing.

'Watch it,' Gloralai said.

'Fuck off,' Ryder told her.

Gloralai caught up with Conner and the two of them marched down with their empty buckets. Out across the jumbled rooftops of Shantytown, a hammer beat a rhythmic tune and a gull cried out. Conner tried to soak it all up, the sights and sounds of home, as he followed Gloralai back into the tunnel.

'You were serious,' she said, eyeing him. 'I thought you were eager to get out of here.'

'Hey, I figure you're itching to go as well. Maybe if I haul a load for you, you'll buy me a beer at the Dive Bar.'

'You think so?' she asked, smiling.

Conner shrugged. At the bottom of the zigzag of warped planks, the groaning monster nodded its sad head and pumped water from the earth. It bobbed up and down while Conner and Gloralai stood in line to get their buckets filled. As the sand heaped in and spilled over, Conner watched a diver emerge near the pump and hand tools up to an assistant. Must have been down there repairing a connector rod or part of the pipeline. That was the life Conner should've had. If he'd made it into dive school, things would've been different. A diver, not a sissyfoot. Just like his brother and sister, out there scavenging and finding the spoils that cities were made of. Maybe then he wouldn't have got worn down, would've spent more time out of the wind, wouldn't be thinking of leaving.

'Get 'er going,' the foreman barked, and Conner saw that his buckets were full. Gloralai already had hers shouldered, was trudging up the planks. She yelled for him to hurry or she'd drink both of their beers.

11

A Date?

C onner and Gloralai dumped their buckets and turned towards town. From the top of the ridge they had a commanding view of the Shantytown slums. Conner could pick out the corrugated metal roof of the small shack he shared with his brother. The dune behind their shack had been creeping; the back half of their home was already buried. Another month and the sand would tumble over the roof and pile up around the front door. They could dig their way in for a while, but then it'd be time to cut their losses and move. Unless Rob was on his own. The dive school would have to take him in, as much promise as he'd shown. Or Graham would make him an apprentice. Or Palmer would have to settle down and stop running around with that asshole Hap. Something would have to change.

Beyond his home and the scattering of roofs and half-buried shops sat Springston with its rows of sandscrapers jutting up into the wind. A lacework of steel beams wrenched loose from similar buildings long buried beneath the sand, some of their squares glimmered with salvaged glass; the others sported sheets of tin or undulating canvas. Beyond the scrapers, Conner could just barely make out the outline of the great wall, which gradually vanished as he and Gloralai made their way off the ridge and behind the dunes. Soon it was just the tops of the tallest scrapers, those misshapen and disjointed stacks of cubes – little hovels and homes and shops built one atop the other with no plan and no coordination. Wisps of sand streamed from their roofs and the wind howled through their eaves. And then the last of the city vanished, and only the location of the dump could be determined, flocks of crows hanging majestically in the air, blacks wings unbeating, riding that rolling zephyr that marched in from No Man's Land and carried with it the thunder of the gods and the sand that was the bane of all their existences.

Conner listened beyond the wind and the crunch of sand beneath his boots and could just make out the distant and beating drums. These were the thundering booms that built and built in men's chests. These were the echoes of rebel bombs that brought back the horrors of loved ones blown to bits. It was the sound that would not stop, the noise that pervaded men's dreams and haunted their waking hours, the torture that drove them mad and madder until they could take no more of it. Until they fled to the mountains and were never heard from again. Or until they staggered into No Man's Land to find the source of this abuse, to beg it to stop. This was why men packed up their families and left for another life elsewhere. Or abandoned them in a shoddy tent.

'You ever dream of getting out of here?' Conner asked.

Gloralai nodded. 'All the time.' She shook the ker around her neck, dumping out the grit.[4] 'I've got a brother in Low-Pub who says he can get me a job in a bar down there. He's a bouncer. But I gotta wait until I'm eighteen.'

---

[4] Sand collected in clothing or in mouths.

'Which bar?' Conner knew what sorts of jobs had age requirements. He tried to imagine Gloralai doing what his mother did, and a rage built up inside him.

'Lucky Luke's. It's a dive bar.'

'Oh, yeah.' Conner ran his fingers through his hair, shaking out the matte.[5]

'You know it?'

'I know *of* it. My sister used to work there. Bartending. You didn't have to be eighteen to bartend back then.'

'You don't have to be eighteen to bartend *now*.' Gloralai led him to the right of a dune and onto a path. A group of kids sledded past on sheets of tin, screaming and laughing. 'You gotta be eighteen to work in the brothel upstairs,' she said.

Conner choked on sand. He fumbled for his canteen, even though he knew it held the barest of splashes.

'I'm only kidding,' she said, laughing. 'My dad just says until I'm grown I have to live with them and obey their rules. Typical parental bullshit.'

'Yeah, typical,' Conner said. But what he thought was how great it would be to have someone else setting the rules. All he and his little brother had were each other. Palmer and Vic had gone off to make their fortunes diving, leaving the two of them to fend for themselves. When their father disappeared, he had left the entire family destitute when once they'd had everything. And their mom – Conner didn't know where to start with her. He sometimes wished he didn't have a mom.

He pushed this out of his mind. Just as he pushed tomorrow's camping trip back to some dark corner. He concentrated on Gloralai there at his side – tried to live in the moment

---

[5] Sand trapped in one's hair.

while he could. Together, they angled towards a half-buried strip of shacks jutting out of a low dune. A generator rattled and smoked on the roof of one. Inside, there was a glow of light, and hanging from the sand-dusted roof was a neon Coors sign with the jagged shape of the westward peaks lit above. Conner nearly pointed out that his sister had salvaged that sign, as he often did when he saw something she'd found and had rescued from the sand.

'Hey,' Gloralai asked, 'are you going to Ryder's bash on Saturday?'

'Uh . . . no.'

She must've caught his accompanying wince. 'Look, he can be a dick, but it's gonna be a good time. Laugh Riot is playing. You should come.' Gloralai held up two fingers to the man in the window and placed a couple of coins on the sill. Conner spotted the small home-made tattoo on her wrist and wondered if she had others.

'It's not because of him,' he said. 'I could give two shits about Ryder. Me and my brothers are going camping this weekend.'

'You and Palm are taking Rob camping? That's sweet.' She handed him one of the foaming jars of beer. Conner took a sip. Cold from the deep sand. He wiped his lips.

'Yeah, it's not really sweet to be honest. It's something we do once a year.' He didn't say that he was dreading it, that he was nervous, that he was packing for a much longer hike. This was too good a moment to spoil.

'So how is Palmer? He moved down to Low-Pub, right?'

'He's good, I guess. He spends his time back and forth. He stopped by last weekend on his way to some salvage job. Probably back at my place right now. Unless he's flaking out on us again.' Conner took another sip of his beer. 'He's the one who's supposed to be looking after Rob, not me.'

'You do a good job. Besides, Robbie can look after himself.'

'Let's hope,' Conner said. He took another sip, then caught the questioning look on Gloralai's face. 'To annual traditions.' He raised his jar.

'Yes, to this date.' Gloralai raised an eyebrow.

'The . . . uh . . . the actual date's tomorrow,' Conner explained.

'Well, to the weekend, then,' Gloralai offered.

'Yeah. The weekend.' They sloshed their beers together. And then a flurry of sand blew off the roof, and they both shielded their jars with the flats of their palms, laughing. The wind carried the puff westward towards the setting sun, and all the dunes trembled in that direction a fraction of an inch, beams creaking, the residents of Shantytown glancing up from their various tasks and distractions at their sagging ceilings.

'Hey, thanks for this,' Conner said, saluting with his beer. He leaned back on the bar post and watched the sky redden, the little people up on Waterpump Ridge marching like ants, the lanterns and electric lights flickering on as shifts changed and day steeled itself for night, and the angry desert whispered right along.

'Yeah,' Gloralai agreed, seeming to know what he meant, that it was more than the beer. 'This is nice. Why can't it be like this all the goddamn time?'

12

Father's Boots

I t was late by the time Conner got back to his place. There were lamps burning higher up his dune, two men on the scaffolding there hammering away at the new home being built on top of his. A scrap of tin fell from the scaffolding and pierced the sand outside his door. One of the men above peered down after it, the scaffolding creaking. He showed no remorse for narrowly missing Conner, no apology, just an annoyed grunt at gravity's tricks and the tiring prospect of climbing down and back up again.

'I still live here, you know,' Conner called out. But one glance at the sand wrapping around his home and he knew this was a complaint with an expiration date.

He pulled the door open and kicked the scrum[6] off his boots before stepping inside. 'Yo, brother! You home?' Pulling the door shut required heaving up with both hands to get the doorknob to latch. Sift[7] fell from the ceiling, and the rafters creaked. There was no sign of Palmer, no boots or track of sand, no gear bag or detritus from a raided pantry. Just a voice calling out from below, muffled and distant.

---

[6] Wet sand packed in the soles of one's shoes.
[7] Fine sand, usually airborne.

Sounded like Rob. The hammering overhead resumed. Conner aimed a middle finger towards the ceiling.

'You had dinner?' he called out. He set his leftovers on the rickety table by the door – half a can of cold rabbit stew from the Dive Bar. His little brother shouted another reply, but again his voice was a dull rumble. It sounded like he was a shack down.

It took four strides to go from the foyer, through the kitchen, and into their shared bedroom with the two little cots on their rusted springs. Rob's bed was shoved off to one side, and three of the floor planks beneath it had been removed. It was dark below. The only illumination in the small house was what little lamplight filtered through the cracked glass set into the front door. A candle by Rob's bed had melted down to nothing. Conner rummaged through the bin by his cot and grabbed his flashlight, turned it on. Dead. He threw it back into the bin. Three strides, and he pulled down the gas lamp from the living room. Shook it and listened to the splash of oil. Fumbled to get it lit. 'You getting the gear together?' he asked.

Rob didn't answer. Conner adjusted the lamp until the room was flooded with light. He sat on the bedroom floor and dangled his feet into the pit, then lowered himself down and reached up to grab the lantern. A pale glow filled someone's former home.

What had once been rafters holding up a roof were now floor joists in Conner's house. Someone else's house stood below theirs, long abandoned and unclaimed. Soon, his own home would be someone's basement and this a sand-filled cellar. And so it went, sand piling up to the heavens and homes sinking towards hell.

Conner swung the lantern around in the small space. He and Rob kept the few things they owned stowed down there.

The bag that held the tent and all their camping gear was undisturbed. It sat right where they'd left it a year ago. It was covered in sift. Conner dusted some of the sand off the bag and wondered where the hell Rob was. He pushed open an old bathroom door and saw more floor planks removed. A light danced below. 'What the fuck're you doing down there?' he asked.

Rob peered up at him through the hole in the old floor and smiled guiltily. He was sitting on a pile of sand one more shack down. It was as far down as one could go, this next buried home nearly full of drift.[8] His brother's hair looked wet, was matted to his forehead, as though he'd been exerting himself. Conner quickly looked away.

'Aw, c'mon, man. You're not down there jerking off, are you?'

'No!' Rob squealed, and Conner peered back into the hole. He saw his brother wiggling back and forth. Rob glanced up at him and bit his lip in frustration. 'Where've you been?' he asked. 'I've been calling for you and calling for you.'

Conner realised now that his brother was in trouble. Crouching down, he lowered the lamp below the floorboards and saw that the sand was up to his brother's hips. There were gouges where Rob had been digging.

'What the fuck have you done?'

'I was just playing,' Rob said.

Conner hung the lantern on a nail and worked his way down another level. 'I told you to stay out of here. Drift can dump through in a flash.'

'I know. But . . . it didn't dump in. I kinda buried myself.'

Conner spotted the wires trailing out of the sand. He

[8] Sand that enters a home.

tried to prise his brother out, but Rob wouldn't budge. The sand around him was as hard as concrete. 'What've you done?'

'I've been working on . . . something.' Rob showed Conner the band in his hand, a cluster of wires trailing off and disappearing into the hard pack. 'I wasn't diving, promise. Not all the way. Just trying to see what I could do with my boots—'

'With your boots . . .?'

'Father's boots.'

'You mean *my* boots.' Conner snatched the band out of his brother's hand. 'Eleven fucking years old, Rob. You're gonna get yourself killed playing with this shit. Where'd you get the band?'

'Found it.'

'Did you steal this?' Conner shook the band. He had half a mind to leave his brother there for the night, just to teach him a lesson.

'No. I found it. Swear.'

'You know what Palm would've done if he found you playing with this? Or Vic?' Conner checked the band. It belonged to an old set of visors. 'Did you find this in the trash? Because that's where this piece of shit belongs.'

Rob didn't say. A scavenger's admission.

'Did you do the wiring?'

'Yes,' his brother whispered. 'Con, I can't feel my feet.'

Conner saw that his brother was crying. And one of his arms was pinned. Rob didn't need to be told how serious this shit was.

'Look,' Conner said, 'you can't leave these contacts exposed like this. They'll work for a while until you get a sweat going, and then they'll short.' He used his shirt to dry the inside of the band. 'Once that happens, everything you try just gets worse and worse. You were tightening the sand by trying to loosen it. All we've gotta do is kill the power and the sand should unclench.'

Rob sniffed. 'I put the power in the left boot,' he said.

'In the *boot*? Why the fuck would you do that?'

Rob wiped his cheek with his free hand. ''Cause I thought I could make a dive suit without the suit. Just the boots.'

'Jesus Christ, how did you make it to eleven?' Conner checked the band, made sure it was dry, and was about to press it to his forehead and release his brother when he thought of his sister and what she would do.

'Hold still,' he said. He pulled his shirt over his head, found a dry patch, and patted his brother's forehead dry.

'I'm not crying,' Rob said quietly, as Conner dabbed his head.

'I know you're not crying. I'm drying your temples.'

His brother held still. Conner checked the dive band to make sure it was aligned right, then paused a moment to admire the tiny solders his brother had made. 'You're a piece of work,' he said. He slid the band down on his brother's head. 'Now listen, I don't want you to just release the sand, got it?'

Rob nodded.

'I want you to flow it down around your legs, okay? Feel it move. Direct it. And then let it push up on the bottoms of your feet. You have to picture two hands down there beneath you, lifting you up. Two hands with good grips on those boots, okay? Can you feel the fingers? The palms?'

'I think so,' Rob said, biting his lip.

'Okay. Try it. Quick, before you start sweating.'

''S' not helping,' Rob grunted. He squinted his eyes and concentrated. Conner felt the sand stir and loosen beneath him.

'Good,' he said. 'Now up.'

Rob yelped as he shuddered skyward. His head nearly bumped into the rafters. The sand lifted him through the hole in the old bathroom, until his boots were high and dry on the pile of drift.

Conner laughed and brushed the spill[9] off his lap. Rob whooped and pumped his fists.

'Awesome job,' Conner said. 'Now take those boots off. You're fucking grounded.'

---

[9] Sand knocked loose from someone's exertions.

13

Son of a Whore

C onner stayed up late that night and waited for Palmer to get home. He finally passed out beside Rob on the tiny cot and woke in the morning to find his own bed undisturbed. He had left it open for Palmer, but his brother had probably got lucky with a girl. Totally flaking out on them again this year, even after promising. After really promising. And now Conner had a crick in his neck for nothing.

He got up and stretched. Rob grabbed the loose sheets, rolled over and cocooned himself. Conner grabbed a white open-front shirt that tied shut around the waist. He stepped into the washroom and rubbed sand on his face and hands, exfoliating the sweat and grime and stink. With some sand in the shirt, he rubbed the fabric together with his fists. The sand in the basin still had the faint smell of the old dried flowers crushed up in there. Damn faint, though.

He shook the sand back into the basin and got dressed, leaving his shorts on and knotting the shirt. Hurrying out into the morning chill, he pissed in the general vicinity of the nearby latrine, steam swirling off in the breeze. After kicking some light sand on the dark sand, he hurried back home.

'Yo, Rob, I'm running out for a fill and to find Palm. Get the tent aired out, will you? And no fucking around down there.'

There was a grunt from the bedroom, and the Rob-shaped mound shifted beneath the covers. Conner gathered his canteens: one on the hook by the door, an old beat-up one of Vic's sitting in the window like a relic or a piece of decoration, and a third he'd hidden on top of the kitchen cabinet. He strung all three over his head, grabbed all the coin he owned in the world – which fitted easily in one palm – and called into the bedroom again.

'All right. I'll be back. Don't sleep till noon, man. I want to get going early enough we aren't figuring the tent out in the dark like last year.'

Conner sat on one of his sister's old chairs and grabbed his boots. Then he spotted his dad's boots where he'd dumped them the night before and decided to wear them instead. Maybe he was already thinking about his trip that night and wanted something of his father's with him, or maybe it was just to keep Rob from getting into trouble while he was gone.

The band and a tangle of wires his brother had rigged up hung inside the right boot. Conner looked for a way to unplug the thing. He glanced into the bedroom, but the glorious Cocoon-of-Rob had not opened and sprouted its precious little butterfly, so he didn't ask. He saw how the band split in two, little metal contacts soldered into snaps, and took it apart. Each half went up a leg of his shorts and out at his waist, snapped back together, and then the band went into his pocket.

He slipped his father's boots on. As he laced them up, he thought of Graham, the dive master and tinkerer who often looked after his little brother after school. Maybe Rob had learned to fiddle with the dive tech from watching Graham. Knowledge of the suits seemed to spread this way, from the gypsies to the south and then into town, from one generation to another. Conner stood and wiggled his toes. It was eerie how well his father's boots fitted. He felt a little older as he grabbed his ker, stepped outside and shook the sift out. He left the door open to let in the light and keep Rob from oversleeping, then set off towards Springston.

His first stop would be the Honey Hole. Palmer would've hit their mom up for money, no doubt. And then he'd try the dive school. As much as he dreaded visiting the Honey Hole, morning was the safest time of day. Not because he minded the patrons and bar fights and the slosh of beer downstairs, but because it presented the best chance of catching his mom when she wasn't working.

The Hole was on the edge of Springston, right between town and the sprawl of shacks and shops that made up Shantytown. The location kept the riffraff who worked and drank there out of the town proper while also keeping the alluring fruit upstairs well within reach of the Lords and the wealthy. No one wanted to walk through Shantytown to find a good time. It would annul the effects of the carnal visits during the long stagger home.

Beyond Springston loomed the great wall where Conner had been born. The towering edifice of concrete rose nearly a hundred metres above the sand, had been erected generations ago by a rare union of the normally sparring and spatting Lords. These gang leaders, who stained the dunes with blood just to control a spring here or a patch of dirt there, had coordinated the most massive of public works projects. It was said that the current wall was far bigger than any of the last and would stand for all of time. It now leaned noticeably westward over Springston, had angled itself towards the nicest parts of town. Any view of the wall reminded Conner of the first six years of his life. The good years. There were the baths he could submerge in, covering his whole body and even his head. There had been electricity and toilets that flushed – no going out to shit in the sand and having to dig his own hole only to find two other shits already buried there. These luxuries he remembered that Rob would never understand, luxuries he had to share with his brother like stories about their dad. They were half-memories of things blurred by childhood and by having taken those years for granted.

Nearer to him, rising up between two of the sandscrapers, was a column of black smoke. The top of the column sheered off into wisps as it rose past the lip of the wall and met the wind. Conner thought he'd heard a rumble in the middle of the night. Another bomb. He wondered who the fuck this time. The self-styled Lords of Low-Pub? The brigands up north? The dissidents there in the city? The FreeShanties out in his neighbourhood? The problem with bombs when everyone was making them was that they no longer stood for anything. You forgot what the fuck for.

He rounded a low dune and approached the Honey Hole, a building no one would ever bomb, not in a million years. The various brothels along the edges of Springston had to be among the safest places across the thousand dunes. Conner laughed to himself. *Probably why the Lords spend so much time in them*, he thought.

He kicked the scrum out of his boots before pulling open the door and stepping inside. Heather was behind the bar, drying a jar with a rag. A lone man sat on a stool in front of her, bent over with his head on his arms, snoring. Heather smiled at Conner before glancing up at the balcony that ran clear around the first floor. 'She should be up,' she called out, not bothering to lower her voice. The man in front of her didn't stir.

'Thanks,' Conner said. *Up* was where he liked to find his mom. Standing. He headed for the stairs and nearly tripped over a drunk sleeping on the floor. Foreman Bligh. Conner resisted a dozen spiteful urges and stepped *over* the man. It was easy to blame people for the misery of life rather than blaming the sand. Yelling at the sand got you nowhere. People yelled back, and at least that was a response. An acknowledgement. Being tormented and simultaneously ignored was the worst.

He marched up the stairs towards the balcony, old wood creaking with each step, and couldn't imagine being one of the drunks who took this walk in full view of their friends. But then men bragged about whom at the Honey Hole they'd bagged the night before. Enough trips up those stairs, and maybe it felt normal. Fuck, he didn't want to get a day older. He imagined sitting down there getting hammered out of his skull one day, a beard down to his navel, smelling like a latrine, then paying someone to lie still while he fucked them.

As much as the entire scene disgusted him, Conner knew that most men ended up right there, hating their life and trying to avoid it. One night of escape at a time. Drowning their misery with a bottle and paying for a brief spasm of lust. It would probably get him too, as much as he hated the thought of succumbing to that. Man . . . he remembered wishing life would rush along, that time would hurry up and he would get older already, but now he wanted it to stop. Stop before shit got any more dreary than it already was. If life would stop moving, maybe he could clear his head. He wouldn't have to run out on it.

He paused outside his mom's room, almost forgot why he was there. Palmer. Right. He lifted his hand and knocked, really hoped he didn't hear a man barking at him to *scram, this one's taken*. But it was his mother who opened the door, a robe draped over her shoulders. She tightened it up and cinched the sash when she saw who it was.

'Hey, Mom.'

She turned and left the door open, walked back to her bed and sat down. There was a bag beside her, a roll of cloth laid out with brushes. Lifting her foot to a stool, she went back to painting her toenails.

'Slow night,' she said, which Conner tried his damnedest not to picture the meaning of. But trying made it happen. Fuck, he hated that place. Didn't know why she didn't just sell it and do something else with her life. Anything else. 'I don't have a coin to spare,' she told him.

'When's the last time I came here asking for coin?' Conner asked, offended.

She glanced over at him. He still hadn't stepped inside. 'Wednesday before last?' she asked.

Conner remembered that. 'Okay, fine, but when before that? And that was for Rob, just so you know. The kid has fucking holes in his kers.'

'Watch your language,' his mother said. She jabbed her tiny brush at him, and Conner resisted the urge to point out that her profession depended on that word.

'I just came to see if you'd heard from Palmer. Or maybe even Vic.'

His mom reached for the bedside table where a curl of smoke rose from an ashtray. She took loud, popping tokes and got the cherry glowing again. Exhaling, she shook her head.

'It's that weekend,' Conner told her.

She turned and studied him for a long while. 'I know what weekend it is.' A column of grey ash fell from her cigarette and drifted to the floor.

'Well, Palm promised he was coming this year—'

'Didn't he promise last year?' She blew smoke.

'Yeah, but he said he was *really* promising this time. And Vic—'

'Your sister hasn't been out there in ten years.' His mom coughed into her fist and went back to work with the little brush.

'I know.' Conner didn't bother correcting her. It'd been eight years, not ten. 'But I keep thinking—'

'When you get older, you'll stop going out there too. And then poor Rob will go out on his own, and he'll make you feel bad for not going with him, but it's *him* you'll feel sorry for, and you'll sit around and wait for him to grow up and figure out what the rest of us know.'

'And what's that?' Conner asked, wondering why the hell he even tried any more.

'That your father is long gone and dead and the more you go on wishing he weren't, the more sick you make yourself for no good reason.' She studied her handiwork, wiggled both sets of toes, and screwed the small brush back into its little bottle. Conner tried not to think where she got little artefacts like this. Scavengers and divers trading for her wares. Fuck, his brain was obstinate.

'Well, I guess I came by for nothing.' He turned to go. 'By the way, Robbie says hello.' Which was a lie.

'Rob,' his mother said. 'Not Robbie. Not Robert. Rob.'

Conner stopped and turned back to his mom. She took a long pull on her cigarette.

'You ever think about what I named you boys?'

She let the smoke drift out as she spoke. Conner didn't

answer. He'd never thought about the fact that she'd named them at all. They just *were*.

'Palmer and Conner and Rob,' she said. 'All of you little thieves. I named you after your father.'

Conner stood rooted in place for a moment. He didn't believe her. It was a coincidence. 'What about Vic?' he asked.

His mom took another drag on her cigarette and exhaled a fountain of smoke. 'When I had Victoria, I didn't know your father was a goddamn thief. That he was gonna run off and leave us with nothing.'

'He wasn't a thief,' Conner said. 'He was a Lord.' He tried to say it with conviction.

His mother took a long, deep breath. Let it out. 'Same damn thing,' she replied.

14

Sandtrap

C onner left the Honey Hole and kicked along the edge of Shantytown. He stared down at his father's boots and thought for the first time on his name and the names of his brothers. *Palmer, Conner, Robert.* What kind of shit was that to learn? And it was like she'd got more blunt over time. Had to be a coincidence. Something her madness had dreamed up after their father'd left. He hoped his mom never told Rob – the kid would be crushed. Would take to calling himself Bobby.

Unconsciously, he allowed his feet to fall into time with the distant booms to the east. *Thrum. Thrum. Thrum.* It was far too easy to allow the pulse of the desert to become his pulse, to power him along to the earth's racing heart. Conner shuffled his feet, mixed up his pace, and tried to be his own man. Not what someone named him.

He crossed a low dune between a freshly collapsed house and a new one under construction. A handful of men were hauling material from the ruin and nailing it back together two dozen paces away, once again forestalling the inevitable. The most disturbing thing about the scene was how normal it seemed, how many times Conner had watched this play out in Shantytown, a ruin serving as the foundation for new construction. But now his mother had him seeing the commonplace in a new way. If anything, this alien view strengthened his resolve for that night's plans. It undid what a beer and rabbit stew with Gloralai the night before had started doing to his head.

He cut through a row of apartments that abutted the back of the dive school. Palmer was probably back at his place right now helping Rob unpack and air out the tent. But still a good idea to check the dorms and see if he'd crashed there the night before.

Ms Shyler waved from her porch as he passed. She went back to sweeping the sand out of her house, when one of her kids stomped inside, transferring some of it back. She turned and yelled at the boy, was her own sissyfoot in a way. They all were. The men building the house from the remnants of a house, all these tasks that required doing over and over with no end in sight, filling canteens and eating, shitting, sleeping, looking forward to a weekend and dreading the week that would come after. Life was lived by sissyfoots, all of them. One bucket of sand at a time.

He had to stop thinking like that. There was progress somewhere. Something better. That's what the slow stagger of men, women and families believed as they marched off towards the horizon. They believed in a life far away from the fighting and the bombs. Away from the riots and the patter of morning gunfire. Away from the shops where sunlight and sand filtered through bullet holes in wrinkled tin. Away from Lords with fickle rules and those who meant to topple them with indiscriminate bombs.

There had to be a reason so many left and never returned. It was the allure of a good life. Or simply no longer being able to stand the sound of the distant drums without feeling an urge, a compulsion, to go see their origin for themselves. That's what his father must've believed. It had to be what he'd felt. Conner's mom was just trying to poison the memory of the man because she hated her own life. That was it.

The door to the dorms was open, letting the light and a swirl of drift in. Conner stepped inside. There were two dive students in the back of the bunkroom, a clatter of dice. They turned when Conner's shadow darkened the pips. 'Have you guys seen Palmer?' he asked.

One of the boys shook his head. 'He and Hap are out on a dive. They're not back yet.'

'Wasn't that a week ago?' Conner asked.

'So it was a long fucking dive. How should I know? They were all secretive about it.'

'Yeah,' Conner said, dejected. 'Thanks.' Another year of disappointment from their big brother. Poor Rob.

'Yo, please kindly shut the fuck up,' someone called from one of the bunks.

Conner apologised and left. The dice clattered against the wall.

Heading home, he realised it would just be him and Rob that night, which screwed up his plans a little. Still workable, though. It would fall on him to lead the talk and to work the lantern. He wasn't prepared. Especially not after visiting his mom. All of his stories had been told and retold to death.

He hiked back through the schoolyard and tried to match his memory of his father with his mother's account. He'd had much more of her version of events than actual time with his dad. He'd been six when his father had left, had spent twice that number of years living in his absence, relying on stories passed down from others. Vic had done her share to muddy his recollection, telling all the stories from when their dad was younger, growing up in Low-Pub, making a name for himself as a diver, the years leading up to his taking over as Lord of Springston, back before his breakdown.

Conner wondered if dredging up the past was even a good idea. It was like being a sand diver in a lot of ways. There were all these rusty hurts buried deep. Bringing them up and trying to oil them, sand them, make them into something they could never be again – how was that healthy? Maybe it wasn't worth it to know who his dad had been. Maybe his mom was right and he should just move on. If their dad did come back, he would be older, weaker, greyer, not the same man. Clinging to an idealised past was a poison of sorts, that bastard Nostalgia, making people think there was a better time and place if they could just get back to it.

He glanced towards the great wall, that towering symbol of his past with its dangerous lean. A distant grumble from No Man's Land could be heard, the faint *boom boom boom* of who-the-fuck-knew-what. The future, that's what. The very near future. The grumble of the unknown, like a hungry stomach that knew it needed feeding, like the hungry soul that needs some new adventure, the *boom boom boom* of a man's pulse when he was scared he wouldn't amount to shit, that if he sat still, the dunes would claim him.

The three canteens rattled emptily by Conner's hip, and he remembered he needed to stop and fill them. He needed to buy some jerky as well. Between Gloralai and his mother and Palm being an asshole, his brain was well and truly scrambled. His father's boots didn't help matters at all. He passed through the low Bleak Wall, which divided Springston and Shantytown in disjointed gaps and divides, a cheap and hasty imitation of the larger wall further east. In the morning shade of the wall, a game of football was being played, shirts and skins. Boys Conner's age ran back and forth, kicking an inflated gooseskin and tackling one another, coming up covered in sweat and sand. There were three skins and four shirts. Guilla, a friend of Conner's, tackled a boy from

Springston. As they disentangled themselves, Guilla spotted Conner skirting the playing field, which was laid out by canteens and shoes.

'Yo, Con!' he shouted. 'We need another.'

'Can't,' Conner said. 'Wish I could.'

Guilla shrugged, and the boys returned to their storm of sand-clouds and scrapes.

Past the wall, there was a line at the cistern. Conner fished in his pockets for three coins and waited his turn. He watched a mother scold her son in the middle of a path, saw Jenkins's dad emerge from their small walled garden holding a headless snake in one hand and a hoe in the other, then march inside their house probably to cook it. He became hyperalert at any gathering like this, saw all the tiny details of normal life humming right along. This was when the bombs came and ripped through crowds. At funerals and weddings and religious celebrations. At cisterns and cafes and protests. Retributions for recriminations. Sins for sins. Territorial squabblings. It was strange how tense one could become while surrounded by the banal. It was the waiting. It made Conner want to flee his flesh, sitting still in that creeping line. It was why he had to go.

Finally it was his turn. He paid his coins and watched the canteens fill. 'To the brim,' he said. The pumpman looked at him with disdain but didn't skimp. Conner put the three straps over his head, the canteens heavy and full on his hip. He headed off to buy some jerky. It would wipe him out, this trip. He reached into his pocket and felt the last of his coins there. Crossing the empty patch of dunes between the cistern and the market, mentally packing for his journey, the ground suddenly shifted beneath his feet—

Conner stumbled. He nearly fell forward, had to throw his arms out for balance, his mind seizing on the idea that it was the damn boots, the band shorting out in his pocket from canteen water. Fucking Rob. But he heard the hiss of flowing sand, and then the laughter of boys, and Conner couldn't move. He looked down to see his legs buried up to his knees, the sand packed so hard around his shins that his feet throbbed. He couldn't fall over if he tried.

'Whadja step in, whoreson?'

Twisting at the waist and craning his neck, Conner could see Ryder and two others behind him. They had sand in their hair and on their shoulders, visors pressed up on their foreheads, had probably been diving in the training dunes near school or had seen him checking the dorms. Conner tried to pull his boots free but couldn't.

'Let me go, Ryder.' He stopped struggling and fought the urge to say *This isn't funny*, because that would only draw laughter. He fought the urge to remind the boys that sandtrapping someone like this was a buryable offence, because that would only bring more threats. Reaching into his pocket, he felt the band there that his brother had made. If only the power weren't in the boots—

'Hey, whoreson, I've got a question.' Ryder stepped around in front of him, grinning. The other two boys flanked Conner to either side. 'When you were a baby, how much did your mommy charge you to suck her tits? 'Cause she charges my dad five coin each!'

The laughter echoed over the dunes. The sun was barely up, but to Conner it suddenly felt like midday. Ryder stepped close. Conner could smell stale beer and onions on the boy's breath.

'I don't want to see you near her,' he said.

Conner knew who Ryder meant. He tried to hold his tongue, but couldn't. He should've told Ryder the truth right then and said he would never see Gloralai again anyway.

That none of this bullshit mattered. That they were kids and the fucking sand didn't care. Instead, he sneered at Ryder, unable to resist. 'That's for her to decide.'

Ryder smiled. 'That's where you're wrong, boy. Ask your mom who decides.' He gripped the back of Conner's neck and squeezed. Conner wanted to punch the bigger boy, but he knew how badly that would go. There were three of them, and his boots were pinched. 'There are men in these dunes and then there are little boys like you. I'm a sand diver, and we take what we find. And I found her first.'

'You're a trainee,' Conner said. 'You're not even a sand—'

There was a flash of rage on Ryder's face – a horrible spasm of bared teeth and wrinkled brow – just before the sands opened and Conner was sucked down.

Conner's mouth filled with grit. The earth had opened for him, dropping him down beneath sand as loose as water. His feet hit something solid below. Swimming with his arms, his head bumped into a wall of sand above. There were walls on all sides. Ryder had made a solid box filled with flowing sand, a death coffin.

Conner sealed his lips, half a dune in his mouth, the loud crunch of grit between his teeth, and fought the urge to swallow or spit. He only had the barest of lungfuls. Had been talking. But his sister had done this to him before, had taught him to be calm, to last a minute or more. If he counted to ten, Ryder would bring him up. He was just trying to scare him. Conner thought this, but part of his brain screamed: *We're gonna fucking drown. Do something, asshole!*

With sand burning his eyes, Conner fumbled blindly at his father's boots. His head flipped upside down. He had to remember which way was up. Had to remember. Goddamn, he couldn't breathe. Couldn't swallow. He hit the power switch under the tongue of the left boot with one hand and pulled the band out of his pocket with the other. *C'mon, Rob*, he thought. *C'mon, brother.*

Conner pressed the band to his forehead, couldn't feel anything, too much sand between the contacts. Damn thing was upside down, that's why. The wires were coming out the top. He tried it again. Could *feel* the sand now. No idea if this would be strong enough. Needed to be stronger than Ryder. Was about to black out. Had to go. Had to go. With desperation, he didn't flow the sand so much as explode it. Arms over his head, expecting a collision, hoping this was up, *that this was up*, not sure – he felt the sandwall above him shatter, felt his arm break the surface, his head and then his entire body rising out of the sand.

The other boys lost their footing in the flow. Conner was on his hands and knees, spitting the grit out of his mouth – grit that had turned to mud. He coughed and wheezed, and the black edges of his vision receded. Arms and legs weak, he fumbled for the band, tried to get it back on his head before they came at him again. Damn – the boots – strong as a whole suit. Shouldn't have been possible. Fucking Rob—

A hand clenched over his knuckles and squeezed into a fist, the bones of his fingers grinding together. Conner dropped the band and grimaced in agony. Ryder was down on one knee, casting a long shadow over him, his face a mask of rage.

'You think you're a diver, boy?' Conner watched as Ryder grabbed the band with his free hand and yanked it away, ripping the wires. 'Patrol would bury you for this.' He shook the band in front of Conner's face, and the grip with his other hand tightened, crushing Conner's knuckles. 'You're lucky I don't tell them. That's your life I just saved.' Ryder spat into the sand and dropped the band. 'I fucking own you. Don't you forget that, whoreson. I own you like every man in Springston owns your goddamn mother.'

A swift kick in the ribs for punctuation. And then the boys were back to laughing. The sand trembled and opened up, and they dived and disappeared.

Conner rested his forehead on the warming sand and took deep breaths. When he spat, it coloured the sand like a sunrise. *This is my life*, he thought miserably. *But not for long*.

15

Sins of a Father

Conner got up and dusted himself off, probed his tender ribs. A sip of water swished and spat got most of the grit out of his mouth. His anger soon abated. It was from looking down – not at the pink sand between his father's boots, but at the old band torn loose and curled amid a tangle of wires.

He stooped to retrieve the band and inspected it again. Ryder would've let him up. Was just messing with him. Damn, he should've just waited it out. But the boots – he remembered how solid the sand had felt the night before, clenched around Rob's legs. Scanning the training dunes, he looked towards the school. He still needed to get jerky, but another quick errand first. His trip that evening had just got more interesting. He needed to show a friend these boots.

Around the corner from the school stood a line of shops that catered to scavengers. Used suits, visors, repair stalls, fins, electronics, all the scraps and tools of the trade. This was an industry honed by abrasive necessity. Practically all of Springston, Shantytown, Low-Pub, Pike and the gardens to the west were built with dredged spoils from beneath the sands. The mounds of dirt that rose up and were in shallow enough sand to reclaim had been discovered by divers. The same divers who went on to do the digging, hauling the soil to the rooftop gardens throughout town, piling it up by the springs that fed the roots that fed the people. Water, gas and oil pumps relied on divers. It was the industry on which all others were founded, which is why the death toll hardly dented the number of enthusiastic volunteers and why most of the kids who dreamed of entering dive school found packs of others standing before them. It was why many never got the chance.

Conner hurried through the bustling Saturday markets in the dive district and down one of the side alleys that kept creeping along with the dunes. He let himself into Graham's, one of the larger shops. An annoying collection of bells and chimes clattered and rang as the top of the door struck them. Inside, the walls were covered in artefacts. Mirrors and clocks, pumps and small motors, coils of wire and tubing and pipe, and bin after bin of bolts, washers and nuts. Across the high ceiling hung the remains of dozens of bicycles. Conner had to duck under a few of these.

Most of the goods that studded the walls and hung from the rafters had been brought up by Graham himself. The rest had been bartered for with something else he'd discovered. Despite appearances and the occasional price tag, hardly any of it was for sale. Convincing Graham to part with a single washer could take weeks of pleading. Trade was the only coin that worked, and Graham always got the better end of the deal. He was a pain in the ass, but had been good friends with their father, which meant getting work done even without an official dive card from the Guild.

'Graham?' Conner let himself through the counter and peered into the workshop. Graham glanced up from his bench. He had a wire brush in one hand and what looked like part of a rifle in the other.

'Con.' He smiled. 'Thought you were off camping this weekend.'

'Tonight. I'm getting some water and a few other things while Rob airs out the tent. Hey, I want you to take a look at something for me.'

Graham pushed his glasses up his nose. 'Sure,' he said. 'You scavenge up something good?'

'You know I'm not allowed to dive.'

'Sand in your hair says you do.'

Conner touched his hair and sand rained down. He stared guiltily at the mess. 'Sorry—'

'Forget it.' Graham shooed his apology like a fly. 'Never gets all the way clean in here. So what've you got?'

'It's this band here that Rob made.' Conner reached into his pocket and pulled out the band. He handed it to Graham. 'The wires are ripped loose—'

Graham gave the band a cursory glance. He leaned over his workbench and studied the wires trailing over Conner's belt, then looked down at his feet.

'Dad's boots,' Conner explained.

'I see that. You got a suit on under there?'

'No, that's the thing. You know how Rob is. Well, I caught him trying to dive with these last night. Wasn't doing too bad a job of it—'

'Diving runs in your family,' Graham said. 'Guild made a mistake not taking you in.'

'Yeah, well, it's just these boots, see? No suit. But I felt what they could do to the sand and I wondered if you'd seen anything like this before.'

'You felt it,' Graham said. 'So how far down did you go?'

Conner glanced over his shoulder, made sure they were alone. 'A metre. Maybe two.'

Graham sniffed. He flipped the band inside out and adjusted the long-armed and multi-jointed light affixed to his desk. 'People have toyed with these before. You can have some fun with a pair of boots. Skate along the sand, dip your toes and whatnot. But they're no good for diving. If you can't keep the pressure off your chest, you can't breathe. And even if you could, you'd be in a world of hurt when you came back up. Did Rob do the wiring?'

'Yeah.'

Graham looked up from his study of the band. 'He's better than you.'

'Yeah, I know.' Graham didn't mean it with malice. He didn't have a cruel bone in his body. But the power of dry observation sometimes felt the same. He made space on his workbench, setting that long steel barrel aside. He plugged in his soldering iron.

'Can I see the boots?'

'Sure.' Conner pulled the wires out at his knees and kicked off his dad's boots. 'He put the power charge in the left sole.'

'Interesting,' Graham said. He grabbed a magnifying glass from his desk and peered into one of the boots, removed the leather insole. He inspected the other one. 'Looks like he made room inside the right one to stow the wires and the band. A visor too.' He glanced up at Conner. 'A metre, you say?'

Conner nodded.

'Hmmm.' Graham studied the ceiling for a moment. 'Could you leave these with me awhile?'

Conner frowned. 'I'm sorry. I wish I could. I was just hoping you could rewire them for me while I wait. I have a few coin.'

Graham grabbed the iron and tested the tip with his tongue. The hiss made Conner cringe and bite his teeth together. Graham began touching the wires back to leads, seeing at once how Rob had rigged the band. 'You're always eyeing that set of visors in the case over there. The green ones.' He didn't look up from his work. 'I'd trade you those visors and a mostly new suit for these boots.'

Conner didn't know what to say. 'That's . . . uh . . . I appreciate the offer, but those are my dad's boots.'

'They were his old boots. Even he didn't care about them any more.' Graham finished his work and blew on the band, smoke curling from the iron. He looked up at Conner expectantly.

'Well, I'll think about it,' Conner said. He reached for the boots. 'What do I owe you for the repair?'

Reluctantly, Graham returned the boots. 'Tell you what, promise me you won't barter these to anyone else, and we're even. Trader's dibs.'

'Okay,' Conner said, knowing it didn't matter. He wasn't going to trade his dad's boots, not after what he'd felt under the sand. 'You got dibs.'

Graham smiled. 'Great. You tell Rob to come by and see me when he gets a chance. Been a few weeks since he's stopped by.'

'Yeah, about that . . .' Conner stuffed the band into the sole of one of the boots. He slipped them on, leaving the laces untied. 'Knowing how useful Rob can be around here, if anything ever happened to me and Palmer wasn't around to watch Rob . . .'

'I promised your dad I'd look after you boys,' Graham said. 'I've told you that. I mean it. Don't you worry.'

'Thanks,' Conner said. He turned to go, then paused by the door leading back into the shop.

'Tomorrow's the day, isn't it?' Graham asked.

Conner nodded. He didn't turn around. Old Graham was too damn insightful. His rheumy eyes could see further into the deep sand than anyone else's. He could tell at a glance how something was wired. If Conner turned to say goodbye, to ask one more question, if he even reached up to wipe the water from his cheek, the old man would know. He would know that tomorrow wasn't just an old anniversary. But the start of a new one.

16

The Long Hike

'Palmer sucks sand,' Rob shouted. He hitched the large pack up on his shoulders, had been complaining about having to carry such a heavy load since they'd left the house. 'He promised us.'

'I'm sure he has his reasons.' In truth, Conner was tired of sticking up for his older brother. It was a full-time job keeping little Rob from being disappointed with the entire family. And here he was about to contribute to that. Just as the sand seemed to pile higher for each generation, so the youngest siblings ended up with the full brunt of familial mistakes. It was a tiring refrain, but Conner thought it again: *Poor Rob.*

He and his brother skirted Springston on their way towards No Man's Land. Avoiding the open dunes, they stuck to the outskirts where they could spend much of the hike in the lee of homes and shops. They kept their kers over their mouths and rarely talked, shouting above noisy gusts of wind when they did. An escaped chicken flapped and clucked across their path, a woman in a swirling dress chasing it, calling its name. In the distance, the masts of a line of sarfers jutted up beyond the edge of town. Conner could hear the ringing bangs of loose halyards slapping aluminium masts. A solitary sail fluttered aloft, caught the wind, and the sarfer built speed towards the west, off to the mountains for a load of soil for the gardens or to trade with the small town of Pike, most likely. Conner and his brother pressed east. He scanned the horizon for other deserters, for families with heavy loads on their backs, but almost no one left town on a weekend. Mondays were days for departure. Wednesdays as well, for whatever reason. Maybe because Wednesdays were those depressing days as far from time off as possible.

When he and Rob got even with the great wall, they tightened their kers and adjusted their goggles and angled off into the wind and towards the roar of distant thunder. Conner took the lead and broke the wind for Rob. Off to the side, he watched the edge of Springston approach. The city sat near to the boundary of No Man's Land – just a few hours' hike – like some kind of dare. But the city also looked afraid. It seemed to sulk in the sand, a towering wall erected to hold back the wind and dunes and fear.

A handful of the tallest sandscrapers tilted sickeningly to the west, ready to topple. One of these towers had been abandoned a few years ago, such were the creaks and quakes felt by its inhabitants. It leaned with a promise of collapsing – and yet a refusal to do so. It had been so long since the place had cleared out that the once-great anticipation had relaxed into boredom. Talk had grown among those now eager to move back in. Conner knew that some squatters already had; pale lights danced up in those forbidden towers at night and could be seen from Shantytown. And the deeds to those apartments had begun to change hands as speculators bet on topple or stability, their moods as fickle as the alley winds.

Conner marched with his head to the side, goggles out

of the peppering sand, and imagined the sound those rickety scrapers would make when they tumbled. The homes in their shadows would be crushed, the people living there buried, the shops and stalls flattened. The poorer people to the west must live in daily terror of what dangerous things their wealthy neighbours built. Those in the shadows didn't speculate with their money but with their lives.

The great wall itself would topple one day. Conner could see this as they passed the boundary of Springston and the wall was viewed edge-on like he saw it twice a year. An entire desert pushed against the wall's back. It had built up slowly and inexorably over the decades, wind howling and sand piling up, spindrift blowing over ancient ramparts to haze the sky with occasional gusts or to dim the afternoon sun with furious blasts. When it went, the sand would loose a hellish fury. He was quite glad he wouldn't live to see that.

'What did you pack in here?' Rob asked, the words muffled by his ker and his voice's upwind march.

Conner waited for his brother to catch up. 'The usual,' he lied. He saw that Rob was practically bent over from the weight of the pack. Conner had planned on carrying it himself so no one would grow suspicious. Which would've left Palmer to carry the tent and Rob the lantern and his own bedroll. *Fucking Palmer*, Conner thought to himself. And for the first time, he considered what his brother's absence would mean for their father's tent. Rob would get back to town easily enough, the wind at his back, but the tent would probably be left to flap to tatters, with no one to help him break it down or haul it home.

'Can we stop for water?' Rob asked.

'Sure.' Conner lowered his large bag to the sand, and Rob nearly fell over backward as he shucked the other pack. Conner could hear the extra canteens of water sloshing in there. Enough for eight nights of marching out and back, as far as he told himself he would go.

'Twelve years,' Rob said. He sat on the gear bag and pulled his ker down, used it to wipe his neck. The cloth had sandworn holes in it and was tattered along the edge. Conner felt like a shitty brother.

'Yeah, twelve years.' Conner pushed his goggles up onto his forehead and wiped the gunk[10] from the corners of his eyes. 'I can't believe it's been that long.'

'It has. It means I'll be twelve this year.'

'Yeah.' And Conner wondered if he'd waited this long for any other reason than to know his brother would be okay without him. And he would. At twelve, Rob could officially apprentice in a dive shop. He could get room and board for what he now did anyway on the side. Graham would take him in. And Conner knew Gloralai would watch after him as though he were her own little brother—

'Why'd we bring so much jerky?' Rob asked.

Conner turned from the horizon and saw his brother rummaging in the rucksack. 'Close that up,' he said. 'You're letting sag[11] in.'

'But I'm hungry.'

Conner reached into his pocket. 'I've got food for the hike here. Now seal that flap.'

His brother did as he was told, didn't seem to have seen everything else in the bag. Rob sat with his back to the wind and chewed on a heel of bread. In the far distance, carried on the breeze, the drums and thunder of No Man's Land could be heard, sounding nearer than last year and nearer still than the year before that. Soon, Conner thought, those

---

[10] The sand that gathers inside goggles and around the eyes.
[11] The sand found in the bottom of any container.

drums would be beating in all their chests, driving them mad.

The sun beat down as the clouds of sand abated. It was one or the other during the day. At night, it was the cold and the howling beasts. The various torments of life worked in shifts so that one was always on duty. Thus was human misery extracted day and night like water and oil were pulled from the earth. Thus was the toll inflicted, the price one paid for being unwittingly born.

'Let's go,' Conner said, getting to his feet and adjusting his ker. He pulled his goggles down over his eyes. 'We'll be making camp in the dark if we keep lingering like this.'

His brother rose without complaint, and Conner helped him with the pack. He lifted the heavy tent with its lantern and bedding and stakes and sandfly, and the two of them left the great wall behind and marched to the thunder. They marched to the thunder, if not in step with it.

17

The Bull and the Boy

Legend had it that the great god Colorado and the white bull Sand had not always been at war. The constellations that hung in the heavens were not always thus, for the stars that outlined man and beast moved like planets, albeit more slowly.

In the olden days, the stars that marked the great warrior had been more closely arranged, the man a mere boy and not fully grown. But even when young he had shown promise as a hunter and a warrior. He and the bull whose tail always pointed north had been great friends in those days. They rode across the sky in defiance of the firmament, laughing and howling, playing and hunting. Together, they ruled all, for the spear and hoof were a keener measure of power than land or title. The world beneath them stood quiet, and water ran everywhere like the softest of sands.

But the white bull belonged not to the boy but to his chief, the One Clansman. Sand was the Royal Bull, protected from the hunt and sacred. So when Sand returned from a long absence with a nick in his hide, it was Colorado's spear that was blamed. Sand moaned and moaned and said this was not so, but none save for Colorado could understand the bull's laments. The others heard only the pain, which stoked their anger.

The One Clansman was pulled from his tent and was asked to make a judgement. He approached his injured bull and studied the wound. When his hand came away red, it painted the sky at dusk. 'It was the boy's spear,' he said.

Outraged, the people of the tribe drove the boy out. They cast stones at him, which broke into smaller and smaller rocks. And still they threw them, until there was stone no more. The boy Colorado wintered by himself beyond the jagged peaks where no rock could reach him. And so began the winter of ten thousand ages. During this time, the belt of the great warrior Colorado never rose above the horizon, as was common in the cold months. The months stayed cold for a very long time.

Rain froze and gathered. The ice grew so heavy, it made valleys where once there were plains. The rocks used to drive the boy out now covered the old world. Sand and ice took turns burying the clan.

Countless moons and a thousand winds passed. Now a man, Colorado chased a coyote up the mountains, following his tracks, which led him over the peaks and down to his people. He had been absent so long, no one recognised him. Not even the great bull Sand, who had grown old, his hide and eyes grey, the scar on his flank a black and jagged mark. Nor did Colorado recognise his old friend of the hunt. The years had been too many. The world was upside down. Ancient maps had been redrawn and relearned.

The only reminder of what had happened was that black scar on Sand's hide, and all the old bull knew of the wound was that the spear in Colorado's hand had made it, and so the bull and the grown boy began to war with one another. Man and Sand were now at odds, could no longer find harmony. A fiction had become truth. Lost was the true story of how Colorado had saved the bull's life. No one remembered the pack of coyotes clinging to Sand's hide, how they'd been felled with a mighty blow from Colorado's spear, a nick made in the bull's flesh as the point caught him as well. The truth had vanished like the sheets of ice. A hide bore a great gash, just as the plains where Colorado hunted held a jagged line in the crust of the earth that marked the boundary of No Man's Land.

Conner knew these legends, but he didn't trust them. He was old enough to know more than one version of these stories. The tales he had learned as a youth had changed, and he imagined they'd been changing for as long as they'd been told. Back when the legends began, the sand that made the dunes had probably been solid rock.

But there stood the valley out of which no man returned. It lay before their campsite as he and Rob staked the tent a dozen paces from its jagged border. It was a hard line, this. The desert floor was cracked, the hide of the bull an open wound. And across this blew the sand. Out of No Man's Land blew the sand. It blew across an injury that would never heal.

No Man's Land. Despite the name, Conner didn't know of a single boy his age who hadn't ventured out to the rift just to jump across and back. It was a dare undertaken in trembling packs of youths, the taboos whispered on long hikes, the false tales each year of a boy who had slipped and had fallen into the chasm and whose screams could still be heard. 'That's how deep it is,' an older boy would invariably warn with a sinister smile. 'You fall in and you fall for ever, screaming and screaming, until you grow old and die.'

Conner had heard these warnings as a boy. Later, he had spoken them to others. When he had gone on his own trek, he had been nine years old and had known that it was the wind that made that noise. And for all the boys who annually seemed to plunge to their deaths, none were ever named. There were never any funerals or sobbing mothers. It was just older kids trying to scare the younger ones.

The chasm itself was a mere two paces across where boys made brave leaps. Once they crossed, they would stand on the other side, trembling and afraid, chests thrust out in defiance of the thunderous drums from deep in the valley, feeling the wind and sand on their faces, thinking on warnings from fathers who had in their youth done the very same. And then they would jump right back, vastly relieved to have this ritual behind them.

And so it was said that no man returned from this land even though all men dipped a toe in unharmed. But Conner knew, as everyone else did, that legends and law did not have such hard borders as these. They were soft things, probed without bursting, until one pressed the point too far. And the danger in life was that no one knew when the skin would give, just as Colorado had not known how to fight an enemy who wrestled with his friend, how to aim true enough to hit only the one.

They set up the tent and made a fire and warmed bread and stew in silence, and Conner thought on these things. They lit the lamp and sipped caps of water and shared stories of stories about the long dead and long absent, and Conner thought on these things. That night, he lay in his father's tent while embers throbbed red outside, and he dwelt on the legends, thinking how a boy might leap across that gap and live, but how no boy truly believed he had entered No Man's Land. Not really. Not for honest. Because this was a place from which no soul returned.

No man, at least.

18

No Man's Land

C onner lay in his bedroll, counting down to the
moment, feeling in his bones what his old man
must've felt twelve years ago to the day. His heart
thrummed louder than the rolling booms in the distance.
He could feel his pulse in his temples. His blood ticked there
like one of Graham's old clocks. And after it had ticked for
what felt like days, he rose as quietly as his father once had.
Slipping from his bedroll, he could feel not only Rob's presence in the pitch black but also Palmer's, Vic's and his
mother's too. He was sneaking out on all of them.

The wind was his noisy accomplice. Conner waited until
a gust shook and flapped the canvas, and just as the breeze
passed and would not blow sand inside, he added to its
nocturnal noise by parting the tent and stealing into the
night.

The stars were bright outside, the sky clear, the air cool.
There was a half-moon low to the west, giving the sand an
even whiteness. That same moon had been high in the night
when he'd left the tent to pee and used this commotion to
remove his pack. He found the bag now by the light of the
firepit's glowing coals. He dumped the scoop out of his
father's boots and sat on the cool sand to pull them on.
Conner shivered and his teeth chattered, as much from nerves

as from the temperature. He felt the urge to pee again but knew he didn't really need to. There was no water in him, only fear.

A wailing lament blew across the Bull's gash, and the coals in the fire throbbed with life as they inhaled the breeze. There was a great and mysterious rumble in the distant earth that filled Conner's chest and throat, a sound of beating drums, that echo eternal. He rose and slung the pack over his shoulders, cinched the truss around his waist to carry the load on his hips, and turned to look back one last time. He studied the dark form of the tent, barely aglow from the coals, his brother sleeping inside, all alone. And he felt a final tug of guilt and doubt before steeling himself and heading off into the noisy beyond.

The moonlight showed him the break in the earth, that dark crack as real as a line on any map. Conner watched sand tumble in and blow past. How many millennia had it done this without filling that hole to the brim? Here was a wound incapable of healing, a slice in need of a stitch. People age day by day, he used to think. Minute by minute, much as a dune is built one grain at a time, much as one region of the desert overlaps and fades gradually into another. But here was a truth keenly felt: that some moments were like great rifts in the earth; some moments as discrete as a young boy's leap. Life was divided into these ages. Here one moment, in the great beyond the next. An eyeblink, and a boy becomes his father.

With barely more than a large stride, Conner crossed what in youth had required a lunge, and this renewed ritual filled him with courage. It was a symbolic break with all behind him. All that was left was the thunder to march into, as so many others had marched before him without coming back. Behind, nothing but sad wails would be left, wails he would not have to listen to. Despite the dread in his marrow, he told himself that this was not final. Four days' march out and four back, that was all. Four days to see what was over the horizon. And then he would return. He told himself this just as he was sure all those before him had. Just as his father had. He hiked towards the drums, promising himself he would return, and the wind picked up and cried at him for being so foolish—

But not the wind. That was not the wind crying. Ahead, in the pale moonlight, some different, anguished wail.

Conner crept forward. He pulled his knife from his belt, expected to find a coyote homing in on his scent or warning him away from its lair. And there, on all fours, sure enough—

But the coyote lifted its head into the moonlight, and it was the gaunt face of a human looking up at him. A boy.

Conner put his knife away and hurried forward. Some stupid kid from Springston. Someone there to dare the gash. He scanned the darkness for the other boys he knew would be there, the friends who had to witness who was courageous and who chickened out. Conner was pissed at having his more serious ritual disturbed by this petty one of youth. And so it was with anger that he rushed to the kid, ready to haul him up and toss him over the meaningless crack in the earth and back to his friends—

But Conner drew up as he approached. What had looked like a boy was a gaunt girl, her clothes in rags, crawling on hands and knees, the remains of a shoe dragging behind by its laces. Reaching ahead, she dug her fingers into the sand and pulled herself forward, seeming not to know Conner was there, simply staring ahead as if towards the glow of the distant fire.

'Be still,' Conner said. He dropped to his knees, and the child saw him at last. She clutched at him. Wide eyes and parched lips and skin pale as milk and moon. Conner held the frail child, the anger in him gone. Drums beat in his chest. Where were her friends? He scanned the sands and saw no one. Probably left her out here alone. Or a coyote had nipped her and scared off the others. She trembled against him, senseless and moaning.

Conner lifted her up – found she weighed less than his pack. He'd have to carry her across, back to the tent, and Rob would need to look after her and get her home. She had played at a boy's game, and look what it had cost her. She was lucky he had been out there. He would get her to the tent, could still vanish while Rob was occupied. This changed nothing. It was simply his first act as a free man. It was a life saved for a life lost. An even trade.

The step across the gap was more treacherous this time with the girl in his arms. It wasn't just the extra weight, it was being unable to see. He shuffled forward until his lead boot felt the edge, extended his other foot, and leaned forward into blind faith. His boot found the far side. And a story leapt up in his mind as he hurried towards the tent, a reason for him being out in the middle of the night.

'Rob!' he called. 'Rob! Wake up!'

There was a glow inside the tent a moment later. Conner started to set the child down outside the tent when the flap parted, his bleary-eyed brother peering out. 'What time—?' Rob began.

'Help me get her inside,' Conner said. And Rob did. The girl was unable to move on her own. The two boys got her into the tent, and Rob closed the flap on the wind. The dive light dangling from the tentpole threw light and shadows across the dishevelled bedding. Conner laid the girl out, then unbuckled his hip belt and shrugged off his pack. He caught Rob studying the heavy load as he set it aside.

'Don't just sit there,' Conner said. 'Get her some water.'

Rob looked up at him, blinked away the fog of sleep, and then lurched into action. He pawed through his bedroll to find his canteen while Conner got a good look at the girl. And the story he had made up in his head was shattered. Not the story he had prepared for Rob about stealing out for a piss and finding kids braving the gap – but the story he had told himself about where this child had come from.

Springston was not so big that he didn't recognise most faces, even if he didn't know their names. But this child was a stranger for other reasons. She was emaciated, her arms like the legs of a bird, one arm folded across her chest, the other bent around her head. Her britches were in tatters and of a strange cloth. The knees of this material were worn through, the flesh beneath torn and bloody and with dark rivulets tracing down her shins. The wounds were black from having dried at least a day ago, but there was fresh wetness on top from where the scabs had ripped and ripped. There was sand buried in all her wounds.

She moaned. Her lips were cracked and dry, her face burnt like a daywalker's. The shoulder of her shirt was missing, torn away, the rest of it barely hanging on. She looked as though she'd been dragged across a thousand dunes, and when Conner saw the bloody stumps of her fingers where her nails used to be, he knew that this poor creature had done her own dragging.

She was half dead and senseless. And Conner knew as a diver does when he raises an unseen relic from the cold sand that this thing at his feet did not come from Springston, nor from any other living world. This child was from No Man's Land. Someone had wandered out. Had crossed that impassable divide.

'How do I make her drink?' Rob asked. He had the canteen open and was looking to Conner for help.

'Just a cap,' Conner whispered, his mind reeling from what this girl meant. 'Give it to me.'

Rob poured a cap, the canteen trembling and spilling, and Conner wondered if his brother knew what he himself knew. Probably. Rob was the smart one.

'Careful,' he said, taking the cap of water. He positioned himself at the girl's side, folded her other frail arm across her chest, and slid his hand behind her neck. Gingerly, he lifted her head and scooted a knee behind her until she rested on his thigh. Another faint moan escaped her lips, a feeble sign of life. The girl appeared to be eight or nine years old, but it was difficult to tell, as gaunt and frail as she was.

Conner dribbled the water onto her cracked and bloody lips. He imagined he heard a sizzle there, as moisture hit the fire of thirst. Her cheeks twitched, a wince of pain, and he had to steady her head. He tried to drip the water past her wounded lips and directly onto her tongue.

'Easy,' Rob whispered.

'I know,' Conner said. He emptied the cap, watched the child's throat bob as her body unconsciously swallowed. 'Fill it again.' He passed the cap back to Rob, whose hand was steadier now as he poured another ration.

This time, the girl seemed to help with the drinking. A weak hand came up and rested on Conner's arm, nailless and bloody fingers curling there, tender and thankful. Desperate.

'Drink,' he told the girl, as if she needed any encouragement. She drank that cap and another, whispered for more, but Conner told Rob that was enough. Too much too fast was a bad thing. He had seen the madness of thirst before.

Her eyelids blinked open. Fluttered. She squinted up at

the dive light, which shone harshly down onto her face. 'Get that away,' Conner told Rob, but his brother was already doing it, was just as keenly aware of the girl's suffering.

Her face dimmed as Rob held the light by her side and out of her eyes. 'Easy,' Conner told the girl. 'We've got you. Everything's gonna be okay.' He said this for himself and for Rob as well. He wasn't sure. 'I want you to rest while I look over your wounds, okay? You can have some more water after I clean you up. I've gotta get this sand out of you.'

He reached for his pack, was thankful for the extra water, for all the emergency supplies he'd brought along that were meant for him and his trek.

The girl made a sound. 'Can . . . near . . .' she whispered.

Conner turned back to the child as she said the words a second time. 'What?' he asked.

The girl clutched his shirt with her small and bloodied hand and whispered it again.

'She wants us to come closer so we can hear,' his little brother said. Rob bent his head to better understand the girl's whispers. 'What do you need?' he asked.

But the girl was looking past him and up at Conner. Her eyelids fluttered open, and for a moment, her cloudy eyes grew bright like a break in a sandstorm. They were half-familiar eyes that bored into Conner as the girl summoned the strength to speak, pulling desperately on the air in that stuffy tent.

'Con . . . ner,' she said again, each syllable an effort, the corners of her mouth curling into the barest of smiles, a smile of some faint recognition and some great relief. '. . . Father . . . sent me.'

And then the light in her eyes went grey again, wounds and exhaustion claiming her. And this girl out of No Man's

Land fell into the stillness of death and sleep, Conner's name echoing softly in his ears, certain that he had never seen this girl in all his life, this girl who spoke of his father as if he were her own.

Part 3 – Return To Danvar

19

The Prodigal Daughter

VIC

All of life was like the deep sand, Vic had learned. From birth to death it was a series of violent constrictions, one after the other, an oily fist gripping hapless souls who popped free long enough to gasp half a lungful before they were seized again. This was how Vic had come to see the world. Everywhere she looked, she saw life squeezing people, forcing them from one tight spot to the next, the cruel palms of misfortune wrapped around hapless necks.

The secret to surviving these sufferings, she had found, was to keep perfectly still in its clutches. Learning how *not* to breathe was the answer. Learning how to find joy in not breathing. The only difference between a choke and a hug was an open pathway. Which was why Vic had taught herself to hold her breath. And then life had become a series of uninterrupted embraces.

At six hundred metres, sand refused to budge. It grew deaf as a selfish lover to her thoughts and wishes. It pinned her and held her helpless. Six hundred metres was well past where divers perished. Long before they reached these depths, most died because they struggled to simultaneously breathe and flow the sand. Wrestling two men at once was futile. Vic knew.

Another two minutes on that lungful of air and she would pass out. Already, lights popped in her vision, the edges growing dim. It would take her thirty minutes to get to the surface from that depth. Thirty minutes to go on two minutes of air. She would be fine. She spotted two of the hard metal cases near one another, the kind with the good seals. The cases stood out bright orange in her vision among the greens and blues of the softer bags. The oval conveyance device from which the bags had spilled was a brilliant white. All that metal, preserved by the deep pack of sand. It would live there for ever, that buried and gleaming steel. Too deep to pull it apart and haul it up. Too risky.

Vic grabbed the two cases, hoped they were the silver kind, the Samsonites, and flowed upward. She left through a gaping hole in what must've been a fabric roof at some point, a tent roof, a tent bigger than half of Low-Pub. She surged up and away from the giant metal birds with their outstretched wings and their hundreds of glass eyes in two neat rows, up towards the flashing transponder at four hundred metres, arriving with just enough air left in her starving lungs.

She found the tank she'd left buried and flowed the sand around the regulator. Slipped it into her mouth. A minimal amount of grit hit her tongue. She stopped thinking of moving and only of that column of sand high above her, all that weight pressing down and from all sides. She deflected that weight and took a deep breath. Another. Her suit thrummed with energy and impatience. It lived for the deep sand.

Leaving the tank and the transponder behind, she flowed upward to the next blinking light. Two more stops to the surface. Ignore the need to breathe. It wasn't the lack of air that made a person panic; it was the urge to *exhale*. It was the poisonous gas building up in her system that signalled her brain to expel the contents of her lungs. Her father had taught her this, had taught her all the mysteries of breathing. The body was not to be trusted, he had said. It could go for a long time without air. Longer and longer the more one worked on one's self-control.

Next stop. Another tank buried in advance. Here, the sand was almost back to normal. As the pack grew less dense, the colours seen through her visor shifted along the spectrum. She had her visor adjusted well beyond spec for the hard pack of near-concrete below. As she rose, the sand around her became like open air, shimmering with purples and unnatural hues. Her suit became similarly amped, even as its batteries ran dangerously low. She could feel a hum there in the looser sand. Her suit was made for the depths; it was revved. Turned up like this, she could feel its energy in her teeth. Here was another secret of the deep dive: you had to be willing to don a suit that felt as though it wanted to kill you. You had to pull on a visor that showed you nonsense. And then you had to dive straight down until the world felt right again.

Vic reached the next buried tank and took a long pull, swallowed some sand in the process. The most important part of diving deep, of course, was convincing everyone else that it was impossible. Part of this was letting people think she never dived on tanks. And mostly, this was true. Other divers had seen her go down to three hundred metres on a single breath. When she'd started staging tanks to go deeper, she had told no one.

The secrecy was important, because if anyone knew it was possible, they would strive until they found a way. All great discoveries were like this. It was the rare souls full of hope who showed the world what could be done; and then came the thundering herds, those doubters and naysayers who had once put up barriers, now shoving everyone out of their way.

Vic realised the truth of this as she breached the surface and felt the rising sun on her face and the wind against her skin. If a man ever reached six hundred metres, no way would he keep that a secret. And then everyone would be down there, scrounging for what was hers and hers alone.

She flipped up her visor and rested on the warm sand for a deep breath. Another. She amped her suit and flowed the loose sand off her gear and out of her hair. It cascaded around her like a morning mist. Reaching into the sand – flowing the dune around her arm like so much water – she hauled out her buried gear bag. The sand in all directions was clear, none of the abandoned clutter and junk that marked popular dive sites. This was the best part of diving deep: avoiding the crowds, not worrying about some scavenger nabbing one of her finds, not dealing with the cranks and topside pirates who dug noisily through the heaps of rubbish left behind.

With her pack out of the sand, Vic powered off her humming suit and could feel her molars again. Low-Pub clattered noisily in the distance. The thrum of generators, the rap of hammers on nails, the sporadic gunfire, the noise of life.

A fitful wind blew across the dunes, carving the tops of them flat and pushing their mounded bulks ever westward. Vic dug her canteen out of her pack, took a long swig and wiped her chin. Now for the payout. She hoped for enough to cover the rent and what she owed Yegery for the tanks and air. She'd rather not put in another deep dive this week, not if it could be helped. Her ribs were sore from being down so long, and her left knee felt tweaked. In the deep sand, all it took was losing flow around a leg for a split second for a foot to get twisted. She'd seen divers come up with arms and legs out of joint, screaming and spitting sand. Or those who got the bends, who forgot to keep the weight around them deflected, and surfaced with bubbles of air under their skin like little blisters, the soreness in their joints, if they were lucky. More often, the divers who lost their concentration never came back at all.

She screwed the cap back onto the canteen and reached for one of the metal cases. There was a silver and a black. The latter had much of its paint scratched off from the trip through the sand. The cases themselves would fetch thirty coin apiece. If the locks worked, her friend J-Mac could file up some keys. Cost five coin apiece but would add fifteen to the price, and Vic knew a couple of shopkeeps in town who needed better safes. As far as she was concerned, both bags were already sold. Here was coin temporarily trapped in the shape of something else.

She started with the black one, knocked the latches with the butt of her palm and jarred the sand inside the mechanism loose. The latches were stuck. She had a dull metal rod for this, pulled it out of her boot and rested the case on its end. With a swift stab, she slammed the two latches, and both popped open. She put the rod back into her boot and set the case flat, was about to open it, expecting the typical jumble of clothes to pop out, when the sand rumbled beneath her—

Before Vic could slap her suit on, she and the two cases dropped down into the desert floor. The sand hardened all around her, leaving just her head and neck free.

Panic surged in her chest and sand blew into her mouth;

it mixed there with the adrenalin taste of metal. She had filled her lungs by reflex – had expanded her chest – so she could still breathe. Her hand had flown towards her suit's power switch, was nearly there. She strained against the packed earth, wiggled her shoulders and arm, just needed another inch—

In a fountain of sand, Marco emerged beside her. He floated up to his feet with a twirl and a flourish and shook the sand out of his dreadlocks. Vic averted her head as far as she could and squinted against the flying sand. 'I'm gonna fucking kill you,' she said.

When she opened her eyes she found Marco lowering himself down beside her as if to do a push-up, until his grizzled face was just a few inches from hers. 'Did you say you're gonna fuck me?' He lifted his thick eyebrows, mocking her.

'I said I'm gonna *kill* you.' Vic spat sand. 'I'm counting to three, Marco. One—'

Marco lowered himself and crushed his lips against hers. Vic bit his tongue and Marco pulled away, laughing.

'Two, motherfucker.'

Marco pointed a finger at her. 'Now that's totally not fair. I haven't fucked your mother *once* since you and I started going steady.'

'Three, asshole.'

Vic got her finger to the switch, and the power in her suit surged. The rage of being pinned down exploded through her, that same rage she often felt when Marco got too rough in bed and would laugh and hold her wrists, that feeling of helplessness, of wondering when play became abuse, biting on her lip to keep from crying in front of him, remembering the last men who had held her down.

With her suit humming and teeth shivering, no one could hold her down.

A ram of buried sand flew up from beneath Marco and slammed into his chest, launching him and the two cases into the air. Vic heard an 'oomph!' escape from Marco's lungs. She flowed herself up to the sand's surface as Marco shot skyward, yelping now, waving his arms fruitlessly, an explosion of clothes around him like a flock of startled birds. Fuck. She'd hoped to send him up three feet. Marco went up thirty. Asshole was gonna break his neck.

Vic knelt and slid one hand into the sand. With her other hand, she adjusted the band around her forehead. She watched Marco plummet back to the earth, screaming like a crow, half a clothing shop raining down around him. He hit the flowing sand with a splash, and Vic had to avert her face from the grit. She flowed him up to the surface, but he was face down. Using the sand, she rolled him over, worried he'd blacked out, but Marco was spitting grit and coughing, his face up towards the sun. She froze him like that, partly submerged, shoulders pinned in hard pack, and crawled across the sand to lean over him.

'Fuck me—' Marco whimpered.

'Wow,' Vic said. 'Still in the mood?' She ran her hand across the sand until it was over his crotch. 'Maybe a few sand needles will take the edge off?'

'Please—' Marco said. 'My ribs—'

Vic put a finger to her lover's lips. 'What I want to hear right now is the most goddamn convincing apology that pretty little mouth of yours has ever uttered. I want to fucking believe you. I want tears in those big brown eyes of yours. I want you to shed water for me. Say something to make my heart flutter. Go.'

A pair of trousers struck the sand right by Marco's face, knocking more sand into his mouth. He spat and sputtered and closed one eye.

'Not very convincing,' she said.

'I'm fucking sorry,' Marco told her. 'It was goddamn stupid of me. I wanted to surprise you, just wanted to hold you down and kiss you so fucking hard because I love you. You're the only one for me. I swear on all that's holy I'll never do it again, and I'll rip the balls off anyone who tries—'

A pair of pink panties, caught in the wind, fluttered down and struck Marco in the face like a bright bird dive-bombing his worm-pink tongue. Marco yelped, the sound muffled by the underwear, and began to shake his head, trying to get it off. He spat and made blowing sounds. The panties fluttered but stayed in place. Vic covered her mouth and howled. She pounded the sand with the flat of her palm and rolled onto her side, doubling over with laughter.

Marco screamed for her to help. He shook his head back and forth, but Vic could barely see. She had a brief panic at the thought of not being able to stop laughing – ever. It was more difficult to breathe right then than it had ever been in the deepest of sand.

'Goddamnit,' Marco shouted through the underwear. 'Help me!'

Vic managed to sit up straight. She wiped her eyes and looked down at her fingers. 'Holy shit,' she said, laughing and disbelieving. 'You fucking made me cry.'

20

A Scrounger's Trade

Vic was still laughing fifteen minutes later. It took that long to round up the clothes scattered by the wind. She shook the sand out of every piece of underwear she found and asked Marco if he needed a new ker. While she howled, he ignored her. He seemed morose as they lugged the bags and her dive gear over a dune and to his sarfer. Marco had laid the mast back to make it hard to spot. A mast upright in the middle of nowhere was a homing beacon for other scavengers – or a warning to a girl that her boyfriend was gonna fucking prank her instead of just picking her up at the dive site as she'd asked. But she had got the last laugh. Was still laughing as they reached the sarfer.

'It totally isn't as funny as you're making out,' Marco said. He loaded her dive gear into his haul rack. 'Maybe if the bag was full of *clean* clothes. Maybe then.'

'Oh, shit.' Vic grabbed his arm. She hadn't smelled the clothes to see if they had been worn or not. The seals in those Samsonites were really that good.

'Yeah,' Marco said. 'Shit is right.'

After half a minute, Marco had to help Vic up from the sand. Dabbing her eyes and seeing the tears there, she told Marco, 'This is the happiest day of my life.'

'Yeah, you suck. Lesson learned and all that. And Jesus, can you please take it easy on who you tell?'

Vic smiled at him.

'Ah, fuck, Vic, I'm gonna hear about this for weeks.'

'Oh, hell no. This is going to last a lot longer than that. And if these clothes fetch a coin less for all the sand you got in them, that's coin you owe.'

Marco looked like a kicked dog. Vic almost felt sorry for him. Almost. She loaded the black bag into the haul rack, and Marco did the same with the silver. Behind them, twin sets of ruts streaked their way across the dunes. Already, the lines in the distance were fading, filled in by the wind. Vic marvelled, not for the first time, on all the wheeled conveyances she'd seen buried beneath the deep sand. To think there was some distant past or place where wheels made any sense—

'You ever think about the old world?' Vic asked.

Marco cinched the haul rack straps across the first bag. 'All the time,' he said. 'I think about digging it up and selling it.'

'No, I mean, do you think about what happened to it? What went wrong?'

Marco used his ker to dab sweat from his brow. 'Who says anything went wrong? The sand piles up. That's what it does. It's still happening.'

'I don't think so,' Vic said. 'There's stuff down there that's . . . too different. Like from another people.'

'Different Lords, different times,' Marco said. He secured the second bag and tugged on the handle, made sure it wouldn't bounce free during the ride into town.

'Is that what you think? Lords come and go, Marco, and nothing changes. Not like the difference between this world and the one down there—'

'Nothing changes?' Marco turned and tugged the ker down from his mouth. 'How can you say that? So what're we fighting for?'

Vic laughed. 'I'm not fighting. I come to your meetings for the free booze. And the solid dating pool.'

Marco looked genuinely offended. 'You don't mean that.'

'Sure I do. C'mon, you don't think it really matters who owns that spring or patch of dirt or cistern, do you? Or who owes retribution to who? It's all bullshit. There's not a soul in the Legion who remembers the original offence—'

'You're wrong. We didn't start this—'

'Nobody did. That's my point. It's boys blowing up markets as far down as I've dived. And nobody dives deeper than me, Marco. So what was the old world fighting about? And how come the things we bring up are nicer than the things we make today? You ever think about that? Where are we heading if all the nice things are buried in the past? Where's any of this getting us?'

'It's too early for this shit,' Marco said. 'Give me a hand with the mast. And pull your ker up. All that flapping is letting sand in—'

'Ho, Marco!'

Vic stopped herself from telling Marco what he could do with his own mouth. She turned and followed his gaze, the pair of them shielding their eyes in the low morning sun. A figure stood atop a nearby dune, a silhouette with a tall lance in one hand, the other arm raised in salute. The mast of a sarfer could be seen jutting up beyond the dune, the sail tightly furled.

'See?' Vic said. 'While you were screwing around, trying to scare me, someone spotted your sarfer.'

'Shit.'

'Wait, is that Damien? Oh, he's gonna love this.'

'This what? You mean the underwear thing? Please, Vic, I'm begging you. At least wait until we get to town. Or tonight when everyone's drunk and no one will remember. Don't let him be the first to know. Not Damien.'

Vic squeezed Marco's neck and laughed. 'Some freedom fighter you are.'

Marco tensed. 'That's just it. I'm a *fighter.*' He made a fist, and his great tan biceps bulged, scars and tattoos straining.

Vic stopped smiling. 'I was stressing the *freedom* part. You forget that, and all you are is fighting. I'll tell who I want, when I want. Freedom, Marco. Don't get like these assholes and fall in love with the fighting. Then you're just setting off bombs because you like the noise they make.'

Marco didn't say anything as Damien glissaded down the dune towards them, causing a gentle avalanche and using his spear for balance. He stomped over with a grin, and his eyebrows lifted when he spotted the two bags in the haul rack. 'Jesus. Nice find, guys.' His eyes went to the trails left in the sand, quickly filling. 'How the hell do you two score every time you go out? And way out in the middle of nowhere?'

Vic didn't say that it was usually *her* scoring while Marco watched their things on the surface. 'Just lucky, I guess.'

'Clothes?'

'Mostly underwear,' she said. And before Marco could respond, she added: 'For the *ladies.*' She fought off a bout of giggles.

'Hey, my wife could use some. Maybe hook me up before you sell to Jimbo or Sandy and they get their squeeze. I'll pay what they pay.'

'Slow down,' Marco said. 'Don't be in a rush to get our panties off us.' He laughed.

'Maybe they're for *him*,' Vic said, teasing Damien.

'Yeah, fuck you two. And here I was getting ready to do you a favour. But I guess you can wait until you get to town to find out the news yourselves. To think I was gonna ask you to tag along.' He turned and marched back towards his sarfer.

'Wait. Tell us what?' Marco asked.

Damien held up his middle finger and kept walking.

'Tell us fucking what?' Marco demanded.

'I'll trade you,' Vic called.

Damien slowed. He turned and glanced at the bags. 'Trade for what?'

'Give me the news, and I'll tell you the funniest story you've ever heard in your entire fucking life.'

Damien waved his hand and spat sand. 'News like this don't go for a joke.'

'Don't you fucking dare,' Marco hissed, but this only seemed to get Damien's attention.

'It's not a joke,' Vic said. 'It's a true story. And I promise you won't be disappointed. You'll be getting the good end of this bargain, I swear.'

'I dunno . . .' Damien said, walking back their way. 'There ain't *never* been news this big. But fuckit, I'd rather you hear it from me than from someone else.'

'You first,' Vic said. In truth, she didn't care about his news. She was just rehearsing how best to tell this story, a story that would get many retellings.

Damien took a deep breath and searched their faces. The two sand divers waited. The clatter of Low-Pub spilled over the dunes, and sand rode through the sky above their heads.

'Fucking Danvar,' Damien finally said. 'Somebody found it.'

21

Buried Alive

PALMER

I t was a crypt for a king. His friend Hap had left him to die in a crypt for a goddamn king – this tomb of untold riches. Palmer was going to take his last breath in a manor no Lord of Springston could refuse. A place where a truly great man should be laid to rest.

And it'll do for me, he thought morosely.

The air in the buried sandscraper tasted stale and seemed to be growing thinner. But it had outlasted his water. Palmer had poured himself half-caps for what felt like five days. He had eaten both strips of jerky one tiny nibble at a time, like a mouse trying to win the cheese from a loaded trap. Now all of that was gone, along with fifteen or twenty pounds of himself. He hadn't been eating that well even before the march north. The stress of a deep dive always messed with his appetite. No . . . it hadn't been the dive. It had been the camping trip coming up, the anniversary. He never ate well before that trip. Had bugged out the year before. Damn . . . maybe he'd already been down there a whole week. Con and Rob would go without him, just like last year. Con and Rob. The thought of his younger brothers shook him. They would never hear from their big brother again.

Or maybe it hadn't been so long. He had counted five days – five urges to sleep – but maybe it was four. Hell, it could be ten days or ten *hours* since Hap had abandoned him. His mind was playing tricks. He heard noises and voices. Had a dream about his father that seemed so real, Palmer had truly thought he was dead and in heaven. Ah, a crypt fit for a king, and where was his asshole father buried? His father's bones had ground to sand in No Man's Land, that's where. A pauper burial for a Lord. A place for desperate dying. It was as ironic as Palmer's lavish crypt.

But Palmer had been old enough to remember a Lord's life. He had bawled when his mom had pulled them away from the wall. Had bawled when he had been put in a different school with strange kids who smelled bad. Had bawled harder when he could no longer smell them because he had begun to stink as they did. What he wouldn't give to have all those tears back. Just a capful.

He licked his cracked and burning lips. The dream about his father made sense now. Some part of him had been dwelling on the anniversary. He'd let Con and Rob down again. He was a shitty brother and a shitty son and did not deserve to die in so fine a place as this.

Such were his wild thoughts as he left the conference room where he'd been imprisoned by his hope of Hap's return. He staggered out and through the dark building, his dive light as dim as he could make it, its staid old battery down to rations as well. Maybe he'd find a pool of water where a spring had flooded or where trapped moisture had drained down through the impossibly tight pack. But there was little hope of that. He left the conference room to get away from his nightmares and his failures. To let his body wander instead of his mind.

Before he died, he should go out into the sand one last

time. Better to perish there and be discovered by another diver as they came to pick the bones of this city. He still had a good charge in his suit, might see how far he could make it before the sand filled his lungs. But some naive part of him kept thinking Hap would come back, that Brock would send others, that he would be a fool to go out and die when there was still air in that building to breathe. At any moment, Hap could burst in with a second set of twin tanks, laughing and saying he'd only been gone two hours and here's the coin those scroungers paid and all the beer and pussy in Springston would be theirs.

Palmer kept thinking this, but the hope had grown as stale and thin as the oxygen. The hope that had kept him prisoner in that room with the chairs and the great table and the brewing machine had weakened. Gone was the need to be there when the divers came for him. And as that hope waned, he left through the door that had damned him, that heavy door that Hap had slammed shut on his face, and with his dive light barely aglow, he nosed around his crypt for the first time.

He had seen many crumbling office buildings full of sand outside Springston, but never on such a scale as this, never so pristine. The buildings he had seen had been scavenged for centuries. Men with mastery over the sand had ripped out great holes and had salvaged almost anything worth taking. But Palmer now strolled through a perfect re-creation of that long-dead world. It was a museum for the buried gods and the world they had lived in. His fragile mind tallied stacks and stacks of coin as he felt his way down the hall. There were clocks; pictures framed and behind perfect glass; recessed lights and miles and miles of copper wire; unbroken tile; wood countertops. Coin everywhere.

Other divers would come and claim these things. Probably

not Hap, for the guilt would gnaw at him. At least, Palmer hoped it would. No, it would be some other diver who would find his bones. They would remove Palmer's skeleton from his suit piece by piece and marvel that he still had a charge left, that he had been too scared to make for the surface, and someone would point out that he didn't have tanks, and some other asshole would say that there was a girl from Low-Pub who could've done it, and none of them would know that these bones in their hands belonged to that girl's brother.

He tried another room. A bathroom. Porcelain fixtures and indoor plumbing. He felt insane for twisting the spigots, but no one was watching.

The next room was a jackpot. A bonanza of riches. A small room no bigger than a bed but full of tools. Brooms and mops and much else. He picked up one of the brooms. Synthetic bristles. Plastic. As good as the day it was made. Palmer kicked some of the scrum from his boots to the marble tile and whisked the sand around with the broom. His mother – the mother of his youth – would've loved such a broom. Palmer flashed back to chasing Conner through the house when they were boys, giving him a beating before his sister caught up to them both and dispensed *two* beatings. Back in the closet, he shook bottles of liquids, cracked the cap on one of them and took a sniff. His nose burned. If he needed an easier way out than the sand, here it was.

He surveyed all the useful things packed into such a small space, enough coin to retire on, and closed the door. Someone else would come and take these things. They would figure out a way to dive deep and bring it all back. Wouldn't bother with him, though. Palmer thought of the city that would be built above these dunes on all that was stolen from the past. There would be an orgy of excess. A gold rush like the old-timers used to tell of Low-Pub's founding. No one would remember the first person to set foot in that scraper. He pictured Hap in the Honey Hole at that very moment, blisteringly drunk, delicious golden beer everywhere, telling the gathered that he'd been the first one inside, that he'd discovered Danvar all on his own. Fucking Hap.

The next room was an office. Palmer checked the drawers, hoping for a canteen, even though the ancient peoples seemed rarely to use them. Dry pens. Knick-knacks. A silver key, which Palmer couldn't help but slip into his belly pocket. Folded paper. He pulled this out and held it close to his dive light. A map. Dark lines and place names. The word 'Colorado' caught his eye. Palmer slipped this into his pocket too. When they found his body, they would find something useful. Find that *he* had been useful.

In the centre drawer he found raw riches. Coin. An entire pile of them jumbled together as if they'd been swept inside ages ago. They weren't even locked up, just left among paper clips and pens and other worthless artefacts as if these trinkets were as dear as money.

Copper and silver, they were unscratched by sand. Palmer studied them one at a time before throwing them into his stomach pocket with the key. There grew a jangle by his belly to go with the grumbles, a two-man band. He would die wealthy. Starving and wealthy. Whoever found him would bury him well and pour a beer into his grave. A note! Palmer would write a note to go with the coin, a note to his pall-bearer and one to his sister Vic. He would brag about being brave in the first message and admit to being an idiot in the second. He rummaged for a pencil, found one, pulled out his dive knife and scraped the point sharp. It felt good to have something to do, something as simple as sharpening lead. He slipped the knife back into his boot and found a pad of paper. Eaten through by worms, but it would do. He scratched out instructions for his burial and a quick note to Vic saying he was sorry. He signed his name and started to write a date, was just going to guess, but then wrote the anniversary of his father's disappearance instead. Probably not right, but it was close enough and there was poetry to it. Poetry was better than truth. He folded both notes and stuffed them in with the heavy sag of coin. Hopefully it wouldn't be Hap who found him. Hap wouldn't come back. Unless he was arriving right then and Palmer was missing him.

In a panic – despite the days of staring at the drift of sand with no sign of Hap – Palmer imagined his friend coming back right then, seeing that Palmer was gone, and leaving him for a second time. Palmer rushed back to the hall, hands on his belly to keep the coins from sloshing around, and he heard a noise. The creak of an old building with the weight of a world on its head. Coming from across the hall.

'Hap?' He called out his friend's name, felt a little delirious. How long had he slept the last time he'd lain down? Was he still dreaming? 'Father?'

There was a noise on the other side of the door. Palmer looked up and down the hallway, the dim red glow of his dive light barely penetrating a dozen paces. He tried to get his bearings. Was this the room he'd been wasting away inside of? Did he get turned around? The darkness beyond the feeble reach of his dive light made everything seem distant and full of quiet potential. He tried the door and found it unlocked. A single door. A different room. He stepped inside and saw rows of desks, those flat plastic screens on each. Several of the desks were jumbled together; they had been shoved away from a large pile of drift pushing its way into the room.

Palmer's brain wrestled with possibilities: an old breach, a building giving way from years of the crush. It was on the opposite side of the building from his approach with Hap, so he hadn't seen it. He might have swum right in if he had.

Perhaps other divers had made this. A new hole. They had come here while he had slept. Brock's men – with Yegery, the old dive master, to confirm the find and salvage a few things. Yes, there were signs that others had come. Bootprints of sand. Two desks cleaned off and pushed together, away from the others. Yes. The plundering had begun. Divers must be descending on this place as he stood there. *He would be saved.*

Or was it Hap? Maybe Hap had come back for him, hadn't found the other way in, had made a new way, and had left tanks of air for him so Palmer could save himself. Yes! There were the tanks, a triple set, sitting beyond the reach of the sand like a gift from the gods. Unless he had gone mad. Unless this was an apparition like his father. Unless he was still dreaming as before.

Palmer staggered through the desks and towards the dive tanks, wanting to touch them to see if they were real. All the possibilities for how this drift of sand had breached the building, and the true answer never occurred to him. Never occurred to him even though he should've remembered. Should've remembered that he and Hap weren't the first to be sent down to discover Danvar. And they hadn't found the bodies of the other two divers in the sand. All of this would come too late. It would come to him as the animal shot out from behind a desk, claws out and teeth bared, hell-bent and determined to kill him.

22

A Fight with Madness

The man was naked. He was all bones and ribs and snarling mouth. The front of him was caked in blood, a smear of charcoal black in the dim red glow of Palmer's dive light. There was just a flash of this grisly image before the man crashed into Palmer, knocking him to the ground, desperate hands clenching around his throat.

Palmer saw pops of bright light as his head hit the floor. He couldn't breathe. He heard his own gurgles mix with the raspy hisses from the man on top of him. A madman. A thin, half-starved and full-crazed madman. Palmer fought for a breath. His visor was knocked from his head. Letting go of the man's wrists, he reached for his dive knife, but his leg was pinned, his boot too far away. He pawed behind himself and felt his visor, had some insane plan of getting it to his temples, getting his suit powered on, overloading the air around him, trying to shake the man off. But as his fingers closed on the hard plastic – and as the darkness squeezed in around his vision – he instead swung the visor at the snarling man's face, a final act before the door to that king's crypt sealed shut on him.

A piercing shriek returned Palmer to his senses. Or was it the hands coming off his neck? The naked man howled and lunged again, but Palmer got a boot up, caught the man in the chest, kicked him. He scrambled backward while the man reeled. *The other diver. Brock's diver.* Palmer turned and crawled on his hands and knees to get distance, got around a desk, moving as fast as he could, heart pounding. *Two divers. There had been two divers.* He waited for the man's partner to jump onto his back, for the two men to beat him to death for his bellyful of jangling coin—

—when he bumped into the other diver. And saw by his dive light that he was no threat. And the bib of gore on the man chasing him was given sudden meaning. Palmer crawled away, sickened. He wondered how long the men had been down here, how long one had been eating the other.

Hands fell onto his boots and yanked him, dragging him backward. A reedy voice yelled for him to be still. And then he felt a tug as his dive knife was pulled from its sheath, stolen. Palmer spun onto his back to defend himself. His own knife flashed above him traitorously, was brought down by those bone-thin arms, was meant to skewer him.

There was a crunch against his belly. A painful blow. The air came out of Palmer. The blade was raised to strike him again, but there was no blood. His poor life had been saved by a fistful of coin.

Palmer brought up his knee as the man struck again – and shin met forearm with a crack. A howl, and the knife was dropped. Palmer fumbled for it, his dive light throwing the world into pale reds and deep shadows. Hand on the hilt, his knife reclaimed, he slashed at the air and the man fell back, hands up, shouting, 'Please, please!'

Palmer scooted away, keeping the knife in front of him. He was weak from fitful sleep and lack of food, but this poor creature before him seemed even weaker. Enraged and with the element of surprise, the man had nearly killed him, but it had been like fighting off a homeless dune-sleeper who had jumped him for some morsel of bread. Palmer dared to turn his dive light up so he could see the man better.

'Sorry. I'm sorry,' the man said. 'Thought you were a *ghost.*'

The blood on the man's chin and down his neck made Palmer's stomach turn. 'Did you think I was your partner come back to get you for what you did to him?'

The thin man pointed a bony finger at Palmer. 'You're a diver. Did the others send you? Oh, thank the heavens. Thank the heavens!' He glanced down at his naked form. His eyes shot between the desks where the corpse lay. 'No, no. I didn't kill him. He died out in the sand. I brought him in here. I was . . . I was starving. Oh, God. Food. Do you have food? Water?' He staggered forward.

'Stay back,' Palmer said.

The man hesitated. 'Juice,' he said. 'I used up all my juice on the way down. Did you bring a charge? I've got a tank of air, but no juice. Help me.'

'You tried to kill me.'

'I thought you were a ghost.' He took another step forward, wild eyes on Palmer's dive light. 'Give me my knife back,' he said, baring bloody teeth. 'I found that. Found it in your boot. In *my* boots.'

The man screamed and lunged, a bloodthirsty cry, naked limbs all bone and sinew, a mad and desperate creature in the red throb of Palmer's flickering, dying light. The two men crashed together. A clatter as metal fell to tile, a single coin spilling out of the gash in Palmer's suit, a sound two scroungers knew well, the price of one life saved and another taken as bare flesh impaled itself on a dive knife and a belly opened like a purse, a cost far graver than coin spilling to the floor.

23

Missing Treasure

VIC

Vic and Marco sailed back into a Low-Pub that had transformed into chaos. It was not the sleepy town they usually found after their pre-dawn dives; this was a town startled into frenzy, a transformation jolted by the electricity of rumour. The tale of Danvar's discovery had sent the diving community into a tizzy, and along with that community the rest of the small southern town. Those who rummaged scrapheaps, the welders who reshaped old steel, the women who catered to men's lust, the shopkeeps and barkeeps and everyone with a love of coin, all seemed to be out in the streets gossiping or packing their sarfers or checking their gear before they ventured out to find the great and untouched city said to be buried a mile deep.

But confirming a legend may have heightened its allure without any promise of bounty in return. Damien had warned them that no one knew exactly where the city was, only that a couple of divers were said to have found it. Some drunken brigand had flapped his gums in a crowded bar, claimed to have been there to witness the discovery, and now that same brigand was said to be dead. It had sounded to Vic like the sort of unsubstantiated nonsense that scavengers and conspiracy theorists were drawn to. And even as she and Marco pulled into the marina and began to voice doubts about the veracity of these Danvar claims, other sarfers were flying out in all directions at once. They could hear rumours being shouted from one deck to another over the whistling winds, each diver seizing on the location that made the most sense to them. It was clear from the chaos around the marina that no one knew where Danvar was, but that wasn't going to stop anyone from being there when it was uncovered. It was madness. Vic was about to tell Marco this, when he voiced madness of his own.

'So where should we start?' he asked.

Vic moved to the foot of the mast and helped him flake the sail against the boom. 'What do you mean, "start"?' she asked. 'You don't believe this nonsense, do you?' She lashed the sail to the boom and saw that Marco was tying slip knots while she was using reefs. As if he planned on heading right back out and she was looking to stay.

'It's probably a load of shit, but what if? You'd rather sit here and miss the find of the century?'

'No, I'd rather sit here than chase my tail around the thousand dunes. If there *was* a find of the century, I'd go. But we both know there isn't.' She rolled her eyes as Marco undid one of her reef knots and looped in a slip. 'You do whatever. I've been up and diving since four while you've been napping in your sarfer. I'm gonna shake the sand out of these clothes, see what's in this other case, and then get some sleep.'

Marco looked hurt.

'If you find Danvar,' she added, 'come and wake me.'

'Well, I need to run to my place and grab my tanks. But yeah, I'll catch you later.' He leaned over the boom for a kiss, and Vic obliged.

'Later,' she said. She hopped down to the sand, her knee still a little sore, and slung her gear bag over her shoulder.

She grabbed the two cases from the sarfer's haul rack and extended the handles. Dragging them to her house on those small and useless wheels, she cursed the madness the old world's allure made in men. The promise of buried treasure warped their minds. Vic liked to think she was more rational than that.

But of course, her mind was prone to dreams of sudden riches too. And she had her own guesses about the location of Danvar. She wasn't immune to the idea of seeing a city untouched by time and scavenge. Even with the craziness around her, the hysteria, the fun she might poke at Marco and these people off their rockers, she knew her own rocker was prone to tipping too. It tipped right back, that feeling of vertigo as some momentous event loomed underfoot, until she was the one asking herself: *What if it's real? What if?*

But only a fool runs around shouting 'A find! A find!' when they haven't seen it in their own visor. Right? She tried to convince herself. Because the greater fool sits in a bar alone, nursing a warm beer, while hauls of coin start coming into town and the stories that will one day be legend fill the pub. It's a fool either way, so it's all about cost. Which fool would she more loathe to be?

She dragged her two bags across the sand. It was early morning, but so many people were out and about. Divers who would've normally asked where she'd found the cases rushed right by in a hurry. Shopkeeps who would've begged her to come pop those latches on their counters were too busy haggling over the rising price of a fuel cell or the use of a generator or the purchase of a haul net. Vic slid through the throngs to her house. She set the cases down outside her shack and fumbled in her pocket for the key. Out of habit, she tapped her toes on the kickplate along the bottom of the door to knock the scrum from her boots loose. The gentle raps caused the door to swing open, hinges squealing. Vic pulled her hand out of her pocket. She was damn sure she'd latched it when she'd left.

'Palm?' she called.

Her brother often treated the place like it was his, had started spending as much time in Low-Pub as Springston and liked to take advantage of the fact that Vic spent most of her nights over at Marco's. He was the only other person with a key. There was no answer from inside. She studied the door, saw the scratch marks from someone jemmying the thing open with a screwdriver, which brought back memories of the dozens of times she'd jemmied the damn thing open with a screwdriver. She hesitated before going in, wondered if maybe the latch just hadn't caught that morning. It'd been dark and she'd been groggy when she'd left.

'Hey, Palm? You asleep?'

Vic reached into her boot and pulled her latch-break out. She used the metal rod to push the door all the way open. It was dark inside, the west-facing windows getting little of the morning light. She didn't hear anyone. Must've not pulled the door shut when she left. That was it. She lit a candle and checked the bedroom and bathroom, was satisfied with her theory. She went back for the two bags, brought them inside and kicked the door shut.

Two days, max. That's how long before they'd know if Danvar had been discovered. No harm in waiting and getting in on the action late. No harm in that. She had plenty of places she could dive that no one else could. Hell, it might get nice and quiet around Low-Pub for a couple of days once everyone cleared out. That would be a pleasant change.

Vic stood under the beam she used for pull-ups and jumped up and grabbed the palm-worn wood. She held herself with one hand while she patted for the key. Securing it, she dropped back down and removed the padlock from the hatch in the living-room floor. Grabbing the black case full of clothes, she lowered it down to the slope of drift below. The silver case she left out; Vic wanted to take a peek before she got some rest.

Opening her icebox, she grabbed half a shrivelled lime and a jar of homebrew, squeezed the former into the latter and sipped on her breakfast. She set the Samsonite up on its edge and tried the latches. Stuck. Both of them. She took another swig of the beer, stale but cold, and was wiping her mouth when there was a knock at the door.

'Begging won't make me change my mind—' she started to tell Marco, when the door opened and two men barged into the room. Brigands, by the smell and look of them. Vic recognised one of the men. Paulie. He used to run with the Low-Pub Legion. Couldn't hack it as a diver and took to muscling people. The red Legion ker was gone, though. Both men sported the golden kers of the northern wastes. Vic wondered what the hell these guys were doing this far south. And then she saw that the bigger man had a gun on his belt. Probably didn't work – as most of them didn't – but the problem was in the *probably*.

'Hey, wrong house, assholes.' Vic stood up and blocked the view of the Samsonite. 'If you're looking for Danvar, it's not in my cellar—'

'Save it, Vic,' Paulie said. 'Where the fuck is Palm?'

'How the hell should I know? And you guys are tracking sand in.'

The larger man with the gun stomped towards the bedroom and peered inside.

'He's not here,' Vic said. 'You've got the wrong fucking house.'

'Well, we hear he spends time all over the place.'

'He's probably in Springston,' Vic said, trying to throw them off.

'We already checked Springston,' Paulie told her.

'Yeah? Look, I don't care what he owes you. Dusting up my place is gonna get you in *my* debt—'

'Chill with the tough act,' the big guy said. He pointed a finger at her. 'Where the fuck is he?'

'Even if I knew, I wouldn't tell you.'

The large brigand made a move in her direction, but Paulie held the man back. 'She don't know. She's just fucking with you.'

The brigand spat at Vic's boots.

'Lovely,' she said. 'I'll tell my brother you boys are wanting him to come out and play.'

'Do that,' Paulie said. 'Seriously. Your brother is tied up in shit beyond your comprehension. If you see him, tell him to come in. It'll go easier on him this way.'

'Shut the door behind you,' Vic said.

The large brigand took one last look around the room. His eyes fell to the locked hatch. But Paulie guided him back towards the front door and the large man relented. They left the door open. Vic crossed the room and shut it. She spun the latch and rested against the hammered tin. What the fuck was her brother into this time? It was that asshole Happy. Gonna get her brother killed, running around with that group, trying to impress people. She'd talked to Palmer about that, about needing to find a different dive partner. And what the hell could he have got into that would have brought a couple of scavengers this far south? That would have them running all over Springston and Low-Pub when everyone else was out looking for Danvar—

'No way,' Vic said. She paced a small circle around her living room. 'No fucking way. Palmer, you *didn't*.'

She glanced at her dive bag. Damn, she was tired. Too tired for this. But her brother had come to her a week ago asking if he could borrow her visor. She'd laughed and told him to fuck off. He'd then asked her about a two-tank valve, which she'd given him. She remembered the conversation as if it were yesterday. Remembered the way he'd hugged her before he left. He never did that. Couldn't remember the last time he'd done that.

'What've you done, Palm? What the fuck have you *done*?'

Vic crossed the room and grabbed the jar of stale beer with its shrivelled green lime. She chugged the bitter breakfast down and grabbed her dive bag. Damn, she was tired. But hopefully Marco hadn't left town without her.

A Mad Dash

PALMER

D
ive light and diver were extinguished as one. Palmer felt the wild man sag lifeless to the ground, and the light around his neck threw out one last spurt of red rays before it too gave up the ghost. He was left shaking and terrified in the pitch black. His dive knife felt heavy in his hand.

Palmer wiped the blade on his thigh and placed a hand over his belly, holding the coins there. He remembered that a coin had spilled out, and bent down, patted the floor until he found it. There was a tear in his suit. He felt to see if any of the wires had been severed – couldn't be positive but didn't think so. The knife went back into his boot. He arranged the folded map in his belly pocket so it was against the tear, outside of the coins, staunching the costly wound.

Reaching for his dive light, he switched it off, shook it and tried it again. Popping the battery out and touching its leads to his tongue didn't resurrect it. He felt for his visor, wanted to check the charge in his suit, then remembered it getting knocked off. Palmer felt around in the darkness and tried to retrace his steps. The air was fucking awful in there. It was the stench of the dead mixed with the stale and too-weak oxygen. His knees were wobbly. He bumped into a desk. Felt around the corner. Went too far and placed a hand in the gore of the other diver.

'Fuck. Fuck!'

Palmer backed up, wiped his hand on the ground, wiped again on an office chair, was bumping into things and making noises, ghosts everywhere. He practically crawled on his belly, swept his arms across the floor, found random knick-knacks, lost a coin from his pocket and chased after it, wasn't able to find the damn thing, when he bumped into his visor.

Tank of air, the madman had said. *Tank of air but no charge.* Palmer had some battery left but no air. Fucking Hap. He tried to remember where the tanks had been. Couldn't see shit. Couldn't see his hand in front of his face. His fins were back in the other room. Vic always made fun of him for using fins, said only beginners wore them, that once you really learned how to flow sand you could do it in your boots. You could do it barefoot.

Palmer strained with his other senses. He listened for the sound of sand tumbling across sand, the drift settling, little tiny rocks the size of pinpricks whispering in diminutive avalanche. He searched for that noise which plagued his entire goddamn existence: sand on sand.

He heard a sigh. A hush. Barely more than a rustle, maybe the sound of him breathing or his heart thrumming or the brush of fabric between his trembling knees.

But no – it was sand moving. Sliding towards him.

Palmer slid towards it in return.

He crawled through the desks, straining to remember the layout of the room, where the tanks had been, where in relation to the drift. There were chairs and desks everywhere. There were tangles of wires and a keyboard. Palmer considered trying his visor, using it to navigate, trying to see by the pulsing purples of open air, but the dead dive light around his neck was a reminder to not waste his charge. His suit had held enough juice to get him down to that building and back to the surface, and he was only halfway through that dive. This is what he told himself as he fumbled around in the darkness: *he was only halfway through this dive*. He had stopped for a few days, a few hours, who knew how long? He had starved at the bottom of his plummet, had scrounged longer than any living soul ever had, and he wasn't through. Weak and exhausted and terrified, he wasn't through.

Palmer felt sand beneath his palms. He nearly bent and kissed the stuff, those cool granules that reminded him of home. He turned to the side and kept one hand in touch with the slope of drift, the other waving out in space, shuffled along on his knees, when his fingers hit that cool metal.

The tears came. Palmer cried out in relief. But he dared not hope, dared not hope, not until he knew. He felt around the dive tanks for the valves – everything in a different place, a strange arrangement, a different model, three damn tanks to lug, to flow around. No way he could lift all three. He cracked the valve at the top of one tank and felt down the hose to the regulator. With his heart pounding, unable to breathe or think or swallow, he touched the purge button in the centre of the regulator.

Nothing. Empty tank. He tried the next. Prayed. Really fucking prayed to the old gods, the ones he didn't believe in, but he promised them now that he would. He would. He would believe. Just give him some air.

But the regulator made no sound. He tried sucking on the mouthpiece to make sure. Nothing.

Last tank. There was no hope now. No promises to the gods. Nothing but weariness and despair. Anger and fear. And then – a blast of air.

A blast of air, goddamn you. He thought this to Hap, to his friend who had left him for dead, who had promised to come back for him, to save him. Well, Palmer would get out of there and he would find Hap, would return to him like a vengeful ghost. He would kill that motherfucker. That's what he would do. And this gave him the courage to go. To go. Palmer fumbled for the webbing straps and the buckles that held the tanks in place. He removed the two empties, shoved them aside with clanks and bangs, set them off to roll into invisible furniture and warn away the ghosts.

He slipped his arms through the webbing straps on the harness, the single tank lopsided on his back. His visor wouldn't be able to interface with the regulator and tell him how much air he had, but that didn't matter, did it? There was enough or there wasn't. The dead diver would've turned back if he had got too low. Palmer told himself this. He told himself this. Pulling his visor down and powering both it and his suit on, he bit down on someone else's regulator, took a long pull of someone else's air, and he crawled up that slope of drift. He told his suit to vibrate outward against the world, against the hard pack, shiver it until it moved like water, and then he sank down, was enveloped by the deep dunes, the purples becoming oranges and reds, and he could see again.

25

The Risk of Believing

VIC

Vic found Marco back at the marina, loading his tanks into the haul rack. His was the last sarfer in sight. There were sails and masts out across the dunes, but all were heading away. Everyone was looking for Danvar. Vic wondered how to explain to Marco that they needed to use his sarfer to look for her brother instead.

'You heading out alone?' she asked.

Marco turned from his sarfer and smiled. He moved his goggles up to his forehead. 'Thought you needed a nap.'

'Naw. When I need beauty rest, I just blink.' She batted her eyes to demonstrate.

'Prettier by the moment.' He helped her with her gear bag and lashed it down with the tanks. 'So I thought we'd head south. One of the rumours floating around is that Danvar is in a line with Springston and Low-Pub. A lot of people are going west where the sand isn't so deep. I think that's a mistake.'

'I think we need to go north,' Vic said.

'You would.' Marco studied the wind generator at the aft end of the sarfer. It howled as it spun in the breeze. He checked the charge on the batteries. 'If I'd said north, you would've told me we needed to go south.'

'No, I think we need to find my brother.'

'Palm? To cut him in on this? Shouldn't we find the joint first?'

Vic followed Marco to the boom and helped him tug the slip knots loose. 'I didn't get a nap because a couple of assholes barged into my place as soon as I got there. Paulie and some other guy.'

'Paulie? Is he back in town?'

'Yeah. Looking for Palm.'

Marco shook his head. 'You gotta tell your brother to stay away from those guys.'

'I have.'

Marco lowered his goggles and unwrapped the dock lines from the hitching post. The sarfer rocked in the breeze, felt eager to get moving. The wind generator whirred. He lowered the rudder against the sand and tested the tiller. 'How about we shoot south just to see if anyone's found something, and then we go look for your brother?' He nodded at the mast. 'If you raise the main, I'll pull us out of here.'

Vic stepped back towards the cockpit instead. She raised her hand and steadied the boom as it moved in a gust of wind. 'I don't want to find Palmer to take him diving with us,' she said.

'Good. Let's get going.'

'We need to find Palmer because . . .' She wasn't sure how to say this. 'Goddamnit, Marco, I think he might be the one who found Danvar.'

26

A Long Way Up

PALMER

Palmer slid easily through the loose bank of drift inside the building, but the hard pack he found outside was a shock. As he pushed his way back into the world, the earth he encountered there pushed back at him. He didn't quite get a full breath of air before the strain around his chest and neck made another gulp impossible. He could've turned and forced his way back into the building to escape the crush, but a slower death beckoned there. And he might never have got up the courage to go again.

His mortality was suddenly everywhere at once. Never before had it registered with him that *this was the moment. Now. Right now. Here was where he would die and where his bones would lie, never to see the stars again.*

With half a lungful, he turned skyward in desperation. He only knew which way was up by leaving the tall building behind. Fighting against the squeeze, fighting against all that pressure, he struggled to flow the sand and at the same time to breathe. But still he could not prise the hands of those deep dunes from around his neck. He had a tank of air strapped to his back, but he couldn't draw on the regulator, couldn't force his chest to expand, needed to go *up* in order to win a breath.

Palmer kicked and flowed the miserable sand. He should be around three hundred metres. There was no depth reading in his visor. *Go by feel. Move fifty metres. That should be enough to get a breath*. Battery in his beacon must have been dead. *Doesn't matter – just kick*. The depth would show when it sensed the surface. Should've been able to breathe but couldn't. Too weak. Too exhausted. Too hungry and thirsty and terrified.

The sun does this every day, he heard his sister say. Palmer felt consciousness slip through his fingers. He was back on a dune with Vic, learning to dive in the loosest of sand, afraid he wouldn't have the knack, that he wouldn't have the special talent that made diving possible, was afraid all of his dad's skill had gone to his sister.

Look at the sun, she told him. The sun was just coming up. He'd been in her too-big dive suit for hours and hadn't been able to so much as slide a hand into a dune. He was growing frustrated. He didn't want to hear another lecture from his older sister.

'Every day,' Vic told him. 'Every day, the sun rises out of the sand without effort. It glides. It burns. It melts all in its path, and then it shows us how it's done in the evening as it bores straight down through the jagged peaks. Through solid rock, Palm. And all you've gotta to do is move the *sand*.'

The sun. His father was calling. His father, who told him he would be a great diver one day. Sitting on his lap, Palmer's earliest memory, back when his father had been a great man and a ruler, telling his firstborn son that he would be the greatest of divers one day. Nearby, Vic listened, ten years old, sitting in the same room and unmentioned. Unmentioned.

No shadows cast, not from this son. No, this son *lived* in

shadows. Lived in the dark and cool sand. Watched his sister dive and rise up again, basking, radiating glory, a rebel and a pirate and a scrounger and a great diver. But Palmer . . . who saw Danvar when it was a legend . . . who spilled the life of a man with his dive knife . . . who would die with a tank of air on his back and a quarter-charge in his suit . . . his white bones at three hundred metres—

Three hundred metres. The depth reading flashed in Palmer's awareness like the appearance of a mother's face in the midst of a burning fever. Like a knock at a door in the middle of a nightmare. A small part of his brain yelled at the rest of him, saying: *Hey, you might want to see this.*

But he'd been going up. Should be less than three hundred metres. His lungs were straining. And then he remembered the bowl they'd dug, the deep shaft in the sand they'd made, the extra two hundred metres. Fuck, he'd only got started. No way, no way, no way.

Palmer stopped moving. He worried less about the flow and more about breathing. The sand held him, but he was able to draw air through the regulator. A breath. A sip. Life. That surreal feeling taking him right back to the day Vic had taught him how to dive, had told him to *breathe* while his head was under the sand, his body telling him this was impossible, his brain saying not to do it, his sister yelling at him, her voice distant and muffled, to fucking breathe.

And breathing.

Palmer managed a gulp. He peered down at the now-faint image of the sandscraper below. Up was the other way. Away from Danvar. He kicked; he grunted with effort, the sounds of his screams trapped in his own head, his own throat. So far to go. Where was he? There were no trans-ponders, no beacons, but his visor was getting his depth now, so the surface was up there somewhere. No beacon to show him the way. And the shaft they'd descended, that Brock's men had made, that bright yellow needle deep in the earth, was missing. That's why so deep.

It grew harder to breathe, even as he pierced two hundred metres. Should be getting easier. Air was running out. Fuck. Air running out. Only enough to get back to the bottom of that well. No. Not this close. He wouldn't die this close. He felt the resistance of the dry tank, that fruitless tug on a bottle sucked dry, and his air was gone. Maybe he could get fifty metres on a lungful. Maybe. Two hundred metres to go. He kicked anyway. He wouldn't make it. This registered as bright as metal in loose sand. He wouldn't make it. Could feel himself blacking out. Still another one fifty, as deep as many divers dared to plunge, at the bottom of most dives, and he was down there with a lungful of nothing but toxic exhalations.

An orange spot in the sand above. Thirty metres away. Something to steer for. A dying light. An island in the vastness. His body needed to breathe; his body told him to spit out his regulator and suck down sand; it was that impulse at the end of asphyxiation, the urge to get something into the lungs, *anything*, even the soil. Whatever it took to *breathe*. To *gasp*. Just fucking do it. Clog his lungs with sand and end the pain. He would. He would. But an orange spot. A body.

Palmer ran out of energy. The sand would no longer flow. There was a diver there beside him, and he numbly, distantly, in some corner of his diminishing soul, knew why Hap had never come back for him.

Hap had never made it.

Palmer spat out his regulator. He tasted the sand on his tongue. He could see Hap's face, the way his body was twisted out of shape, something wrong about that. Something wrong.

A frozen look on Hap's face, mouth and eyes wide, regulator dangling. Palmer's regulator. *Palmer's regulator.*

Palmer flowed the sand around the regulator and grabbed it, placed it into his mouth. No hope. No hope. But air cares not for hope. It is or it isn't. And here it was. *Here it was.*

Air.

Energy flowed into Palmer's cells like electricity. He blinked away the tears behind his visor. Vic and his father were yelling at him. His mother was yelling at him. His baby brothers. Hap. All yelling at him. *Go. Go. Fucking breathe.*

A hundred metres to the surface, to the bottom of that slowly filling bowl of sand. No time to switch tanks. But this was sand he could handle. Even as he could taste the wet metal on his tongue that let him know this other tank was running dry, this tank and regulator he knew so well running dry, he also knew the loose sand. He knew this dead diver. Palmer was a scrounger, a sand diver, one who brought back heavy loads from the past and saw the sun glint off them for the first time in generations. He flowed the sand upward, pulling Hap's lifeless body and his tank with him, rising through the last hundred metres of sand as his air ran out, but he knew and Vic told him that he could make it. And he believed.

27

Mother

VIC

Vic and Marco sailed north on a steady breeze, the sail taut and full, the lines singing and happy. Marco had found a good trough through a line of dunes, which meant very little tacking. It was the kind of sailing that coaxed a mind into wandering. Just the vibration through a riveted hull of piecemeal steel as the sarfer crossed those patches of sand with the little channels the wind made, those striations like the wrinkled hands of the elderly. There was the shushing sound of metal runners on hard pack, the creak of lines in burdened wooden blocks, the groan of a happy mast bent before a gathering wind.

Vic watched the great wall approach in the distance, the tallest of the cobbled scrapers looming over the far dunes. It was not yet noon. They had made excellent time, hard to believe she had been on a dive before dawn that same day. Her thoughts went to Palmer, the idea that her brother may have been a part of this find of finds. Their father had been right all those years ago when he'd said Palmer would be the one. Vic was the scrounger who made fortunes. Fortunes she spent just as quickly. Spent them chasing the next score, her prospects rising and falling with the moon, always looking for that truly impressive discovery, the one that would mean never gambling again. But Palmer was the one.

Marco tapped her arm. He was in the webbed seat next to her. He motioned to the tiller and then pointed towards the bow, needed to go forward. Vic took over. She enjoyed the way the tiller hummed in her hand. The same technology found in her dive suit allowed the sharp rudder to pierce the sand and flow through it like water. She steered and watched Marco work and realised her mother had been as right about her love life as her father had been about her diving prospects. Her mom had said she would end up with someone dangerous, someone who took too many risks, and that this would be the end of her. 'Nothing but brigands and bastards in your future,' her mom had said. As if she knew what she was talking about.

Vic watched Marco wrestle with the hanks on the foresail until a wrinkle was out and the shape of the jib was better. Instead of returning to the cockpit, he stood on the bow and gazed out towards approaching Springston. Whatever he was thinking was hidden behind those dark goggles of his, was lost in that mane of knotted cords, those tattoos and scars and wounds from fighting for some ideal that she didn't think either of them could even remember. What were they fighting for?

And what would she do differently if she went back and did it all over? If she thought her parents were right, what would she change? Vic couldn't think of a thing. The ink and the sandscars on her body would never disappear, and she didn't regret them. She would be proud of Palmer if he went down as the one who found Danvar. Proud of him and his friend Hap. Glad for them and in love with her brigand boyfriend and damn her parents if they'd been right about everything. Damn them. After her big score, when she had kids of her own and sent them out into the world, she'd tell them the things she'd learned and then say that they would have to learn these very same things all on their own. Every generation did. Trying to prevent this was like shouting at the wind and hoping it stopped.

Ahead, the clean northward trough ended. Vic steered around a dune and through a break until she found another trough. She had to adjust the sails as she did so. Marco seemed at peace on the bow and made no effort to come back and help. Probably knew she'd be pissed if he tried. He held the forestay with one hand and continued to gaze towards the horizon, thinking on his own riches, possibly. Or busy naming their kids. Or dreading the day their mother told them about the time their dad was nearly killed by an undergarment.

Shantytown rose at last, after the scrapers and the great wall. A scrabble of low huts with bright steel roofs gleamed in the rising sun. She had to search hard to spot the marina on the south side, for it was nearly bare. Just two sarfers parked, neither of them fitted with masts, otherwise Vic was sure they'd be out among the dunes as well, looking for Danvar.

The traffic they'd seen between Low-Pub and Springston had been unprecedented. She and Marco had passed dozens of parked sarfers among the dunes with their dive flags up. Dozens more had been spotted with their sails billowing as they raced all points but east. Vic eased the sheets to drop some speed and steered into the marina while Marco lowered the jib. It felt good, this ride between Low-Pub and Springston. The anxiety of the chase for treasure had lessened. She just felt an urge to find her brother and share in the excitement with everyone else. Nothing wrong with being second or tenth. Just a pang that her father wasn't there to be a part of it. To hear that Palmer had maybe been first.

She guided the sarfer into an open flat of sand, loosed the mainsail, and realised this would be her first trip into Springston in almost a year. God, today was the day, wasn't it? Or was it yesterday? She knew it was coming up. Conner and Rob would be out camping. Maybe that's where Palmer was as well. Hell, maybe he'd had no part in locating Danvar. He'd just been camping, had done whatever two-tank dive he and Hap had had lined up and had gone out to No Man's Land for the weekend. Doubt crept in after getting Marco's hopes up. She may have sailed them in the wrong direction.

'I'll stay here and watch the sarfer,' Marco said, snapping her from her thoughts. The noise of the wind and the skids was gone, leaving a residual roar. They would both be shouting at each other until it went away.

'No, you're coming with me.' She coiled the mainsheet before tugging her gloves off, then nodded to the small shack beyond the mooring posts. 'I'll give the dockmaster a coin to watch our stuff.'

Marco shrugged. 'If you insist.' He wrapped a line around one of the posts so the sarfer couldn't break free and run under bare pole. They flaked the mainsail and left the mast up so they could get out of there as soon as they found Palmer. Vic tied back the halyard so it wouldn't clang a racket, then checked their dive gear in the haul rack to make sure nothing had come loose. She took a long pull on her canteen, dreading the hell out of this, dreading it worse than any deep dive, then led the way towards the Honey Hole, Marco having to jog to catch up with her.

28

No Room for Breathing

The brothel, with its noisy generator and bright lights and balconies hunkered under juts of corrugated tin, stood between two shovelled dunes in that never-where between Shantytown and Springston. Vic couldn't decide which town the building belonged to. It was as if neither side wanted it but neither wanted to lose it. It was that last piece of rotten snakemeat begrudgingly fought over by two starving but half-hearted men, each secretly hoping the other might win the struggle.

The sun pounded the back of the Honey Hole by day, baking it until noon, then allowed it to revel in all its lurid glory as it slowly set to the west. This was when the idle women left their idle beds and leaned over railings from their balconies, their breasts drooping seductively in fire-red lace and midnight-black straps as they smiled down at the men who went twelve dunes out of their way home from work to ogle what they could not afford. Or as they shoved their way inside and paid anyway for what they could not afford.

Vic avoided the place like no other spot in the high desert. She would just as soon venture into No Man's Land after her father or swim through a viper's nest as set foot in the place. This distaste was an inconvenience when in Springston, for quite a bit of a diver's business was conducted around the mismatched tables of the downstairs bar, men leaning heads together over smouldering ashtrays to consult expert maps scratched in charcoal on the faces of napkins. It was a blessing, in a way, that her mother owned the place and worked there. It gave Vic an excuse to shun the joint. Otherwise she would have to explain herself, would have to admit that it had nothing to do with her mom. Without this excuse, the men who dominated the world of diving would think her craven and unworthy.

'You go in,' she told Marco, holding up outside the front door. 'Ask for Rose and tell her to meet me out back.'

'Why don't you just come in with me?' Marco asked, wagging his eyebrows, mocking her. 'You really have such a problem with what your mom does?'

Vic hesitated. 'It's bad for business,' she finally said. 'When I walk in there, all those drunks take one look at me and they decide they don't want nothing else for a week. Bad for business, and it's my mom's business.'

Marco laughed. 'Jesus, whatever. I'll go book an hour with your mom for you.'

'Yeah, fuck you—'

But Marco was already through the door. The Honey Hole belched a blast of noise as it swung open for a moment, the early-morning crowd unusually alive, probably because of the news of Danvar, or still going strong from the night before. Vic took advantage of the lee of the three-storey building to pull out her tobacco pouch and roll a smoke. Getting low. Would need to ride out to the gardens at some point and hit up her supplier—

'Why don't you smoke that in bed after we're done,

honey?' A face and two breasts leaned out over the rail above. 'Twenty coin for you. Special rate. Whaddya say?'

Vic clicked her lighter, fired up her cigarette and blew smoke towards the balcony. 'Fuck off,' she muttered. She left the shelter from the wind and stepped around the building between the dunes that were daily carved away from this most sacred and protected of buildings. She thought of her little brother Conner as she considered how the sand here was eternally dug away just as it was from other wells of nourishment.

At the back of the building, there stood a low wall around a service door where drunks and garbage were dragged out. Vic enjoyed her smoke, the deep inhalations calming nerves jangled from being near the place. Rusted hinges full of sand screamed as her mother stepped out, an unlit cigarette in her mouth, the white robe Vic's father had brought up from beneath Low-Pub fluttering around her knees.

'Got a light?' her mom asked.

First words exchanged in a year, and Vic was pretty sure they were the same words she had last heard from her mother, standing there in that very place. She cupped her hand tight around her silver lighter and her mom dipped her cigarette into the flame. It came out aglow and smoking.

'New tattoo?' her mom asked. She pointed the lit cigarette at Vic's arm.

'Yeah,' Vic said, resisting the urge to look down at her arm and see which one she was talking about. The sun was just breaking over the highest scrapers. She could already tell it was going to be a hot one. 'Look, I'd love to chat, but I just need to find Palmer. Have you seen him?'

Her mom inhaled, nodded, turned to the side and blew smoke against the sandblasted door. 'Saw your brother last week. Needed money for a set of visors. Said he would *really* pay me back this time.'

'You know where he was heading?'

Her mom shook her head. 'Nope. Didn't care. Don't you wanna ask if I gave him the money?'

'No, I don't. Did he say anything about the job he was taking?'

Her mom shrugged. 'He said he would stop back by on his way down to pay me back. That's all. Conner came by yesterday looking for him, so there's another broken promise.'

'Did Conner say why he was looking for him?'

Her mom's eyes narrowed into slits. 'Because he was supposed to go camping with your brothers last night. Why? Is Palmer in trouble?'

'No. I think he's in the *opposite* of trouble. All the commotion around here this morning, it's because someone found Danvar.'

Her mom exhaled noisily. 'I heard. You honestly believe that? Someone's always finding Danvar. And it always turns out to be some no-name town full of half-rotten debris that was already known about. More people will go broke than make anything, you watch. Good for our business for a few days, and then a ghost town after that.'

'I think this time is different,' Vic said.

'It's always different. And look, unless you want to come in and talk, I've gotta get out of the sand. I can't afford to take an extra shower today just because you don't like what I do here.'

'Okay. Whatever. Good to see you.'

'Same.' She flicked the cigarette into the sand. A crow dived down to take a look and peeled away, screaming at being fooled.

'Hey,' Vic said, as her mom opened the door. 'Did he get the visor?'

Her mom looked sad for a moment, a frown of wrinkles around her mouth. 'I gave him the money, yeah.'

'Who was he buying it from? Graham?'

'Go ask Graham,' her mom said. She stepped back inside and the wind and sand helped slam the door.

29

A Soul's Weight

'Well?' Marco asked. He was waiting for Vic out front.

'Danvar is north of here,' she said. 'I think.'

'You *think*? Did your mom say that? She know where your brother went?'

'Not exactly. But Palmer told her he would stop back by on his way *down*. Plus, I don't think he would've come this way just to head south or west. They were passing through Springston from Low-Pub, and he stopped to hit her up for money. We need to run to a dive shop real quick. I've got one more person to ask.' She grabbed Marco by the shirt and pulled him close for a deep kiss. One of the women on the balcony whistled.

'What the fuck was that for?' Marco asked, smiling.

Vic wiped her lips. 'Making sure you didn't have any lipstick on you. You're clean.'

'Oh, is that right?' He followed her as she set off towards the dive school. 'I'm clean, huh?'

'Yeah, but your breath tastes like panties. That could mean anything, though.'

'That joke's gonna get real old real fast,' Marco said. He ran to catch up. 'So what dive shop are we going to? You've got a lead?'

'Yeah. Family friend. A guy my dad used to scavenge with. Name's Graham—'

'Graham Siler?'

'Yeah, you know him?'

'I know *of* him. If it weighs a Graham, he gives a damn. A hoarder, right? I know a guy who came across one of his buried caches once. Said there was a hundred thousand coin worth of artefacts two hundred metres down out in the middle of nowhere.'

'Bullshit. Those are legends.'

'No, he was for real. But he wouldn't touch any of it. Said he'd heard Graham booby-traps the caches. I'm not kidding. This guy still goes out there sometimes, dives down, and just looks at it. I've tried to get him to take me.'

'He won't take you because they don't exist. He's just a junker like my dad was. Hey, did that sand up there just settle? Like it was moving?'

Marco peered at the dune she was pointing to. There was still a small cascade of sand sliding down the face. 'The wind,' Marco said.

'Felt like someone was watching us. C'mon, there's a back way to his shop through here. We can stay out of the market. It sounds nuts over there.'

'Yeah . . .' Marco lagged behind, was still studying the dune. Vic turned down a narrow path and into a tight alley where shacks jutted out of the high sand and roofs met overhead to form a dark tunnel. Cracks in the tin allowed thin lines of sift to fall in golden veils. Vic ducked her head as she passed through one. She found Graham's by looking for the shack with the billiard ball for a door handle. A perfunctory knock, and she pushed her way inside, bells overhead ringing.

'Graham?'

There was no one at the counter. A lantern flickered with the breeze swirling through the door. Marco kicked his boots on the door jamb and joined her inside, closed the door, which upset the bells again but stilled the shadows. 'Look at those bikes,' Marco whispered.

Vic ignored him. She ducked under the handlebars of the suspended bicycles and peered into the back. The workshop was empty. 'Graham? You still in bed?' She had gone up two rungs towards his loft to check his mattress when she saw the body behind his workbench. Graham's stool lay on its side. 'Marco!' she called. She scrambled down from the ladder and hurried around the workbench. An electric light on the bench was still on. She swivelled it towards the floor so she could see better.

'You okay?' Marco asked.

'Fuck,' Vic said. She moved the stool, which lay across the body.

'Is that Graham?'

'No. Never seen this guy before.' She reached up and adjusted the light better. 'Damn. Look at this.'

There was something wrong with the man's face. It was stove in, as if he'd been hit with something, perhaps a bat, but there was almost no damage to the skin, just rivulets of blood streaking from his nose. 'What the hell?'

'Hey, I know that guy.' Marco knelt down beside the man. He lifted the man's hand and bent his arm around, studied a tattoo and a knot of sandscars on his wrist. 'Danger,' he said. He looked up at Vic, saw the confusion on her face. 'His name. That's what he went by, anyway. Used to be in the Low-Pub Legion. Muscle. Blew shit up. Whatever you needed, he did it for a price. Went north when the price got better.'

'Cannibals?' Vic stayed away from the wastes as much

as she could; there was a grove of trees up there and a couple of sources of water, some nice dive sites, but the dunes were generally unsafe.

'No, a new outfit. One of our bomb guys hooked up with them as well. Word is they're fast and loose with their coin. Haven't taken credit for any attacks, but that don't mean they aren't trying. What happened to his face?'

'Looks like he was hit with something.'

Marco reached down and touched the dead man's cheek. The flesh moved like rotten fruit.

'Fuck,' Marco said. 'It's like a sponge.'

Vic held her hand over the man's face, careful not to touch it. She just lined her palm up over the damage. 'Graham must've had his dive gloves on. He powered his suit up and shoved your friend here in the face, probably when he came back around the bench to threaten him.'

'You think he hit him with his suit?'

Vic nodded. 'Would've powdered his skull. Turned it into sand. I think that's his brains leaking out his nose.'

'Aw, fuck!' Marco stood up. 'And he just left him here?'

'Well, either Graham took off in a hurry or Danger here wasn't alone and Graham was hauled off. Weird of him to leave the place unlocked and unmanned like this. He's weird about his shit.'

'Yeah, well, it was weird of whoever took him to leave that kick-ass visor just sitting there on the workbench.'

Vic turned to see what he was talking about. 'Don't even think it,' she said, watching him reach for the set.

'Just want to see them.'

'A friend of mine might be in trouble.'

'So what're we supposed to do? And what do you think Danger wanted? Your guy owe him money, maybe?'

'What do you think, you goon? You think maybe we're

not the only two trying to track down Danvar by following leads rather than bumping over the dunes with our sails flapping in all directions? Someone else thinks Graham knows where Danvar is. Or . . . shit.' Vic stood up. 'Maybe someone else knows that Graham knew where *Palmer* went. Maybe we're two steps behind . . .'

'No, no, no.' Marco paced up and down behind the workbench, shaking his finger at the dead man on the ground. 'I've got it. Oh, fuck, I've got it. You were right. It's north of here. There's this guy Brock, the one I told you about, the one who's been hiring up talent and throwing coin around. I bet that's who financed all of this. Yeah.' Marco stuck the end of one of his long dreadlocks into his mouth and chewed, lost in thought. Vic gave him time. For all the grief she gave Marco, she had fallen for his brains before his good looks. 'What if your brother didn't discover Danvar?' he asked, reasoning something out.

'I'm listening.'

'What if they think he's the one who leaked the news?'

'Damien said that guy was dead.'

'Well, maybe he ain't. Maybe it was your brother, and now they're after him to shut him up. Maybe they thought your family friend here could track him down. I think they just want him dead.'

'I don't like where you're going with this.'

'But it makes sense, right? Otherwise, where's your brother? No one's seen him or his friend, right? I bet they're both in trouble.'

'Or they're over Danvar right now, diving and hoarding. Or they're both shit-faced drunk. Either way, we should check with this guy you know. The two assholes who barged into my place were wearing kers from the north—'

'Who, Brock? I don't know him. Only heard about him.'

'What've you heard?'

'Conflicting stuff. I heard he grew up in Springston and came from money. But a friend of mine says his accent ain't like the Lords, that he had to be from up north. Supposedly he has a camp up there in the middle of the wastes. I know a guy, Gerard, who quit their group. Came back saying he couldn't live that far from an adequate supply of pussy—'

'Lovely.'

'In fact . . . shit, Gerard disappeared on a dive a week or so after he got back. And nobody found his body.'

'We need to go talk to this guy.'

'To Gerard? I'm pretty sure he's buried.'

'No, idiot, to Brock. His camp, you say it's in the middle of the wastes? You know where?'

'Not really.' Marco chewed on a dreadlock. 'It's near the grove, I think. I remember Gerard talking about lavish campfires. West of the grove but south of some big spring. I only remember 'cause he was bitchin' about having to haul barrels of water down from—'

An explosion of bells rang out as the front door was thrown in. There was a shout, and then the stomp of heavy boots. Vic turned and looked for somewhere to hide, started to yell for Marco to c'mon, to get out the back door, but then two men with guns joined them in the workshop, silver weapons gleaming, one swinging at her and the other at Marco.

'Hey, whoa—' Marco said. He held up his hands, and Vic found herself staring down the barrel of one of those ancient and unreliable killing machines.

The two men looked down where a pool of light spilled on a dead man. The guy training a gun on Vic, a bald man with tats on his face, snarled at her, rage in his eyes, as he pulled the trigger. There was a click and a curse. She and

Marco still hadn't moved, were both rooted in fear and surprise. And then the other gun went off. And Marco moved for the very last time. One side of his skull erupted, his body sagging downward. There was another click, but Vic was moving now. Moving and screaming, staying in a crouch with her arms over her head, unable to breathe or think straight as she dived for the back door, another gunshot ringing out behind her.

30

Into the Starry Night

PALMER

There was no sun waiting on Palmer's arrival. No people or encampments. Just the vast and jewelled clear desert sky.

Small gulps of that sky passed through Palmer's sand-specked lips and filled his desperate lungs. He lay on his back, gasping, the sand collecting against his side and filling his windward ear and his hair as he breathed in the loud, laborious, grateful way a newborn does.

His friend Hap lay lifeless beside him, partly submerged in the sand. Somewhere, a coyote howled at this sudden scent, and the wind skittered across the dunes with the sound of a thousand snakes flicking their tongues.

Palmer scraped the sand off his tongue using his teeth. He spat out the grit and with it precious fluid. He turned to Hap, whose shoulder and knee were out of the dune. A boot as well, but not in the right place. He could see Hap's canteen strap on his shoulder. Exhausted but mad with thirst, Palmer slid his hand into the sand and floated Hap up the rest of the way. His visor beeped with a battery alarm. His suit was nearly dead.

He reached for the canteen, saw that it was tangled and

pulled out his bloodstained dive knife. He cut the strap. A quarter full. He was too weak to ration and took great gulps. The water burned his parched lips. His stomach churned, was startled to have something to do. Palmer twisted the cap on and sat with his back to the wind, studying his dead friend.

It wasn't the canteen strap that'd been tangled, he saw. It was Hap's body. Palmer covered his mouth. The grumbling in his stomach grew worse and he feared he might lose what little fluid he had just taken in. Hap's leg was twisted beneath him. Where the thigh meets the pelvis was torn the wrong way. An arm was shattered, white bone pointing up at the stars. Palmer tried to make sense of this. He had seen bodies snared in the sand before, had seen them trapped in silent and peaceful repose. This was not that. This was a life that had met a violent end. His brain whirled as the clues fell together. His homing beacon was in a mesh pouch on Hap's thigh. Palmer had found his friend a hundred metres down, right beneath the dip in that great bowl Brock's men had dug, right where their dive had begun. Hap had made it back after all.

Maybe the walls of that strange shaft had crushed him. Maybe Hap had got back too late, right as they'd given up on them both, and when they'd released the held-back sand, the walls had pushed in violently around him. But no, there would be damage everywhere. It would be even. Hap had been hit on that side, there. A fall. A great fall.

It was the visor that told the story. Hap's visor was gone. It would have a recording of his dive. Of Danvar. Of the location of every building, maybe even the streets below, every block of that buried legend.

Sand blew across Hap's body and ramped up against his side. His mouth was packed with grit, his nostrils clogged, his lifeless eyes dusted. Palmer saw now that there was never any coin in this for either of them. This had been the plan all along. Get a layout of the land, see where to dig, where to put their efforts, and keep the location of all those vast spoils to themselves. He saw in Hap's open and horrified eyes what had happened, imagined him pulled up by the ropes, maybe saying that his friend was still down there, that there was a pocket of air in the building, that they needed to go back. Or maybe Hap telling them that it was no use, that his friend was dead.

Palmer scooped a handful of loose sand and placed it over Hap's eyes, duning them shut. It was no wonder they were never told what they were looking for when they'd taken this job. If Palmer and Hap had known they were diving for Danvar, they would've wondered why they weren't blindfolded for the hike north. Hell, they would've known right then and there that this was a one-way trip. Of course. Otherwise, they would've *begged* to have been blindfolded. They had marched north from Springston as dead men.

'You saved my fucking life,' Palmer told his dead friend. 'You betrayed me, and you saved my fucking life.'

And who knows, maybe Hap would've come back for him. Who was to say what decision he'd made, what had gone through that mind of his, what he had told Brock and the others? Yes, he would've come back for him. Palmer was sure of it.

He was also sure that his life was now in danger. Not just because he was in the middle of the desert and starving, but because he knew what Brock didn't want anyone else to know. Palmer reached up and touched the visor on his forehead, needed to make sure it was still there, that his dive was still there, that it had happened.

As exhausted and weak as he was, he needed to do

something about Hap. Not relishing the task, he patted his old friend's pockets, pulled the two transponders out of his hip pouch, then reached into Hap's belly pocket for his death note and the few coins there. With his suit's charge dangerously low, he flowed the sand beneath Hap and sent his body straight down. No way of getting the distance exact, but Palmer planned on being long gone before anyone realised the body had moved.

He took off the tank he'd stolen from the other diver and stretched his limbs, pulled his hiking goggles out and adjusted them around his eyes, stowed his visor away. He would have to carry the tank a few dunes away and bury it. Couldn't leave anything behind, couldn't flow it down with Hap where it might be discovered, where Brock's next foray into the sand would reveal that they had a problem.

Rising on unsure legs, he peered up that slope of sand from the bottom of the great pit Brock's men had dug. There was no generator running; the sand was no longer loose; the metal platform had been taken away. He could see the sand rolling down in the darkness to fill that great dip in the desert floor. Dreading the climb, he took one step at a time. The night wind would mask his departure. His bootprints would be erased by morning. He could put the breeze on his left cheek, keep the Pole Star at his back, and head due south until he reached Springston. But he knew he would never make it that far. He was starving – only had a few swallows of water sloshing around in his dead friend's canteen – he wouldn't make it two days' march, much less five.

At the top of the arduous hike out of the bowl, Palmer faced the wind. He tried to remember the route he'd taken to get to the dive site from the brigand encampment. And oddly, strangely, crazily, he prayed that Brock's men were right where he'd last seen them. They would be the only ones with food and water for miles around. On weary legs and with little conviction, he marched off towards the men who in all likelihood wanted him very much dead.

31

A Bounty

There was a glow beyond the dunes. Voices mixed and carried on the wind. Palmer used the tall sand for cover and worked his way towards the light. When the voices seemed too near to dare march any further, he snuck up a sloping dune, crouching as he got higher, then crawling on his hands and knees before finally squirming on his belly to the wind-blown peak. He peered over the lip and down into the camp where he'd spent his last night above the sand.

The encampment had shrunk. Palmer had expected an explosion of activity – the rest of Brock's men descending on the site of the find – but many of the tents from earlier were gone. The large tent where he and Hap had been shown the map was still there, throbbing with the light of a lantern inside. Beyond this tent, the embers of a fire glowed and sparked, a column of smoke dulling a patch of stars. There were two men around the fire, animated silhouettes. The smell of food cooking made Palmer's empty stomach knot up. His belly tried to convince his brain that these people didn't want him dead, that Hap's mangled body was an accident, that he could just stroll into camp and be hailed a hero, the discoverer of a lost land, with coin and a feast for his efforts.

There was laughter in the darkness – one of the men around the fire – but it was almost as if someone were mocking his belly's wild thoughts, someone daring him to come down and announce himself.

Palmer lay still behind the crest of that dune, his ker over his nose and mouth, his goggles pelted with sand, just watching and thinking and starving. The sun would come up soon. The stars were already dim over the horizon. He was wasting time. He needed to eat. There were several dark tents he might try to surface inside of, to scrounge for food or water, but the danger of waking someone was too great.

An hour passed, lying there, the stars marching the width of a hand, the horizon faintly glowing, Palmer unsure, undecided. His aching stomach told him he had to go. He chose a tent to raid, figuring it was better to be caught and buried than to starve on the back of that dune. He removed his hiking goggles and fumbled for his dive visor, got the band around his forehead, when a commotion erupted in the distance – and Palmer thought he'd been spotted.

He ducked down and began to scoot back, then watched as the two men by the fire rushed off, casting long shadows. There were voices, shouts. Palmer looked in the direction the men were running and saw swinging flashlights between the dunes. A marching party. A nearby tent filled with a brightening glow as someone woke. Several silhouettes left the larger tent where the lantern was burning. Everyone was moving away from Palmer and towards this arriving party.

Now, his belly commanded. *Now, goddamn you.*

Palmer obeyed. He scampered over the crest of the dune and glissaded down the other side on his back, the loose sand following him. He found himself half in the lee of a smaller dune, the sand no longer pelting his face. The large tent stood nearby, the fabric flapping noisily. Palmer remembered the barrels of supplies in this tent. There had been a table in the middle. He could go down and pop up under the table, have a look around.

Hurry, his belly told him. The marching party was approaching. How long would they sit around the fire and swig liquor and smoke tobacco before returning to their tents?

Palmer took a chance by creeping around the dune and hurrying in a crouch towards the back of the large tent. He needed to get close. There was danger in entering the sand with the charge in his suit low. The only thing a diver feared more than running out of air was running out of charge and feeling the sand stiffen around their body. Movement was life in a way no lungful of air could match. If you could move, you could get to the surface and win a breath. A full lung and an empty cell were what nightmares were made of. This gave a diver time to die and space to do it in. And so Palmer ran in a crouch as far as he could, hoping he had enough juice for a quick dip.

He reached the back of the tent without being noticed. All attention was on the people returning to camp. Listening over the wind and the flap of canvas, he heard nothing inside. Palmer powered up his visor and his suit and lay flat on his belly to minimise the drain. Damn, he was weak. Hungry. Limbs quivering. He flipped his visor down, eyed the red blinking light in the corner of his vision, his suit telling him that it was nearly done. *You and me both*, Palmer thought to himself.

The sand accepted him. Palmer held his breath and slid down a full metre in case the floor inside dipped. He slid to where the centre of the tent should be and peered up at the wavering purple overhead. Open space. Nobody standing there. A few patches to the side that might be his barrels of food and water. He came up slowly with his head tilted back, breaching just his visor and ears, ready to flee if anyone spotted him. Bringing one hand out into the air, he flipped his visor up and took a deep and quiet breath. The table overhead blocked the lamp, keeping him in shadow. He flowed the sand so that it spun him around slowly and silently, giving him a scan of the entire tent. No boots. No lumpy bedrolls. No voices approaching. He rose out of the sand in a crouch and powered his suit down quickly, conserving whatever he had left so he could get out again without going through the flap.

He crawled first towards a stack of crates, some part of him aware of the tracks he was leaving in the sand. The lamp overhead swayed, the shadows in the tent stirring menacingly. Burlap covered one crate. Palmer could only think about food, and when he lifted the burlap, he saw loaves of bread sitting there. Bright white loaves. He retrieved one, caught a whiff of something like chalk and rubber, and realised these loaves were too small, too heavy, not bread at all.

His mind was playing tricks on him. Palmer held the object into the light. Explosives. He'd seen bombs like these once before, when a sandscraper in Springston had had to be demolished before a dune pushed it into its neighbour. He checked the crate and saw that it was full of white loaves like that. He had seen the after-effects of rebel bombs. Everyone who grew up in Springston had. The red stains on the sand, the trails of gore, the boots with bloody stumps, men and women and children unrecognisable. He felt the same fear holding that loaf, that tingling up the back of his neck, that he felt at any funeral or wedding or celebration where there might be reprisals, where a loud roar would be the last thing you'd ever hear.

Palmer scanned the tent. Brock and his men were losing the look of scroungers and pirates out for a score. Something else was going on.

His belly told him to focus. *Food*, it said. The explosive went back with the others and the burlap was put back as he'd found it. There were barrels on the other side of the table. The metal hook of a ladle gleamed over the lip of one barrel. Palmer's mouth ached for a drink. He shuffled towards the barrel, shaking the sand loose from his canteen, and peered over the side to see a dim, murky but glorious reflection at the bottom. His gaunt face wavered in the inky puddle. Palmer uncapped the canteen and leaned over the lip, plunging the vessel beneath the surface, the water on his arm cool and invigorating. The canteen gurgled twice, pockets of air bursting through the surface, and then a shout erupted just outside the tent. Laughter. Voices approaching.

Palmer yanked his hand out and whirled around. His limbs and organs desired to go in all directions at once, which left him rooted to the spot. The laughter grew near. He fell to the ground as the tent flapped open. Wiggling on his belly, he got under the table, dribbling water, pairs of boots kicking their way inside.

'Fucking hell!' someone roared. 'This thing's heavy.'

There was the thud of a palm slapping someone's back. A smell of cooked meat, a hot meal in someone's hand. Palmer powered his suit on and sank his knees and feet into the earth, pivoting his legs down while keeping his shoulders and arms clear. He worked the cap back onto the canteen, didn't risk taking a sip, could feel water dripping off his right hand. He pressed his wet palm to his mouth and sucked what moisture he could without making a sound. Seeing the tracks he had left behind from crawling under the table, he used his suit to flow the ground level, as careful as a man tucking in a sleeping baby. Something heavy thudded down right beside the table, a large metal cylinder, and there was a shout to be careful. Packs and other gear knocked overhead. Someone brushed the sand off the surface of the table and it rained down around Palmer, a veil in the lamplight.

Palmer started to sink himself beneath the sand to get out of there, to wait and come back later when everyone was asleep, but a fragment of a sentence caught his ear.

'—any sign of the other diver?'

The laughter and noise died down. Palmer held his breath, certain that his heartbeat could be heard.

'No, sir.' It was Moguhn speaking. Palmer recognised his quiet but commanding voice. 'We scanned down two hundred metres, as far as we could, and there's no body but the one.'

'And no chance he surfaced?' This was Brock again, the one who had asked about the diver. There was no mistaking his strange accent. He must've been away from camp. Just returned with the hiking party. But from where? Palmer listened.

'No chance at all.' This time it was Yegery, Palmer was sure of it. 'One diver out of four can go that deep, and that's what we've got. One in four of them made it. The sand down there makes it impossible to breathe and move at the same time. Besides, it's been four days. He's gone.'

Four days, Palmer thought.

I tried to tell you, his belly said.

'So is this heavy-ass thing what we were after?' someone asked. They sounded doubtful. Disappointed. Palmer couldn't see what it was they were referencing.

'This is it,' Brock said.

'How far down was it?' someone asked.

'Not far,' Yegery said. 'Less than a hundred metres.'

'So what took you guys so long? Was the map off?'

'There's nothing wrong with the map. The map was perfect, once we got Danvar located. It was getting through the damn hatch—'

'Now that we've got what we came for,' someone interrupted, 'does that mean we can break camp?'

'Yes,' Brock said. 'First light, and then we head south. We leave no trace.'

'And you're sure this thing does what you say it does?'

'Let's see it,' someone said.

'Set it on the table,' Brock ordered.

Two sets of hands drifted down right in front of Palmer to grasp the large metal cylinder. Palmer took a deep breath to expand the sand around his chest, then powered his suit down. He couldn't have more than a trickle of a charge left. He was buried up to his armpits, but he could still breathe.

'You sure the table will hold it?'

'It'll hold.'

Above Palmer, the metal table creaked and strained from the weight of the thing. He had only got a glimpse of the object in the lamplight, but it looked like old tech, something scavenged, a cylinder with wires and small pipes, made with precision and expensive-looking. Expensive and old.

'Damn thing's heavy,' someone said as the table somehow didn't buckle. Palmer kept a hand on his chest, ready to dive at any moment. He could feel that object overhead like a dark thought.

'Looks busted to me. Wiring's fucked. And look at this here. Ain't no fixing that.'

'Ignore that,' Brock said. 'It's what's inside that matters. The rest of this is for setting it off, but we don't need that.'

The men grew quiet as they studied the object. The scavenger in Palmer grew intensely curious.

'It's a thing of beauty,' Yegery whispered.

'But how docs it work?' Moguhn asked.

'I don't know,' Yegery admitted.

There was an uncomfortable shuffling of heavy boots.

'I mean, I don't understand the principle, the science. But the book says one of these can level an entire town—'

'An entire town,' someone scoffed.

'Shaddup,' Brock ordered. He told Yegery to go on.

'It's just a little sphere in there. That's all the stuff on the inside is. It's inert enough. The book says it stays good for hundreds of thousands of years. All you do is tighten that little ball real quick, like turning a fistful of sand into a child's marble, and everything goes boom. This thing will send dunes to the heavens and turn the desert to glass.'

'And you're sure about that?' someone asked.

'Yeah, but it's fucked,' another said.

'It'll work,' Brock said. 'Trust me. We could level all of Low-Pub with one of these.'

'What about Springston?' someone asked.

'We stick with the original plan for Springston,' Brock said. 'We blow the wall, and then we hit Low-Pub. If there's anything left of either of them, we'll go back for another of these. Now that we've got a reference point for the map, we can grab as many as we like. Before long, there won't be a structure standing south of our dunes, and the Lords can rule over the flat sand we leave behind.'

There was chuckling at this, which grew into laughter. Someone bumped into the table, and there was the clink of a jar tipping on its side. 'Fucking idiot,' someone grumbled. There was a rush to remove gear, the scrape and slide of bags and swords and guns. 'Get the map,' Moguhn said. A rustle of paper and boots stomping into action. Palmer wondered when the fuck they were going to get out of there so he could grab something to eat, and then an object hit the sand in front of him, a dagger, plunging blade first. A hand dropped down to retrieve it and gripped the hilt. And then a stooped head. Eyes flashed in the darkness.

'What the fuck?' the man said.

And then an angry roar as the pirate pounced at Palmer.

32

Run

Palmer barely got his suit powered on as the man scrambled under the table after him. There was a blow to his head, the swipe of a hand and sharp nails, and his visor was knocked off. He reached for it, got a hold of the headband, felt the visor snap off, lost. Dazed, he took a quick breath and pulled the band on, flowed the sand in order to sink down, and got his eyes closed just in time. He was blind and weak and on a sliver of a charge and barely a lungful of breath. In a burst of inspiration, he dropped the sand in the tent a metre and hardened it. It was a killing offence to use the sand against men, but these men wanted him dead anyway.

He moved sideways as fast as he could to clear the tent walls before rising towards the surface. There was drag in the sand, as if something were wrapped around his feet, were wrapped around his entire body. The sand grew thick. Dense. His fucking suit was dying. Or the band had been damaged when the visor was ripped free.

He went up as fast as he could, blind, half a breath in his lungs, and came up flat, was partway out, his head clear, when the sand froze around him. No more charge. Palmer grunted and worked his shoulders back and forth until he got an arm free. He began to dig himself out of the sand, the stars twinkling serenely above, while two metres away, men were hurling insults and curses and shouting for help as they tried to dig themselves out.

It was a race. Palmer got his other arm out. He kicked with his weak legs, twisted at the waist until his hips were free, was only in ten or so inches of sand, fucking close. A metre down, and he would've been buried. A few inches deeper, and he would've been trapped. He heard the stomp and crunch of sand in the distance as men were summoned from their tents. Palmer got up and ran, keeping the large tent between him and the rest of the camp as the men inside yelled at the others to fucking dig them out, to get out there and find that diver, to kill him fucking dead.

With his heart in his throat, a canteen sloshing a quarter full, his visor with the proof of his dive and discovery of Danvar gone, and hardly anything for his efforts but the life in the marrow of his bones, Palmer ran. He kicked sand in the darkness, keeping to the well-trod valleys where the shuffle of feet would make it hard to follow, and he fucking ran.

33

Not Happening

VIC

Vic burst through the back door of Graham's shop and ran across the hot sand. Gunshots rang out behind her. It sounded as though both men had their weapons working now. Fountains of sand erupted from the face of the dune ahead of her; there was a zing off a metal roof, an explosion of sand near her feet, and then some wild animal took a bite out of her calf.

Vic sprawled forward in the sand, her leg on fire. Someone yelled that that was his sister, goddamnit, don't fucking kill her. Feet stomped in her direction. Vic could feel them coming, could feel a thrumming in the sand. But the thrum wasn't from the boots chasing her down.

The sand opened and swallowed her. Vic was too startled to take a breath, only just got her eyes closed in time. A regulator was pressed to her lips. She accepted it and took a deep gulp of air, felt the sand around her stay soft so she could breathe, could feel movement through the earth as she was hauled sideways like so much scavenge.

The regulator was taken away for a moment. She was left with only blackness and motion. The regulator was returned. Someone was sharing their tank with her. Vic clutched this person, knowing they had saved her, hoping it was Palmer. The agony in her leg faded to a dull throb, and the sight of Marco's head erupting filled the back of her eyelids and played over and over again – a bang and a fountain of what she loved best about him, a profound hollow in the pit of her soul, so that when she was brought up through the sand and into the open air, she was unaware of this, didn't know she was out of the sand, couldn't feel the hot sun on her flesh, wasn't aware that there was air to breathe even as it filled her lungs, wasn't aware of anything but that Marco was dead.

There was just fact like an all-encompassing blackness. A cool pit in the centre of her chest. Her cheeks were dry and dusted with sand, Graham holding her, calling her name, asking if she was okay, her leg colouring a dune like a sunrise.

Graham worked on the wound while Vic sat there numbly. She gradually realised that they were on the back of a low dune in the training grounds, where at least it was legal to use a dive suit. Though they were long past legality. People were trying to kill them. No find was worth this. Danvar wasn't worth this. Vic could feel the senseless violence of retribution attacks, that blank stagger when people would mill about the dunes after a bomb had interrupted a funeral or a wedding or a queue at the cistern. *Bang*, and the world stopped making sense. *Bang*, and mothers were wailing. *Bang*, and body parts mingled. *Bang. Bang. Bang.* The lucky would make it out to mourn. For the lucky there would be a click, a misfiring of fate, a dud of doom. Vic was there on that slope of sand, and Marco was dead. Life was capricious and cruel and totally fucking random and there was no hope of finding meaning in a nightmare. In a nightmare at least her enraged screams would come out a hoarse whisper, but Vic could not manage even that. Could not manage even a whimper. There was just the thrum of her leaking pulse and the distant growl of whatever the hell made that noise way beyond No Man's Land.

'You're lucky,' Graham said. He was winded. Was tying off her calf with a strip of her own bloody trouser leg, had torn it without her realising. 'Missed the bone. Damn lucky.'

She just stared at him. She could taste blood in her mouth. She hoped it was hers and not Marco's. Hers from falling face first into the sand, from biting her tongue. *Don't let it be his.*

'I don't have air enough for both of us,' Graham said. 'Not for long. And my suit's not on a full charge. But we need to get you out of here. They're after me.'

'They're after Palmer,' Vic said, thinking out loud. Her voice had returned, but it was distant, as though it were being carried to her on the wind from some faraway place.

'Yes,' Graham said. 'Do you think you can walk? I haven't taken us far. You should get out of here if your leg is okay.'

'What about you?'

'I'm going to bury those two.' He said it like a man announcing his intention to take a piss. 'And I can live in these dunes longer than they can search for me. If you want to stay here, I can try to snag a tank from the market. I know where there's an extra suit—'

'The marina,' Vic said. 'My suit's there.'

Graham nodded. 'I can get you partway. They'll never catch you if you can stay moving. You should lie low for a few days. Get way out of town for a while.'

Vic thought of her two brothers out camping. She wondered where Palmer was. Life had been simple and good an hour ago. Click. Boom. It couldn't happen like that. It couldn't.

'Hey, Vic, are you with me? You're not going into shock, are you? You've lost some blood—'

'Marco,' she said. She focused on Graham's face for the first time. He was the nearest thing she had left to a father. 'I loved him. He's dead. Marco's dead.'

'Well, let's worry about you, then. You've got a sarfer in the marina?'

She nodded.

'I'll get you there. You just need to figure out where you're going once I do.'

'Brock,' she said. She remembered Marco's words. Remembered his voice. His face. 'The northern wastes. West of the grove, south of a spring. That's where I'm going.'

And Vic became aware of the sun on her cheek, the grit in her mouth, the wind in her hair. She came alive as one returns from sleep. Alive but different. An empty husk capable of thought, of hearing, of processing. Of wanting men dead.

That Final Embrace

PALMER

P almer kept the wind on his left cheek and pressed south. He'd never felt so weak, so tired, so ready to lie down and succumb. Three nights of staggering in the dark, a lengthening furrow of sand trailing behind his shuffling feet. Three nights of marching and three mornings of sleeping in dwindling dune-shade. Three days of high noon spent roasting, trying to cover himself in sand to protect his skin. Three afternoons of watching the shade slowly form again, giving him somewhere to starve in peace.

His black dive suit was too hot to wear in the day, so he kept it draped over his head to cast a little shade. At night, the same thin suit couldn't keep him from shivering. Whenever he stripped it off, he wept at the sight of his emaciated frame, his ribs jutting out like rolling dunes, his pelvis that of a dead man, his legs too frail to carry him one step further. It'd been a week or more since he'd had a meal, but he would thirst to death before he starved. Wouldn't be long. Wouldn't be long.

And yet – knowing this – he took another step. Didn't know why. Just did. His left foot dragged and left a furrow behind. The sun was coming up, the stars fading one by one until it was only Mars up there, ready to war with him another day. Have to peel his suit off soon. Last time. Palmer wouldn't make it through this day, could no longer feel the hunger. The gnawing had become distant. He would die on the hot sand. This day – he was sure of it. Another two or three nights to Springston at that limping rate. The crows would get him. He could see them circling. They knew.

'Caw,' he whispered, the word choked back by his swollen tongue. 'Caw.'

The sun topped the hill to his left and its naked rays struck his cheek like an open palm. A lucid memory of his father. Palmer remembered the only time his father had ever struck him. It had been a joke. Just a joke. Second day with a dive suit on, wanting to show what Vic had taught him, had been gonna do a full submerge, had thought he was getting the hang of loosening the sand, making it flow. He'd opened a soft patch beneath his father's boot and closed the sand around it, had thought he'd be proud for the trick, had thought he'd laugh.

Palmer remembered the bright flash of light and the crack like wood splitting. The fire on his face . . . He'd been knocked to the sand, had lain there with the taste of blood in his mouth. His father standing over him, yelling at him, telling him to remember the code, the code he'd learned just the day before, what happened to any diver who made a weapon of the sand. What the other divers would do to him.

It was the only time he'd ever hit him. And it was the last time Palmer had tried to make his father laugh. He'd been ten years old. Just about Rob's age. Rob. The kid was too damn curious. Mom said he got it from their father. If it led to danger, whatever it was, it came from their father. What little good they had in them came from her. Her side of the story. Only left with her side, her version of events.

That's what Dad got. His doing. His fault for leaving. Poor Rob. Too curious, that boy. Causing trouble. With only Conner to look after him.

And Conner . . . who just wanted to be like his older brother, who wanted to starve like his older brother and stagger along, a sack of skin draped on bones, shuffling across that hot sand before he was eaten by the crows. A diver. A dream of being buried without a marker. Lost in the sand. Chasing his misfortune. No . . . camping. His brother wasn't a diver. He was camping. Four days under the sand. Three nights marching. A week. He would die the day his father had. The note by his belly was truth. Poetry and truth.

'Caw,' Palmer whispered to the circling crows. He reached down and shook the canteen as if it might have filled itself. Still the chance he might come upon a spring. An oasis. He marched for hours and hours, thinking on his brothers, on his life ending, amounting to nothing, watching for an oasis. The sun cooked the sand, and this day he didn't stop. Didn't pull his dive suit off. Didn't bury himself in the sand. Wouldn't make it to evening. Wouldn't make it another step. But then he did. He doubted every step and took another. The crows cried in disbelief. Palmer tried to laugh, but his throat was closed tight, was swollen shut, lips cracked and bleeding and bonded together. When there, on the horizon, in the wavering heat of the afternoon sun, a tree. A solitary tree. A sign of water. Another mirage to stumble through, to kick up dry sand right through the middle of, but maybe this would be the one.

He veered towards the tree. Hoping. Moving with what vigour his bones had left. The tree was getting closer. Faster than his stagger ought to make it. The tree was rounding a dune. The mast of a sarfer. The crimson sail of rebels. Brock and his men.

Palmer tried to run, his brain remembering back to when that was possible. But his damnable body reminded him of more recent events by collapsing onto the sand. Palmer spat grit. He coughed – his swollen tongue in the way. Peering to the side, he saw the sarfer speeding towards him. Maybe they didn't see him. But the damn crows, circling and diving, a cloud of swooping arrows, betraying him. *Here, here*, they cried. And the sarfer came.

Maybe to save him. The rebels would save him. Palmer nearly stood and waved his arms, and then he saw Hap's gaping mouth full of sand, his body twisted out of shape, heard the shouts inside that tent to catch him and kill him dead. Two more nights of walking and he would've made it to the outskirts of Springston. This is what his fevered brain thought as he began to scoop sand over his head. On his knees, his forehead against a dune, ass in the air, the wind offering little help, he scooped handfuls of sand and dumped them on the back of his neck, sobbed for help, sobbed beneath the gyring crows, trying to bury himself before someone else did.

There came the approaching crunch of a sarfer's foils carving the desert floor, and then a spray of fine sand as the wind-powered craft slewed to a halt. Palmer kept his forehead to the ground and bit down on his whimpers. His back remained arched up into the sky, his dive suit hanging loose around him, sand spilling through his hair and down the cuff of his neck.

He heard the whir and zip of a line passing through gloves and wooden blocks. The creak of boom and mast and the noise of a sail depowered and left to flap in the wind. Boots landed on the sand and crunched towards him. A sword to spill him or a canteen to fill him, he didn't have the courage or energy to look. Palmer had left his wits and senses a thousand dunes behind.

Someone asked him to show his hands, wanted to see his palms. They asked again. He tried to raise his hands but couldn't. It was the sword. The sword was coming for him.

Strong hands fell on his shoulders and rolled him over. Sand fell from his hair and across his face. 'Palm,' the voice said again. 'Palm.'

The mirage of his sister. A hallucination. His sister, the red flapping sail of a rebel sarfer behind her. His sister, tugging her gloves off, wiping the sand from his cheek, the mud from his crying. She was crying as well. Fumbling with her canteen, hands shaking, a mask of horror on her face from the sight of him, Palmer unable to speak.

She lifted his chin, crying, 'Palm. Oh, Palm.' Precious water was tipped over blistered lips and around his fat tongue. Palmer's throat was a clenched fist. There was no swallowing. No swallowing. He felt the water evaporate in his mouth, slip inside his tongue, become absorbed. Vic poured more. Her hand shook, canteen and eyes leaking, whispered his name. She had come looking for him.

The water sat in his mouth until it disappeared. Another cap, and something like a swallow, a loud and painful gulp, a body remembering how.

'Danvar,' he croaked. 'I found it.'

'I know you did,' Vic said. She rocked him back and forth. 'I know you did.'

'Might be trouble,' Palmer hissed. He needed to tell her about Brock, about the bombs, about getting out of there.

'Save your strength,' Vic said. 'Everything's gonna be okay.'

She wiped her cheeks, and Palmer watched as more tears spilled from her eyes. The loose sail flapped nearby, the crows watching to see what would happen. The drums grumbled far to the east, their growling voices carried on the wind, and Vic told him over and over that everything would be okay, even as she started sobbing, even as she clutched him in her arms, whispering it would all be all right. But Palmer knew this was just a story, just a story told over a sputtering lantern in a family tent, and that it wasn't true. Never had been.

PART 4 – THUNDER DUE EAST

35

Oasis

The sarfer crunched across the sand and slowed to a stop. Sand hissed against the bright red sail and spilled over the edge of the boom in a veil. Vic lowered the sail and studied the depression between the dunes. A handful of stumps poked feebly towards the sky, but whatever tall trees had lived there had long ago been butchered. Between the stumps there was a dark spot of sand, almost as if the sun were casting a shadow. It was no oasis, but it would do.

She jumped down to the sand and helped her brother out of the haul rack. The small bimini she'd made to keep him in the shade was already tattered and threadbare from the half-day of sailing due south. Part of her wanted to press on to Springston and get there before dark. The rest of her felt sure her brother wouldn't make it that far without water.

His head listed from side to side as Vic gathered him in her arms. He weighed little more than a tank and a gear bag. Vic lowered him to the line of shaded sand by the sarfer's hull and grabbed Marco's dive suit from the gear she'd crammed into his helm chair. She folded the suit several times, lifted Palmer's head, and slid the pillow between him and the sand.

Palmer asked for water. Vic slung her canteen around from her back and shook it. Empty. 'Hang in there,' she said. 'I'm getting you some.'

She left him in the shade. Back at the helm, her own dive suit was plugged into the small wind generator that poked up from the aft of the sarfer. She unplugged this, stripped down in the hot sun, grabbed scoops of sand and rubbed it over her armpits and her sweaty chest, then brushed herself off as best she could. She tugged on the dive suit, which was hot and smelled like melting rubber. Tears wetted her cheeks. She cursed these and wiped them away. Her brother was dying. Her brother was a pile of chapped and sunburnt bones. It horrified her to see him that way. Horrified her to think of Marco, her lover, dead. Killed right in front of her. And now she was going to lose a brother, too.

She dug her visor out of her gear bag, wiped her cheeks again and promised herself that it wouldn't happen. Not Palmer. Through clenched teeth, she promised. No one else would die that day. No one. She slung Marco's canteen over her head. It rattled emptily against hers and Palmer's. 'I'll be right back,' she said. She scanned the horizon for sarfer masts, had seen dozens in the distance on the sail south, but none right then. Supine on the sand by the sarfer's hull, Palmer looked peaceably asleep. This is what she told herself as she powered on her suit and disappeared beneath the sand.

Palmer lay alone on the warm sand and stared at the dark patch his sister had vanished into. The minutes ticked by like hours. The crows that'd followed them as they'd sailed south circled overhead. His sister had taken his canteen. Hap's canteen, the one with his name etched into the side. Palmer remembered the dive they'd been on when Hap had carved his name there with his dive knife. They'd left their gear buried in the sand. Hap had been worried they might get their canteens mixed up. Same models. Both new. So young then. Worried about what was whose. Worried about sharing. Tenuous friends. A lifetime ago.

More minutes went by. Palmer stared out over the desert sand. Vic had emptied her canteen into his mouth one cap at a time. His stomach was in knots. Springston and hope felt so very far away. And where could they go once they got there? People wanted him dead. He remembered the way Hap's body had been twisted out of shape. What the hell had he got himself involved in? And for what? Some coin?

A crow swooped down and lighted on the sarfer. The mainsail flapped, and the bird flapped back. It pecked the aluminium with its beak, the reaper rapping to be let in. Palmer waved his arm and begged it to go. He wondered what he would do if Vic didn't come back. How long before the sun slid overhead and his shade dwindled to nothing? How long before another diver or a brigand found the sarfer with its flapping sail? How long?

The crow startled and with a beat of its black wings laboured into the sky. Palmer heard a deep gasp. He turned to see Vic sliding up out of the ground, sand cascading off her and catching in the breeze. She took deep breaths. Rested on the sand for a moment. And then she flipped up her visor and startled Palmer with the barest of smiles.

36

A Note from Father

ROB

'We're gonna put a tear in Father's tent,' Rob warned. He could see at once what his older brother had planned, could tell by the way he was knotting the ropes. It wasn't going to be good for the tent.

'This is *our* tent,' Conner said, correcting him. 'Yours and mine. Not Father's. And we can't very well carry her all the way to town.'

Conner went back to his knots, and Rob watched his brother work in the pale light of the starry sky. The horizon was beginning to lighten beyond No Man's Land, out where the sporadic bootfalls of stomping giants could be heard. The sun would be up within an hour by his estimate.

He turned back to the girl and watched her sleep. They had moved their bedding and the girl out onto the sand in order to collapse the tent. She lay flat on her back with her head to the east and her feet to the west. Sand gathered in her hair. She might have appeared to be dead were it not for the almost imperceptible rise and fall of her chest, which lay partly exposed by the rip in her shirt. Rob reached over and pulled the fabric shut, covering her pale flesh. He had watched as Conner had cleaned her wounds. His brother had two extra canteens of water and all kinds of bandages and supplies in his pack. Rob didn't ask about these things. He knew what they were for. He didn't ask why Conner had been out of the tent in the middle of the night. He knew where Conner was going. It scared him to think of being alone, but that's what Conner had planned. Rob kept all this to himself. He often saw how things worked, how they fitted together, and had long given up on explaining these things to those older than him. Adults just looked at him with strange expressions when he spoke his insights, as though they didn't believe him. Or were frightened of him. Or both.

'If you're done fondling her breasts, you can grab my pack and stop this damn tent from flapping.'

Rob grabbed Conner's pack. No point in telling him he hadn't been fondling her breasts. It would just sound as if he had been. Silence would sound the same way too. Didn't matter either way, so he saved his breath. He carried Conner's pack and set it on the folded tent opposite where his brother was knotting the lines. The fabric stopped flopping around in that pre-dawn breeze.

'Make a pillow for her. Up here where her head will go.' His brother sounded annoyed. No, something worse than that. Conner wasn't being himself. He sounded scared and unsure. Rob didn't like that.

'We should put her head back here and drag her feet first,' Rob told his older brother. 'To keep the wind and sand out of her face.'

Conner studied him for a moment. That look. 'Whatever,' he said. It's what adults said instead of: *You're right*.

The girl was moved onto the sand for a moment. The bedding went onto the tent, and then the girl went back onto the bedding. All their gear was arranged on the flat canvas, which was now like a sarfer with no skids and no sail. Just two sets of lines to shoulder. It was a long way back into town, but neither Rob nor his brother complained as they adjusted their kers, draped the ropes over their shoulders and leaned into the task.

'What if she dies before we get there?' Rob asked.

'She won't.'

'But how do you know?'

'I just do, okay? Now shut up and do your share or we'll go in circles.'

Rob pulled. He counted his steps. Whenever he could, he counted anything that could be counted. A few years back, he and Conner's camping trip had come on a windless night, and when the fire had died down to coals and the stars had burst bright, he had counted five thousand, two hundred and fifty-eight stars before he couldn't be sure if he was counting the same ones over again. Numbers calmed him in a way that words couldn't. If he thought with words, they went around in circles and crashed into each other and grew more dire and terrifying, just like they were right then as he forgot to count steps and remembered that camping trip and worried that they were dragging a dead girl across the sand.

'She made it out of No Man's Land,' Conner finally said, as if he could sense Rob's worry. 'She'll make it to town.'

Rob didn't argue. He dug his boots into the sand and tried to do as much work as his brother. He could feel a blister forming on the back of his heel. He was tired. They'd only gone to sleep what felt like a few hours ago.

'What're the chances someone would show up on this night?' Rob asked his brother. 'This night of all nights?'

'Not good,' Conner said. 'The same as dropping a grain of sand and then finding it again. Those are the chances.'

Rob thought so too. 'She said she had a . . . a message

from Father.' He grunted between words from the effort of the haul.

'She was delirious. Keep quiet and pull. Let's head to the right a little and around that next dune. Get in the lee.'

Rob obeyed. He kept his thoughts to himself. Which meant he couldn't know if Conner was piecing together all that *he* was piecing together. Coincidences didn't make sense, but if they did happen, they could get you thinking really strange thoughts. He knew a boy in Shantytown – a kid in his class – whose roof had caved in twice, both times on his birthday, six years apart. It had buried him in drift both times, but they had dug him out. Now he slept under the stars every birthday and wouldn't listen to sense about it. He also hated the number six. And as much as Rob found this silly, he was pretty sure he'd be the same way if that had happened to him.

And now his brain was whirling with all kinds of new facts. People came out from No Man's Land. That wasn't supposed to happen. So maybe Old Man Joseph wasn't so crazy after all. Old Man Joseph claimed to have been to the other end of No Man's Land and returned, but no one believed him. But maybe. And maybe Father was alive out there somewhere. Maybe he had sent this girl to them. And if so, he had sent her to arrive on the night he and his brother would be there. But there was something else about what she had said—

'Hey, Conner?'

'Jesus, Rob, what the fuck is it?'

'She didn't say "your" father. She just said Father.'

'Save it, Rob. I'm thinking.'

Rob felt the blister on his heel go. Raw flesh began to rub. Sand would get in, and then the real hurting would begin.

'I'm thinking too, you know.' He bit his lip and tried not to limp, tried to be strong. His brother took a deep breath beside him.

'I know. I'm sorry. What're you thinking, little brother?'

'I'm thinking the way she said Father, it was like hers and ours are the same one.'

They reached the lee of a great dune, and the whispering wind fell quiet and the rushing sand was no longer at their ankles but high above their heads. Conner eventually answered.

'I've been thinking the same thing,' he finally said.

37

The Sand-filled Screams of the Dying

ROSE

A pad of paper spelled out the bad news in a single column of numbers. There was more subtraction than addition taking place. Rose would've been happy to break even, for every dollar earned to be a dollar spent. But rarely were such balances kept. If there was a zero-sum game, it was played among a host of winners and losers. Businesses like hers going under – literally, more often than not – while riches piled elsewhere to the heavens. Coin was like sand in this way: it only flowed in one direction. And to compound the misery of those to the west, these two currents of woe ran counter to one another. The poor shipped off their coin to the east and got buckets of sand in return.

It was the damn water prices. The cost per litre had nearly doubled that year, which meant a near doubling in the price of beer. And the Ladies of the Balcony still needed their showers. Not so much for their clients to stand them – clients who could hardly be expected to nose their wares over their own stench – but so that the ladies could stand themselves. Rose had put it off longer than she should have. She'd have to jack up the price of a pint and hike the room rates again. There would be bitching and moaning when she announced both; people would act as though she were gouging for the fun of it. Truth was, the whole place would shut down if they had another month like this.

The din of activity beyond her door, of people spending money, served as temporary comfort. News of Danvar's discovery had the divers in a mood. Even the Lords seemed interested. They were already scrambling for who might have title based on mineral claims, arguing and spilling beer on ancient maps. Rose had seen this play out before. There would be a frenzy of spending all the spoils one *hoped* to make. This would be followed by the lean times of those same gamblers asking for loans and handouts. People hardly took a breath between these extremes. It was the stagger home of a drunk who could hit every dune on either side as he lurched in a thousand paces what he might've crossed in ten.

But Rose knew a slow rise could lead to just as precipitous a fall. She had married a man who'd decried such fits of gluttonous frenzy. Her husband had made his gradual fortune, had gone from filling tanks for other divers as a boy, to learning to dive on his own, to discovering springs for Lords, to claiming a spring for his own and fighting to defend that claim. She remembered him as a gangly teen who could barely grow a beard, had watched him climb a slope of infamy up those sometimes peaceful dunes to the heights of the great wall, and then had watched him step off just as neatly. All he might have left her had been snapped up by villainous thugs who gave themselves title and who thought a bath and a clean robe made them natural-born princes. She had been left with nothing but the Honey Hole, which her husband had won in a game of dice.

It had only been a place to stay on the night she was

tossed out with her children. But then it had been a business to manage, her only source of income. She took care of the girls and tended the bar, grew some vegetables on the roof, whatever it took to keep the water flowing. But each passing week drew the noose tighter and tighter around her neck. She looked for a buyer, but who would buy a place that barely broke even? Everyone else got their pay, she made sure of that. The drunks who swept up in the mornings for a pint made more profit than her. There was nothing left for Rose after the school fees for the kids, after the dive gear Palmer and Vic needed in order not to lose their spots. There was nothing left to help them start a life of their own, help them open a business, rent a stall in the market, anything. Nothing but mounting costs. Piles of coin transmuted into piles of resentment. Resentment that left her bitter towards her husband for bolting in the night, for leaving her a tent and a whorehouse to choose between.

For a long while, she'd only tended to the men at the bar, only slaked *that* thirst. But there had been long hours of thinking how tight the money was, and the joking offers had come fast and loose. They had been made with a laugh, but there had always been the dangle and jangle of coin. 'Hey, Rose, I give you fifty to go upstairs right now.' 'Hey, Rose, one hundred. Just scored big time down in Low-Pub.' 'Hey, Rose.' 'Hey, Rose.' 'Hey, Rose.'

There had been one night where a hundred and twenty coin had been enough. This was the cost. Enough to pierce some membrane within her, some barrier she would've sworn could not be crossed; but it had been worn down over months and months of lean times. Worn so thin the right words could make it through.

The offer had come from a customer she'd known well enough, might have dated if they'd been sitting on the same side of the bar, if they'd been around any other bar, in any other place, at any other time. She would've had sex with him for nothing, the way a respectable woman does. Instead, she'd let him pay. And it hadn't been bad. He'd cared. Asked her if that had felt okay. Had done all the work. Hadn't hit her or spanked her or asked if he could choke her a little. Had pulled out and even cleaned her up with his shirt. She would've done it for free. Had nearly told him so as he'd left stacks of coin on her dresser. Fragile, wobbly things, all that coin. Like the tall scrapers to the east.

And then he'd gone back to the bar, and Rose had sat and stared at the towers of coin sitting on the dresser her husband had left her, and it had been a different woman who'd walked out that door. She would survive, she'd realised. But it would be a different her. It would be someone *else* who did the surviving, who would drag memories of a former self along, a tiny echo of a woman somewhere deep in her skull, a small voice of who she used to be.

When Palmer had come asking for a little help the next day, it had felt different. He had been fourteen back then, and Rose had thought he could tell. She'd thought he knew. *She* sure as hell had, and the same ten coin that he had asked for and always got had suddenly weighed the same as ten thousand. Palmer had pocketed it too readily. As if it had been the same coin. But it'd been too hard won for that. Not to slide away so easily. Not to just disappear. And here had been when the gulf with her children had opened. It had opened not the day her legs had, but the day her palms had. It had been the only way, she'd told herself. There had been no other. She would earn her keep the only way she could. And the cost of dispensing that keep could only grow.

It had been inevitable that her children would find out. Men don't just talk, they brag. They brag about rented love, even. And children hear everything. They are echo chambers. And they take what they learn from their parents off to school more readily than they haul anything of merit home. A father's boast becomes a way to torment a peer. And so the boys had heard about her new line of work from the worst source possible.

No, not quite. Vic had heard about it from someone even worse than the boys. A client. A young man who had made a flippant comparison, who'd thought it might be taken as a compliment, who had said in the heat of passion that the daughter was more expert than the mother.

Vic had already stopped coming around the Honey Hole, wouldn't even approach the place. And after this, she wouldn't agree to see Rose anywhere. Not for three long years. And so her children had begun to wither like the roof gardens did when showers and beer water took precedence. They had begun to die to her and she to them. Even as the small voice she carried deep within her soul relented now and then and dispensed with hard-fought coin. Even though some part of her left her pillow wet in the morning as it leaked out in quiet sobs. Leaked out, but never emptied.

All this and more, her husband had taken the day he'd run off. All this and more he had stolen. But she would survive. Rose told herself this as she studied the column of numbers where more was subtracted than added. There was a knock at the door. She checked her watch. It was her six o'clock.

Oh yes, she would survive.

38

No Place for a Girl

CONNER

The sun was up by the time the boys entered Springston and swung around the edge of the great wall. There was still shade in that part of town where people could afford to delay the rising sun and be sheltered from the creep of sand. And though it was early and a Sunday, Conner felt something was amiss. There was that nervous buzz about town, like after a bomb had gone off – but bombs rarely went off so early in the day. The young men who caused violence were as lazy as any youths when it came to getting out of bed. And besides, there were no columns of smoke. No wailing mothers. Instead, there were the sails of sarfers spread out to the horizon. There was an empty marina with bare hitching posts jutting out of the ground and only the wind passing through. There were people in front of their homes, talking with neighbours, out and about, even though the markets had not yet opened.

'Head left here,' Conner told his brother. There was a doctor on the edge of Springston who sometimes took people in from Shantytown. He might help them. He might be trusted if he found out where the girl came from.

Where the girl came from. Conner chanced a look over

his shoulder. She could be sleeping or dead. She could be someone who had wandered into No Man's Land with her family and had turned back after two days of hiking. But she had spoken his name. Had mentioned his father. If she died, would anyone believe their account of things? Or would he become Old Man Joseph, standing at the intersection of the great dunes, holding a sign, screaming to frightened kids about No Man's Land?

These were the thoughts swirling in his mind long before the sun came up. Conner couldn't stop thinking of all the girl might know, might say, if she survived. Their father might still be alive. Twelve years of camping on the edge of No Man's Land, twelve years of listening to the wind moan across the Bull's gash, twelve years of Shantytown, of their mother selling herself, and their father might still be out there.

Conner outpulled Rob, his legs pumping as his thoughts raced. They rounded the corner and stopped outside Doc Welsh's place—

'Closed,' Rob said.

There was a sign on the door. Half the stalls they had passed were closed, but a glance at the sun told him it was after nine. They'd been hiking for almost five hours. 'What in the world is going on?' Conner asked. He dropped the line and went back to the girl on the tent. Rob was right about the wear on the canvas. Conner could see where it was tearing. He pulled his canteen out of his pack and knelt by the girl to give her more water.

'Is it a special Sunday?' Rob asked.

'Not that I know of.' Conner poured a capful there in the shade of the doctor's office. 'Bang on the door,' he said.

His brother did. A woman with a load balanced on her head hurried past. 'Hey,' Conner called to her.

She slowed. The load wobbled as she turned her head. 'You know if Doc is out on a call?'

The lady looked at them both as though they were from the northern wastes. She gave the girl lying still on the folded canvas a brief glance. 'Probably out looking for Danvar,' she said. 'Haven't you heard?'

'Danvar?' Conner asked, quite certain he'd heard wrong.

The lady didn't dare nod. 'They found it,' she said. 'Half the town's out there now. The other half is scrambling for their coin. I've gotta go.'

She and her load turned and headed off.

'Wait!' Conner called out. 'This girl needs help!'

'Good luck,' the lady called.

Conner turned and beseeched the next couple who hurried past, two men with dive tanks on their backs who made a concerted effort not to look his way, not to even glance at him for fear of the guilt they might suffer. Rob looked as if he were on the verge of tears. The cap of water disappeared into the girl's mouth, but she didn't swallow. Conner tried to feel for a pulse but he didn't really know how. Maybe that was his own pulse in his thumb he was sensing.

'What the hell?' he asked. He studied his hands, which were raw from the haul. His legs ached from the long hike with the weight of the girl and the tent. There were doctors deeper into Springston who he couldn't afford, but he could tell them what the girl promised. What she might mean. Or he could go door to door in Shantytown and beg for help. Hope someone might know more to do than give her water and clean the sand out of her wounds.

'What about Mother?' Rob asked.

Conner's hands shook as he twisted the cap back onto the canteen. He peered up at his brother, who had tears streaking down both cheeks. It was the worst idea either of them could possibly have. But it was also likely that their mother was the only person who would take the girl in, who might know what to do for her.

'Goddamn you,' Conner told his brother. He cursed him for being right.

39

A Rose on the Pillow

ROSE

The leak in the pipes had not been fixed as the plumber had said. Rose could see that the brown stain had spread across the white-painted ceiling, had grown. It was a stain within a stain within a stain, three concentric brown patches of varying hue, one patch each for the three times the plumber had ripped her off, one patch each for the three times the plumbing to the upstairs basins had leaked precious water. Drip, drip, drip goes the coin.

The crack up there was getting worse as well. Widening. A zig at the end that used to be a zag, moving its way back and forth across that warped surface. The sands were shifting, the walls twisting, a house out of shape.

And the springs. The springs of the bed needed oiling. They sounded like the mad call of some crazed bird, some animal that chirped over and over, waiting for a response, for a hint of life, for awareness from some other, but only getting a rhythmic silence. A pause for every squeak. *Week, week, week, week.* Years piling up.

Her husband had brought her the bed triumphantly, had raised it from nearly four hundred metres, or so he'd bragged. And it was heavy. She could attest to that. Rose had moved it with a friend when the palace had fallen. It was all she had left in the world: the bed, that dresser, this brothel. It was fitting how her husband had left her prepared for her new life. Other men concerned themselves with getting their family up on their feet. Rose had fallen for a man who had left her on her back.

'How was that for you?' the man asked. He had evidently finished. Was now looking down at her expectantly, sweat dripping from his nose to splash between her breasts. His arms – muscled but layered with fat – trembled. There was more hair on his shoulders than his head, and his beard was full of sand.

'Oh, you're the best,' Rose told him.

'Ah, you're just saying that.' He grunted and fell to the side, a flock of startled springs chirping.

'I'm not,' Rose said. 'You know you're my favourite.' She prayed to the gods he wouldn't ask her what his name was. *Please, please, please don't ask.* They always wanted to hear it, to make it personal, to own more than just her time. But he didn't ask. Worse: he started snoring.

Rose groaned and moved gingerly to the washbasin. She pulled the sewn intestine out from between her legs and washed it in the shallow puddle of water. The milky swimmers swirled on the surface with the others before slowly settling to the bottom. Rose draped the intestine over the lip of the basin with two others to dry. With a towel, she wiped off what had leaked out and had dribbled down her inner thigh to her knee. She dressed while the man snored. She would charge him rent for the bed if he stayed more than an hour. Serve him right.

Leaving the room, she stood on the narrow balcony walkway that circled the inside of the Honey Hole. It was dead quiet below, early in the morning, but the remnants of a noisy evening were scattered everywhere. Drunks sleeping on the floor, curled around bar-stool legs like lovers. *Spent as much time on them as on any woman*, Rose thought. A card game had been abandoned, the pot and players missing but the empty jars and cans and glasses standing in a crowd around the discard pile and folded hands. There were two puddles in the middle of the floor to clean up – piss or spilled beer. Idiots wasting their coin on fluids they couldn't get in them, or on fluids that would pass right through.

Another of the doors opened down the catwalk – or the 'Esplanade of Pussy', as one of her regulars called it. Diana stood in her doorway and suffered a deep kiss goodbye, and then her client waddled down the stairs towards the bar, fumbling with the laces on his fly as he went.

Diana and Rose exchanged weary and knowing glances. They peered over the railing at all that needed cleaning before happy hour that night. Weekend hell. No sleep for the dreary.

Rose tried to remember a time before this routine. She felt like a speck of sand in an alien land, confused as to how it had got there. Carried on the wind from one dune to the next, each getting her closer to a destination she never would've chosen if there had been some way to make the wind listen.

There was no one behind the bar. Off for a piss or gone home. That bar had been the first dune, Rose thought. She remembered standing there, drying empty jars, letting the men leer before they went up to give one of her girls five minutes of displeasure. That was the first dune. And it led to all the others. A woman not for sale until the Honey Hole was. But no takers for the latter. Only a few years from being duned over, they said. The books didn't shine too bright, they said. Not enough coin in it, they said. Can't mix business with pleasure, they laughed.

Rose had come dangerously close to simply walking away. The only thing that stopped her was not wanting to be like her husband, not wanting to abandon her children. He had taken even this luxury away from her. Had made her so angry at his abandonment that running away had become a power removed. And so she was trapped.

The door to her prison opened with a squeak, letting some light in. It was her children, Conner and Rob. Just the sort of hour at which she would expect them to burst in, needing something, palms open. She nearly yelled at them, let the mood her client had put her in rain down on their heads, but then she saw what Conner was carrying. Not this. She didn't need this. She rushed down the stairs to send them away, to tell them to find a damn doctor, not to bring their mistakes to her. But Conner's mouth opened before hers could – and out spilled the impossible.

40

Ticking Bombs

VIC

Vic emerged from the moist and heavy sand and took great gulps of glorious air. She rested as long as she dared, the sun beating down on her, before joining her brother in the shade of the sarfer's hull. Palmer had been watching her with obvious relief, a grimace-like smile on his face. But as she handed him her canteen, which sloshed now with spring water, Palmer seemed to catch sight of his blurry reflection in the shiny metal. His pained smile melted into a pained frown. He reached up to touch his cheek.

'I don't look so good,' he whispered. There were tears in his eyes as Vic took the canteen back from him and worked the cap off. Palmer met her gaze. He reached to his swollen lips. 'How do I look?'

'You look like someone who should be dead but isn't. It's a good look.'

'I feel like a blister that's about to pop.'

'Yeah, I was going to say that.'

They shared something like laughter, and Vic handed him the open canteen. Palmer took a sip, his cheeks billowing and contracting as he swished the water around. He laboured to swallow. 'You were gone so long . . .'

'Sorry. Not much of a spring here. Had to go down quite a ways to fill the canteens. There's grit in there, so don't tip it too much—'

'It's okay. I could eat a dune.' Palmer's hands shook as he lifted the canteen to his lips again.

Vic helped him steady the vessel. While he worked the water down, she took a small sip from Marco's canteen, her lips pressed where her lover's once had. 'We'll get you some food in town,' she said, trying to think on other things. 'But we should probably stay here the night.'

Her brother looked past her to the horizon. 'Are we safe? No one followed us here?'

Vic smoothed the hair off his forehead. She remembered Palmer when he was much younger. He seemed much younger right then. Her brother was terrified. 'What happened?' she asked. She had yet to ask him about the dive or the discovery, about the people looking for him in Springston. She had been too worried about losing him, too concerned about finding water and food and nursing him back to health.

Her brother took another swig from the canteen, his blistered hands shaking. He dabbed gently at his cracked lips with the sleeve of his dive suit. Winced. Stared up at the bands of sand swirling on the wind.

'They were never going to let us go,' he said.

'Who was never going to let you go?'

'Brock and his men. That crazy dive master. They brought us there to find Danvar and then to die.'

'But you did find it.'

Palmer nodded. 'Five hundred metres down.'

'No,' Vic said. She situated herself against the hull of the sarfer, blocking the wind for Palmer. 'You didn't go that deep.'

'They'd made a pit and a hole, had the first two hundred

clear for us. I don't know how. Hundreds of dive suits wired up together. It was amazing. And the scrapers down there, Vic. You should see them. Hundreds of metres tall. We hit the tops of the largest of them at five hundred. Was another five hundred or so to the street.'

Palmer must've seen the look of disbelief on her face. 'They'd dug a pit,' he said. 'Did I mention that? But we were down three hundred true. Maybe close to three fifty.'

'You went down three hundred metres,' Vic said. 'Are you out of your fucking mind?'

'You can but I can't?'

She didn't have an answer for that. Not without sounding like their mother. 'Was it untouched?'

Something flashed across her brother's face. 'Not quite,' he said. 'Two other divers had gone down before us, but they didn't make it back.'

'So you were the first to get down and back up? *You* discovered Danvar.' Vic heard the awe and disbelief in her own voice.

Palmer looked away. 'Hap made it back before me. And Hap saw it first. He's the one.'

'But you said Hap was dead—'

Her brother reached up and patted his forehead as if looking for something. 'My visor,' he said. 'They got both our visors.' He seemed to deflate even further with this, seemed to sink down within that too-big dive suit, as if the last juice of life had been squeezed from him.

'Do you think you could find Danvar again?' Vic asked.

Palmer hesitated. 'I don't know. Maybe. If we found their camp, or the remnants of their fire, then maybe. But without the hole they made, it'd be too deep to reach those buildings again.'

'I could get down there,' she told him.

Her brother searched her face, almost as if trying to see if she was kidding.

'Do you know how they found it?' she asked. 'How did they know to dig there?'

Palmer nodded up towards the sky. 'The stars,' he said. 'Colorado's belt. They had a map that showed Low-Pub and Springston and another town in a line, just like the constellation. The third star was Danvar. They knew where it was.'

'A map . . .'

Her brother flinched. A jolt of life and energy. He patted excitedly at his stomach, fumbled for the zipper on his pouch, and out spilled coin after coin—

'Shit,' Vic said, plucking one out of the sand. It was a copper. Untarnished. Beautiful. Thirty or more pieces spilled out and were quickly covered by the rush.[12] Her brother seemed uninterested in these as she gathered them up. He pulled out a folded piece of paper.

'A map,' he said. The paper trembled as he struggled to get it unfolded. Vic helped. She took over. It was a large sheet. It popped in the wind, sand collecting in the folds with a hiss and sliding down into her lap. Vic had seen corners and scraps of maps like this, paper rotted by the sand, by time, by moisture, by being passed from hand to hand. But this was whole and untouched and a beauty to behold.

'You got their map,' Vic said. 'Fuck, Palm, you got their map.'

'No. I found that one in the scraper. It was with the coin.'

Vic bent over to protect the paper from the wind. She

[12] The sand that flows across the desert floor, covering objects and filling tracks.

folded the map in half and then in half again, had to wrestle with the creases, was worried she or the wind might rip it. There were lines and place names and numbers everywhere. Every scrap of a map she'd ever seen or heard about could fit together and not equal even a fraction of this massive, undisturbed sheet.

'Do you know what this means?' Vic studied the square she'd left exposed after her folds. There was a bright yellow collection of squiggles with the word 'Pueblo' written above. But it was a series of rectangles that had caught her eye and had drawn her attention to this part of the map. It was the crooked letter Y the rectangles made at one point, the other part like the letter H. There was a curved structure that stood along the side of them, which she knew had once been covered with a tent but now was full of sand.

'Puh . . . eh . . . blow. Enter . . . national. Air . . . port.' She sounded it out, stumbling over the words, reading them phonetically. She traced her finger from the collection of long rectangles that she had seen in her own visor, that she knew as cracked concrete slabs beneath the sand, to where she knew the ruins of Low-Pub lay. It was the same place. No doubting it.

'What is that?' Palmer asked. His eyes were wide. 'Can you read it?'

'I know this place. I've been here. This is Old Low-Pub, the buried ruins just west of town. Fuck, Palm, this is a gold mine.'

'Old Low-Pub is picked over to hell and back,' Palmer reminded her.

'I know. But this is a map of the *old world*. This thing is ancient. And if it's to scale—' She held three fingers together and placed them between Low-Pub and the dive site where she'd been picking over a cache of bags for months.

Flipping the map around, she refolded it to reveal something else. She measured her way north three fingers at a time. There was an even larger squiggle of lines and place names right where she expected them to be. 'Colorado Springs,' she said. She felt a chill, reading these words, realising it was Springston. Visors were suddenly pulled down over her eyes that allowed her to see through all the sand that choked the old world. She was a god watching from on high. 'This is Twin Rock Path,' she said. She showed her brother the dark set of double lines that ran between Low-Pub and Springston. It was the path their great-grandfather had followed in order to discover Low-Pub. Or so legend had it.

'Enter . . . state . . . twenty-five,' Palmer sounded out. 'The path has a number.' He tried to sit up to see better.

'There are a thousand dive sites here,' Vic said. She felt dizzy, looking at the map. Dizzy and excited. The danger her brother was in dimmed for a moment. But only for a moment.

'The people who want me dead,' Palmer said. 'I don't . . . I don't think they were looking for Danvar to scavenge, Vic. I'm not even sure it was Danvar Brock was after.'

She tore her eyes away from the map. 'Then why would he have you dive down there to find it?'

Palmer situated himself against the hull of the sarfer. He stared out over that dark, damp patch of sand. 'When I got back up, the pit they had dug was already filling back in. And Brock's men had broken down a few of the tents, like locating the old city was all they were after. Like they were moving on. And there was a party that came back, that had gone somewhere. The dive master was with them. They returned the night I went to the camp, looking for water. They'd gone off to find something.'

Vic didn't understand. But she didn't interrupt. Her brother was reasoning something out.

'I remember Brock saying something about us needing to be precise. He wanted us to locate those scrapers, down to the last metre. I think he was using a map the way you're talking about, to find other dive sites. That's how they knew where to look for Danvar. They were homing in on some other spot. Getting it down precise so they'd know where to dig.'

'What makes you say that?' Vic asked.

Her brother turned to her. 'Because Brock found whatever it was he was looking for. I think it was a bomb. I went into one of the tents, looking for water and food. There was a crate of smaller bombs. And then I hid and I heard them talking about this one device – I saw it, a strange-looking thing – and someone said this one bomb could level all of Low-Pub. And I believe them. They were serious. Organised. They laughed about leaving the desert flat. I think they mean to do it.'

Vic studied her brother. She glanced at the map. 'When?' she asked.

'I don't know. It's been three days. They saw me under the table. They probably assume I heard everything. I remember someone saying they were going to hit Springston first.'

'Maybe they'll change their plans because you heard them,' Vic said. 'Maybe they'll call it off.' She was trying to be hopeful.

'Or they'll do it sooner. Vic, we've gotta get to Springston. We've gotta get Conner and Rob out of there. We've gotta warn everyone.'

'There are people in Springston who want us dead,' she reminded him.

'Brock and his men are heading to Springston, and they want *everyone* dead,' Palmer said.

The words stung like a gust of sand. Vic shook her canteen and listened to the contents splash around. She thought of Marco and how fast a life could be taken away, what she wanted to do to those responsible, and knew in an instant that this was why bombs were made, that an unjust blast could still echo while another went off to right that wrong. Even knowing the futility of this, she could feel what Marco must've felt during all those years of fighting, the urge to lash out anyway, consequences be damned.

While she thought of spilling life into the sand, her brother looked away and up at the sky where crows circled and the tops of dunes blew in grey sheets. She knew her brother was right, that they had to warn others, had to catch these men and make them pay. She folded away the map of a thousand undiscovered treasures and slipped it into her pocket. 'We'd better get going,' she said, grinding the sand between her teeth as she helped her brother to his feet.

41

A Smuggled Tale

VIOLET

There was the sting of a wolf biting her lips. A nightmare of burning desert sand and freezing windy nights and a pack of wild beasts tearing at her flesh – all broken by a splash of water against her mouth. And the young girl woke in a strange room.

There was a woman above her. A bed. The young girl was lying on a mattress beneath sheets as clean and white as a child's teeth. Her dive suit and her britches were gone, just a shirt like a man would wear folded across her and cinched with a white ribbon – sweet-smelling and clean. She moved to touch the shirt, and her side screamed out where she'd been bitten.

'Lie still,' the woman said. She placed a hand on the young girl's shoulder and forced her back against the pillows. There were two boys in the room. They were the boys from one of her dreams. 'Can you take another small sip?' the woman asked.

The young girl nodded and a jar was brought forward, the water inside as clear as glass. She lifted her hands to help, but they were bandaged and useless. The water burned her mouth in the best way.

'What's your name?' the woman asked.

'Violet,' she said. Her voice was small in that strange room.

The woman smiled at this. 'Like the flower.'

The older of the two boys moved closer to the bed, and Violet remembered his face from her dream, but it wasn't a dream. Conner. He had picked her up and carried her. She knew where she was, that this was real. She turned to the woman with the water, who was asking about her name.

'Father said violet was the colour he saw when I was born, that it was like seeing the air from beneath the sand. That's why he named me Violet.'

The woman smoothed the hair back from the girl's forehead and frowned, as though this were the wrong answer.

'Can I have more water?' Violet whispered. Her mouth was so dry.

'Just a little,' the woman said. 'It's possible to drink too much.'

Violet nodded. 'You can drown,' she said. 'Like in the river. Or what happens if you drink the bad water from the trough.' She lifted her head and took another sip. The younger of the two boys stood at the foot of the bed and stared at her. She knew who this was. 'You're Rob,' she said.

The boy startled as if someone had stomped on his foot. Regaining his composure, he bobbed his head.

'Father said we were about the same age.'

'Then he wasted no time,' the woman with the jar of water muttered. She sounded upset. 'Where is he now? How far away is your village?'

'How did you get across No Man's Land?' the older boy asked.

'How old are you?' Rob wanted to know.

The woman snapped her fingers at the two boys, and they seemed to know this meant not to talk. And something occurred to Violet. 'You're my second mom,' she said. 'You're Rose.'

The woman's cheeks twitched at this. She shook her head and opened her mouth to say something – Violet thought maybe to say that she wasn't her mom – but instead she just wiped at one eye and kept quiet. The two boys seemed to be waiting for Violet to answer all their questions, but she had already forgotten most of them.

'I don't come from a village,' she said. She rested her head on the pillow and gazed longingly at the jar of water in the woman's hands. 'I came from a camp. It doesn't have a name, just a number, and we aren't allowed to leave. There are tents and fences, and we can see the city from the camp. Kids from the city come to the fence – there's two fences, so if you get through one the other will stop you – and some of the kids from the city throw candy through the fence and some throw rocks – it's usually the bigger kids with the rocks, which means the rocks come harder than the candy, but we're told to stay away from the fence anyway—'

'What kind of camp is this?' Rose asked.

'Like camping in a tent—?' Rob said, but he got snapped at again.

'A mining camp,' Violet said. 'It's where they blow up the ground and grab the worthy stuff out with their nets. That's what the foreman calls them, but Father says they aren't really nets. They have magnets in them. He knows all about wires and magic and stuff. They make us work the troughs for the heavier bits that drift to the bottom. We work with water up to our elbows all day, cold water. It makes your hands and fingers shrivel. People in the camp who come from the south call it the pruning flesh—'

'Water up to your elbows,' Conner scoffed. 'And where's all this water come from?'

It was clear he didn't believe her. Father had warned Violet this would happen, that no one would believe. 'The water comes from the river,' she said. 'But you can't drink it. Some do, and they die. Because of the metals and the mining. The water for drinking comes from way upstream, past all the camps, but they don't give us much of that. Father says they starve our mouths and drown our arms just to drive us mad. But it didn't make me mad. Just thirsty.'

Saying this won her another sip from the jar. Violet felt better. It was the sheets and the roof over her head and the jar of water and people to talk to.

'What's the name of this city?' Rose asked. 'Where's my husband?'

'The city is called Agyl. The people outside the fence call it that, but they talk funny, and Father says I talk too much like them because I was born in the camp. They say it's a small city, but Father says it's bigger than where he comes from. I don't know. It's the only city I've ever seen. Just a mining town. The big cities, they say, are more to the sunrise, all the way to the sea. But that's—'

'What's a sea?' Rob asked.

More snapping.

'Tell me about the people in this camp,' Rose said. 'How many are there? Where did they come from?'

Violet took a deep breath. She eyed the water. 'There are hundreds,' she said. 'Five hundreds? More. Most come from the sunset like Father. Some get there by doing something wrong in the cities. A few of these get let out after so long of working, but more are always let in. Our camp had a big number for a name, which Father said must mean there are lots of them. There are people in our camp who came from the north or the south and were already hungry like us. The ones who come from the sunset don't get let go. Not ever. They have fences and towers where they watch for them and nets to put them in.'

'How is . . . your father?' Rose asked. Her voice sounded funny. Violet eyed the jar.

'Is it okay to have more water now? It's been a while.'

Rose let her take a small sip. It reminded Violet of her father, getting a ration like this, and she started to cry. She wiped the tears off her cheek with the back of her wrist and drank them too. 'Father said you'd ask how he was and to say that he was okay, but Father doesn't always tell the truth.'

This made Rose laugh, but then she covered her mouth and began crying too. The boys fell quiet. Violet thought of what she wanted to say, some of what she was *told* to say with some truth mixed in as well.

'They don't feed us enough,' she said. 'That's what the adults say. And so people come in with muscles and then they go away. Sometimes the people go away all at once. That's when their sheets are pulled up over their heads. I always tucked my chin down like this' – she lowered her chin against her chest and pretended to hold sheets tight up against her neck – 'so it wouldn't happen to me. Father was stronger than most of the men there. Tall. With dark eyes and dark skin like the men from the sunset and dark hair like yours.' She nodded to Conner. 'But I could lay a finger between his ribs while he slept, and his ribs would go out and in, and he gave me too much of his bread.'

Violet thought on what else she needed to say. There was a lot. So much that her thoughts were getting jammed like the trough sometimes did when too much metal came.

'Did he tell us how to get to him?' Conner asked. 'What did he say we should do?'

There was no snapping for quiet. Her second mom wiped her cheeks and waited for an answer.

'He wrote a note—' Violet said.

'A note from Father?' Rob asked.

'Where is it?' Conner wanted to know.

'It was in my suit, against my skin. I think I lost it with my pack. Father told me not to read it . . .' She hesitated.

'It's okay,' Rose said. Her second mom reminded Violet a lot of her first one.

'I read part of it while he was writing it. He made me promise not to read any more. The part I read said not to come for him, to look west over the mountains, and then a confusing part about the sand in the wind and how it comes from the mining they do, that the wind also comes from something bad . . . something with the lands. I'm sorry. I'm trying to remember . . .'

'You're doing a great job,' Rose said. She smiled, but there was still water in her eyes.

'Father used to tell me that it doesn't rain where he comes from. He said the dirt the mining men throw up in the air for the magnets makes the clouds release their water into the cavern, and that's where the river comes from, and that all the rain meant for his people is taken out of the air by the sand.' She licked her lips. Again, the sting of a wolf's bite. 'He used to get really mad and talk about this and watch through the fence as the sun went down. There were always the loud booms out that way that made my ears hurt and blocked the sky up so everything was a haze, but he spent all his time on that side of the camp. The sunset people were the only ones who liked it over there. Father wanted me to stay close, but I'd rather pray for candy and not rocks by the other fence.'

'How did you get out?' Conner asked. And Rob nodded.

Rose said nothing to quieten the boys, so Violet figured it was okay to answer.

'Father gathered stuff. For as long as I can remember, maybe before I was born. Years and years. He said he was going to get us out, just the three of us, and then Mother died when I was six, and he said it would be me and him. He kept stuff in the sand, said it was silly none of the guards looked there, that people would know better where he was from. Bits of wire, a rubber raincoat, batteries, a drill someone left behind because the motor wouldn't work – but Father knew how to fix it. He spent the better part of a year getting a tool for melting wire. It was all so slow. I wanted him to hurry. And then I could place two fingers down between his ribs while he slept and his breathing sounded like he needed to cough all the time, but he said he was going to get us out.

'And then he showed me what he was making, made me swear not to tell any of the sunset people, and I had to wear it under my clothes so it wouldn't be found. He would have me take it off at night so he could work on it, adjust the wires so they didn't scratch me, and then he showed me how—'

'He made a dive suit,' Conner said.

Violet nodded. Rose held the jar to Violet's lips and she took two swallows. She felt selfish after this and dabbed her lips with her bandaged hand.

'There's a big crack in the ground,' she said. 'This is where the muddy river is, where the sand is thrown into the sky and the metals are got out. Bigger than a hundred leaps across and it got bigger and bigger every year. Father said I would have to go under this, that I would have to hold my breath a long time, that it was the only way out. He made me hold my breath while I worked the trough, made me do it over and over, could tell when I was using my nose. I practised until I could do it for long enough.

'I learned to move the sand, and one day I wanted to show him how good I was getting, so I went under the fence and came up the other side towards the city, but he got madder than I've ever seen him and told me never to go that way, that I'd only end up back here and then they'd know what we could do and everything would be worse. I had to go west, he told me, and I had to tell his people to keep going west. That's what he said. There had been a family in the camp when I was too little to remember who shared a story about a sea even past where the sun went at night, where the water wasn't muddy. It never rained there, but there was water as far as you could see.'

Conner grunted at this. Violet remembered how the sunset people in the mining camp hadn't believed this story either. But her father had. And Violet too.

'He said we shouldn't come for him,' Rose said, almost to herself.

Violet nodded. 'There were fights in camp. Some of the people from the city said there were too many of us, more and more coming all the time, that we were making their life bad. But *our* life felt bad. Father said I had to get out, that I was young and strong and that I could make it. He made me dive at night when everyone was asleep. And for months and months, he drank half-rations and filled bladders with the other halves. He caught rats and made jerky. Said it kept him going, all these things. Said it was good to stay busy. Said he never should've come there, never left his people, but that I would make it okay because I would come back and tell about the world that doesn't care for us.'

'And you're a sand diver,' Rob said, his voice full of awe, as Violet paused to catch her breath. All the nights of hiking and thinking and being alone made her want to say every-thing all at once.

'The diving was easy,' she said. 'The walking was the hard part. It was twelve days of walking. It took Father nine, but he said it would take me twelve, that I would have to count and time it right. It was very important, the day I left. Which day. He drew a picture of the mountains and showed me which was the Pike and that I would keep this just left of my nose and the star to the north directly over my right shoulder, and on the twelfth day I would see smoke and on the twelfth night I would see fire, right past a crack in the ground that he said I could leap over at the narrowest—'

'He knew we'd be camping,' Conner said. 'It was our tradition before he left. He knew we'd still be out there, every year.'

Violet nodded. 'He said if I missed the fire, if you weren't there, that I would come to a big wall and a small town, but that if I found the smoke and the fire that I would be home right then. And I was doing good, walking at night and sleeping all day and being careful with my water. Until a wolf came—'

'A wolf?' Rob asked.

'You . . . you call them coyotes, I think. In camp, they had different names for things, talked a whole other language. I grew up with both, so I forget which goes where. Dad used to say my accent was like theirs. The coyote came for the last of my jerky while I slept on the ninth night. I should've just let him have it, but I was scared and so I fought back, and he ripped me good, tore open my pack, and I ran. My last bladder was torn and all the water spilled out, and I ran all day thinking the . . . coyote would come for me, but it didn't. I was real tired and thirsty after that, and I had two days more to find the crack in the ground, and my knees were messed up and my stomach hurt real bad, so I went and went all day and night and then on the twelfth day, I was falling asleep while walking and I would wake up on the sand, and the sun would be hot, and I had bad dreams, and my hands and knees were burning, but then I saw the smoke like Father said, and the night came and I saw the fire, and then I had a dream that you were there.'

She looked at Conner. Took deep breaths. Realised she was winded, that she'd been talking and talking. But there was another sip from the jar for her efforts, and when her second mom Rose wiped the hair off her head and tucked it behind her ears, it was with a different look on her face. Her hand stayed on Violet's shoulder. Everyone else in the room was looking at her with wrinkles of worry, but Violet just rested against the pillows and enjoyed the feel of the sheets and the grumble of her belly around the water. She wasn't worried. She had made it. Just like Father had said she would.

ROSE

Rose left the young girl to rest in a bed too rarely slept in. She made Conner and Rob leave her in peace and pester her with no more questions. Poor Rob had to be dragged away. Both boys had spent the previous day and all night orbiting that bed, waiting for the girl to recover, to come to, to say something. Now they sat downstairs around a table in the slowly emptying bar and slurped greedily at bowls of leftover stew. Rose watched them eat over the balcony rail, her mind in all places at once.

Down the balcony and through a door, Rose could hear a drunk's laboured grunts. Valerie's room. That such baseness could occur alongside events of staggering significance was like a joke from the gods. Rose fought the urge to bash Valerie's door down and slap the drunk off her, to yell at them both, to shut it down, all of it down, not just the Honey Hole but the entire exercise of going through the motions, living life, being there among those dunes. If what the girl said was true – that the elsewhere her husband had disappeared into was worse than this place – then the dream of so many for an easy escape was really just another hell beyond their reckoning.

Rose leaned over the rail, wondering what was taking

Diana so long. She caught Conner staring up at her. Rob looked up as well. They were just boys. Just boys. But they possessed something like protective ownership of the girl. Conner had even referred to Violet as his sister, after she'd fallen back to sleep. Another sister, this girl who would cause a storm. Yes, her story would lead to chaos once it was out. News of Danvar was nothing. The sands would not sit still for this.

Hard to believe it was only the day before that the boys had arrived with the girl in their arms. Rose had nearly turned them away. She had very nearly refused them when they'd shown up. She did plenty of patching after the occasional brawl, and was the one her girls would come to after one of their clients got too rough, but she didn't want it known that just anyone could be brought in with wounds from elsewhere. Then Conner had explained just *how far* elsewhere, had said this girl came from No Man's Land, and that she had a message from their father.

Half of a sentence such as this could fry a woman's brain. The whole had taken over her limbs. Rose barely remembered carrying the child up the stairs and to her room. She barely remembered cutting the foul clothes from her, getting the sand out of her cuts, sewing her up like a pair of torn stockings. It was as though she'd watched another's hands apply a salve and pour water between the girl's lips. Someone else had yelled at her ten o'clock to come back later. No, that had been her. She remembered that. And she remembered telling Diana to get rid of the clothes, which had been little more than bloody rags with bits of wire in them.

Now she found herself asking Diana to track those same scraps down, to get them out of the trash. Rose wanted to know more. She was torn between letting the girl rest and assailing her with questions. What of this distant city? What of this camp? What would her husband of old do if their roles were reversed? She tried to think like her husband the Lord, not the desperate and crazed man who had sent a girl to warn his people away. Not him, but the younger man who had once brought other Lords to their knees. The man she'd never told her children about. Would this man run and hide? She didn't think so. And yet, he was asking *them* to.

And Rose had a terrible thought. What if her husband was still the same man, and he knew in his battle-scarred wisdom that running was the only option? What if he knew that now was the time for lying low, for giving in, for sliding deep beneath the sand? Rose wiped angrily at her cheek, damning him as was her daily ritual.

'I think this is all of it.'

She turned to find Diana beside her, holding tightly to a bundle of scraps tied up in one of the towels from the kitchen. Rose hadn't even seen her climb the stairs.

'Good, good. Thanks.' Rose took the bundle.

Diana glanced at the door. 'Is she . . .? Is that girl okay?'

'She'll be fine.'

'Another attack? Looked like a bomb, maybe, the way her clothes were shredded.'

'No. Something else. Keep an eye on my boys for me. And no appointments for the rest of the day.'

Diana frowned, but Rose didn't care to explain. She let herself into her room and shut the door.

The girl was still sleeping. She held the edge of her sheet with her bandaged hands and kept it up against her neck, chin tucked down. Here was another miserable life her husband had made. Another life ruined, no doubt, in the name of love.

Rose set the bundle on the small table by the window where there was light. She untied the towel and began sorting through the scraps. Her stomach twisted up in knots at the sight of blood on the girl's britches and her dive suit. The rubbery material of the dive suit felt strange – not quite like any fabric Rose had ever seen. It was like the girl's strange accent, with words understandable but the sound not quite right. Everything about the girl was both alien and familiar.

Rose had to be careful not to prick herself on the torn bits of wire as she sorted through the scraps. As a dive suit, the outfit was ruined. But she found the belly of the suit and the pouch there that no diver would be without. Rose turned the large scrap of material into the light. She ran her fingers across stitches her husband had made. And there across them was a neat snip her scissors had left from cutting the material off the girl. Fumbling to open the pouch, her fingers shaking, hoping against hope, Rose felt the folded piece of paper inside.

She pulled out the letter. Unfolded it, hands trembling, not daring to breathe.

The sight of her husband's handwriting blurred the words he'd written:

Rose,

I hope this message finds you well. I have forfeited the right to ask anything of you, but I trust the messenger will be cared for. All that awaited her here was misery and death. I don't have much time left, and so I send her and these words to the gods. I pray I don't write them in vain.

You alone know all the bad I've done. Running from my mistakes was by far the worst. There is a reason no one comes back from this place. They won't let us. They cage us like animals. Don't come for me. They grind the earth to nothing here. They take our water from the sky. Mountains are turned into rivers. There is no talking to them, even those of us who have learned their language. We are the salamander living in a hole beneath the sand. They are the boot that unwittingly buries us. To them, it is just a march onward and onward. To us, it is a trampling.

They know you are out there. They know of Springston and Low-Pub. Others before me have told them, have begged to be released, have begged for help, for water, for any of the small miracles we glimpse of their cities and their life. But no help will ever come for us. Our voices will never be heard. They have lesser problems to worry over.

Listen to me, please. This is not a war to win. It's not one to even fight. They have weapons and technology that seem like magic to me. We have tiny motors that shake the sand. We have dive suits the gypsies taught us to make. We don't stand a chance. So don't let the young there know of this letter. Burn it. You remember how I was. Tell only the old and wise, those with enough scars to fear. Tell the ex-Lords. Explain to them that these people are not evil, which we might understand and combat. Explain to them that these people do not care and cannot be made to, which is far worse. They live in cities bigger than our whole world and will crush us if we dare rise against them. Make our people understand.

Go west if you can. Forget the stories of what lies that way. Forget the mountains. Crush their peaks if you must, but go. Take the children and whoever will listen to reason. Those who will not succumb to reason, leave them behind to rot. Leave them here with me where we belong.

Yours,

Farren Robertson Axelrod – the Pickpocket of Low-Pub

Rose ran her fingers across her husband's name. She could feel the graceful groove the press of his pen had made. A man she had thought dead had written this. She sat there for a long time with that letter in her hands, gazing upon the words, while a young girl lay in the bed beside her, murmuring in her dreams.

Rose remembered a time and a life when things had been different. She read the letter again, hearing the voice of her husband reading it to her, remembering his smell, his touch, the itch of his beard against her neck, the way a man could lie with her and she would want it to last, not end as quickly as possible. Love she would give anything for.

There was no telling how long she sat like this, there in that feeble shaft of light dumping through sand-dusted glass. The sand hissed on the panes. It came in waves with the wind. Her daydreaming of the long ago brought with it more than the sound of Farren's voice. It brought the thunder of drums, which she used to hear from the great wall. Drums like a heartbeat out of rhythm.

The empty water jar on the table shuddered, which snapped Rose back to the present. The drums were real. She could still hear them popping – that unmistakable dull roar of buried bombs being triggered. But too many. She lost count. Rose leaned over the table and banged on the window with her fist, loosening the cake[13] so she could see. There was a noise outside her door, the sound of boots hurrying up the stairs and across the balcony. This was soon muffled by a growing grumble beyond her window, a thunderous din that grew and grew. There was noise everywhere. The door to her room flew open. Rose turned and saw Conner there, Rob standing behind him, both boys winded, eyes wide, looking to the bed and then to the window.

'Mom?'

---

[13] Sand stuck to a window.

Rose turned as the sound grew deafening. She peered through the glass towards Springston. The letter trembled in her hands. The jar wobbled as the violence approached.

'No,' she muttered, realising what was coming, what was happening. The room shook. The Honey Hole quivered. The young girl woke suddenly and began to scream, and Rose yelled at her boys to take a deep breath, to get down. She dived from the window and threw herself across the girl.

And then the sand bashed through the window and buried them all.

43

The Great Wall

VIC

Vic and Palmer spent a night at the buried spring with its tree-stumps, its dark patch of sand, and all that remained of a one-time oasis. Palmer needed time to regain some strength before another day of sailing, and Vic wasn't comfortable navigating the dunes at night. They left at first light in a building breeze. She stopped twice to check on her brother and force him to drink. While she sailed, he rode along in the haul rack, a small bimini flapping above him, his head lolling side to side as he drifted off to sleep.

They arrived at Springston a little past noon, the sun just crossing the mast as Vic steered due south by compass. She took in the mainsheet and sailed the sarfer up and along a ridge of dunes towards the north side of town. Freeing the mainsail and furling the jib, she slowed the craft to a halt. The aluminium hull groaned on its rusty rivets as the pressure on the mast lessened, the sand crunching as the craft came to rest. Vic set her teeth and rummaged through Marco's gear bag – an unpleasant reminder of his absence. She'd always figured she'd lose him on a dive or in some retaliatory bombing, some nonsensical violence, an effort to depose one Lord and replace him with some identical other. She tried not to think of how it had happened. Or the click of that misfire aimed at her own skull. She found his binoculars in his bag and placed the strap around her neck. *Today. Focus on the now.*

'Why're we stopping?' Palmer asked. He had propped himself up in the sarfer's haul rack, Vic's gear bag a pillow behind his head. The bimini Vic had rigged up to keep him in the shade made it difficult for him to see where they were.

'We're stopping so I can get a look at town. Last time I was here, someone tried to kill me, and *everyone* is looking for you. We need food, and I'd like to get word to some friends to be on the lookout for Brock and his men. I'm hoping I can do both at the market on the edge of town here. If it looks too risky, we're gonna push on to Low-Pub.'

Palmer groaned. 'I don't think I can go another dune in this rack, Vic.'

She unplugged her suit from the charger fed by the wind turbine and stood on the deck of the twin-hulled craft. She gave the boom a wary glance, made sure the wind wasn't going to blow it towards her. 'I know,' she said. 'I'd rather not ride any further myself. But I'd also prefer not to get killed, either.'

She pulled her goggles off, wiped the gunk from the corners of her eyes and lifted the binoculars to study the lie of the land. There were a few sarfers parked along the dunes between them and Springston, dive flags flapping high up their masts to warn territorially of activity below. Vic had parked a little west and just north of the line between town proper and the unofficial scattering of shacks known as Shantytown. The last place she'd lived out there had been pushed under a dune a while ago. The morning market on the north side looked as though it had already shut – the tents had been broken down and hauled off. Probably from lack of activity. So many had scattered in search of Danvar. There had used to be a grocer just beyond the market; Vic could always leave Palmer with the sarfer and go check. She had the coin he'd scavenged. She just needed to get in and out without drawing attention to herself.

She scanned further to the east. There was a sandscraper near the great wall that had been abandoned because of its lean. That might be the safest place to spend the night if Palmer couldn't take more travel. The vagrants there would know where to grab an emergency bite. If she got desperate enough, she could make her way beneath the sand and just steal something. Better risk a hanging than starve for sure. Amazing how quickly one could reach such a decision. If it were Marco there suggesting such a thing, she'd be the voice of morality, of caution. But Marco was gone and people wanted her brother dead. She supposed there was a different sort of morality that took precedence. A hierarchy. Life and liberty were the lords of action now.

Focusing past the tall scrapers, she surveyed the great wall. The leaning concrete face was still in shadow. Another way she knew that it was a touch past noon. Vic remembered watching a quiet sunrise from those ramparts when she was a child, remembered not worrying about her next meal or the next cap of water. She licked her chapped lips as she remembered baths, as she remembered braying goats that could be had for their meat as well as their milk and cheese. Her stomach begged her to remember no more.

She spotted people up on the wall, little black specks of privilege. She envied them that home, that fortress that protected bustling Springston. Here was one solution to the winds from the east; a different answer to the same problem could be seen in Shantytown. The problem in common was that the world was in flux. The sands were always shifting, always pushing from east to west. *Progressing*, as her father used to say. Always *progressing* from east to west.

Vic swung the binoculars across Shantytown, where the people moved with the dunes. Not a day went by without a house collapsing. And the rhythmic rattle of hammers there was as constant as the drums beyond No Man's Land. Build and destroy. Destroy and build. People tunnelled through the dunes as they closed in around their homes. Back doors became front doors. A doormat shaken out and relocated. Adapt and survive. Life went on.

People died, of course. Houses collapsed in the middle of the night. Sand rushed through breached walls at any hour. A handful mourned. Hands slapped faces in grief. And then came the rhythmic rattle of hammers, building. The wail of a newborn, breathing.

Change in Shantytown was gradual and continuous. Dunes slid and moved and people adjusted around them. The change was backbreaking and exhausting, but it was a way of life. Each day was much the same as the last. The misery came in buckets, which could be handled. Time. The dunes. Society. The people. They all *progressed*, as her father would say. But Vic didn't buy that. The spoils from the sands told a different story. Things seemed only to get worse over time.

Such were her thoughts as she scanned the line between Shantytown and Springston, dwelling on change and life rather than food, putting off how best to proceed. The high sun beat down on her. She could hear Palmer twisting the cap off his canteen, knew they were both getting low on water. Making a decision with his life in the balance made it difficult to be prudent and wise. She was used to risking only her own life. She preferred diving solo.

'What do you see?' Palmer asked from the haul rack.

'One stall near the market,' she said. 'Might be our best bet.'

She focused the binoculars on the stall, which would have to be their oasis. They could sail over and park close by, get in and out, drop some coin and a warning about Brock's men. She watched a family tend the stall, a woman sweeping sand into piles and two kids hauling it out to the dunes. Maybe she could meet the children there and pay them to bring the food out. She watched them work, not wanting to hurry any one plan, and her mind flitted back to these two ways of managing the dunes, Springston's and Shantytown's. Here was the perfect vantage for seeing how both worked. In Shantytown, the gradual battle with the sand spread misery across the generations. Evenly distributed. While in Springston, people lived protected from the wind, with flat desert and tall buildings rarely swamped by the dunes. Years of woe were stored up behind a teetering wall. That woe missed some generations entirely. It built and built.

And somehow, Vic knew what was happening before it did. Maybe she knew from her life with brigands, from all their plans and boasts, from living with Marco, from beginning to think like them. Or maybe it was the little black figures she spotted running along the ramparts as if something was wrong, chasing some people away. Or maybe the sound came first, and then her brain whirred with such ferocity, such speed, that all the thoughts came next in an eyeblink. It felt as if minutes passed, as if all she considered about the great wall and the coming ages of man flew by between the first thump deep in her chest and the subsequent signs of disaster.

Or maybe it was coincidence. A diver's intuition. Palmer's story about a crate of bombs taking out all of Springston, an old dream of insane schemers and revolutionaries who knew how to destroy but not how to create. Whatever the cause, her gaze was upon the great wall when it happened. And her mind was on the many falls of man.

Thoughts spun. She saw the ages counted by each collapse. Empires that came and went and that made up all of their history and lore. Their ends were both inevitable and unpredictable. The catastrophic nature of each grew bigger with time. No one thought an end would come in their lifetime. People glanced up at the towering wall of concrete and iron bars and reckoned their children or grand-children would see it topple. It would be left to some distant generation to build the next wall, and to build it stronger. Bigger. Like each fall.

Meanwhile, on the back of the wall, the sand grew heavier and heavier. One grain at a time. Like a clock. Like the ticking clock on a bomb. Or a whole string of them – dozens of bombs like loaves of bread – buried along the base of the wall in the middle of the night, placed there by divers with a hellish bent, divers and pirates who had grown weary of that cool shadow that divides one world from the other, that harsh line between those who toil all day and those who can afford to wait.

Those who *think* they can afford to wait.

Tick. Tick. Tick. Sand and second hands. Vic watched from the top of the dune, from the deck of her dead lover's sarfer, a sickness deep in the pit of her stomach, a powerful dread, all of this flashing through her mind as the dull thumps hit her in the chest.

The roars were muffled. They came like drums beating out of rhythm: *boom . . . boom-boom . . . boom. Boom.*

And then the teetering – the unholy teetering. A thing meant to last leaned its sad head. The body shuddered, losing its balance, feet knocked out from underneath. Vic covered her mouth and watched. Sand peppered the binoculars. Palmer yelled at her and asked what that was, his voice muffled by his ker.

The luckiest in life became the unluckiest. Those who lived nearest the wall were crushed. Those who lived inside it disappeared. These were the ones with the most to lose, and they lost everything. The sand they had let build for generations flooded down, finishing what the bombs had started. And a slab of concrete as high as many of the sand-scrapers thudded impossibly flat.

The dune Vic stood on trembled. Sand flowed down the face of every dune in sight as gravity and the trembling of the world made them all lose an inch of height. Vic could feel the impact in the deck of the sarfer, in the soles of her feet. The rumble came moments later, a roar deep in her chest. And then a great wave of sand slid through Springston, a torrent of this unnatural dune finding its rightful level, flowing like water down on the sandscrapers and markets and square, buildings toppling as their knees were knocked out from under them, small black shapes spilling from the upper reaches, these people wrenched violently from their bequeathed homes.

Onward, the sand flowed. It spilled out to the side and caught Shantytown, those few unlucky enough to live along the edge of the shadows, where the summer solstice made the wall's shadow more inclusive for a season. These went too. Only in the distance were they spared. The reckoning of the decades made good in a single moment. Shantytown the new Springston. And the Honey Hole, Vic saw, knocked aside at the far reach of the sand's wake, right along that fuzzy line between town proper and town improper.

Her mother buried. A town lost. A small group of men, somewhere out there, cheering.

The wind stirred. The heavens themselves seemed to adjust to this new world. The sarfer's boom creaked as the mainsail shifted. Palmer was yelling. Vic ignored him and jumped back into her seat. She grabbed the lines and pulled them taut. The jib unfurled with a mighty pop and the sarfer lurched into motion. Vic sailed the craft dangerously down the side of the dune, fighting the tiller, her mind in splinters. She sailed for where she'd last seen the Honey Hole. She had vowed never to return to that place. Now she couldn't get there fast enough.

44

Held Down, Violently

The sarfer raced across the dunes towards a field of debris where homes and shops had recently stood. Over the creaking mast and the taut and singing ropes, Vic could hear shouts for help and screams of horror. Screams from the past. Vic focused on a spot of sand at the edge of the destruction. There was a ridge of heaped tin and metal and wood blocking her path. She slewed the sarfer to a stop on the edge of town – was sixteen again as she jumped to the sand and raced between the dunes. Sixteen again and running half-naked across the desert floor. It'd been night-time back then, and she'd been running *away* from the Honey Hole.

She had only gone inside for a drink. She and two friends. One drink had led to two drinks. She still had had her wits about her, had been able to tell the men no. She hadn't been laughing, not any more. But the rooms had been there, as had been the expectation from those who had learned that anything they saw and wanted could be had for a price. A price. Cheap for them. Rent a room. C'mon, it'll be fun. Firm hands. Friends egging her on.

Tears streaked down Vic's face as she ran across the sand, remembering.

Two men. Laughing. Beer on their breaths. Strong arms

from building and making. Strong arms for tearing and taking. Laughing. Her screams had been funny to them. Her arms weak. But the way she'd squirmed had made them roar. And Vic had been able to hear her friends shouting through the walls, shouting then for them to stop, rattling locked doors, yelling at the people in another room, where similar horrors had been more habit than happenstance.

Loose sand. Vic reached the end of intact houses, the extent of the onrush of that great dune. She ran past people gazing, people watching, people standing still, not helping, not hearing the muffled screams, the calloused hands over pretty mouths, the beer-breath lips crushing down, the feeling of sand piled on, of being buried alive, a pressure against new parts of her, the first time, crushing, crushing.

She hurried up the slope of sand until her legs were sore and would barely obey. She angled for where the Honey Hole used to sit. Vic pulled her band on, flipped her visor down, powered up her suit as she dived forward. She disappeared into the sand with barely a splash. Down where she was free and nothing could pin her.

Bright objects everywhere. The yellow and orange of great spoils, a scrounger's paradise, so much worth saving. There were riches here carried all the way from the great wall. The rich were here as well. Vic saw a form trapped ahead of her, probably too late, but she formed a column of sand beneath the body and sent it to the surface. There were entire homes buried and flattened. There was debris every-where to dodge. And ahead of her, right where she'd been running, was the three-storey building she remembered, the house of nightmares, completely encased by the dune. No one would ever be harmed in that building again. They already had been.

Vic slid through a busted window, hardening the sand

around her to protect herself from the shards of glass. The walls inside were askew. The building had nearly buckled. It might have collapsed were it not for the low concrete wall on the back side of the building to hold back the sand. Vic dialled her visor down to account for the loose pack inside the Honey Hole. Too bright in there. Bodies everywhere. Chairs and tables and the flash of glass jars and bottles. She raced up through the great hall and over the railing – or where the railing had once stood. A purplish pocket of air along the second floor. The sand only got so high. Vic started to move whomever she could towards the air, but there wasn't enough time. Not enough time. Even if the people there had got a lungful when it happened. Even if they had closed their mouths. Dead in minutes. Her mom was gone. Never got to say goodbye.

Vic saw the door to the room where it had happened all those years ago. The door was still intact, still solid, still closed on what had taken place in there. No one knew but those who had been inside. No one. Suffocating.

In her visor, her suit's power glowed a bright green. A full charge. Ready for a deep dive, all that extra juice for holding the world at bay, for holding up that column of sand and air that was always pressing down on her, pressing down. Vic only had breath enough in her lungs for another minute or two. Her heart was racing, burning through her oxygen, not prepared for this. Not ready to see this. Not ready for her mother to die.

She couldn't scream beneath the sand. There were no divers to hear the shouts rising up in her throat. Nowhere for that rage to go. But something inside Vic burst, something like a great wall meant to hold back the years and years. It toppled all at once, anger flowing outward, a power she'd honed in the deepest of sand now surging through her suit. That power exploded; it raged in the deadly spill from that tumbling dune; and the muscle to lift a motor, a car, to rip the roof off an ancient skyscraper, billowed forth.

There was a rumbling in the earth, a swelling, a press of sand from beneath, and the Honey Hole creaked upward, out of the spill, Vic screaming and crying beneath the sand where no diver could hear her, hands curled into claws of rage and effort, the sand spilling into her mouth and onto her tongue, sand soaked in beer and tasting of the awful past, and a grumble, a grumble as the world tilted and walls popped and sand flowed from orifices, out of windows and doors, flowing like warm honey, like blood and milk, draining from that awful place where the past had long been buried, as the Honey Hole rose out of the desert and settled, shuddering, atop the dunes.

The Honey Hole – full of the spitting and coughing and bewildered and dead – was sickeningly saved. And Vic, exhausted again in that place, terrified and weeping, collapsed to the ground outside her mother's door, her mother's open door, blood coming only from her ears and nose this time.

Part 5 – A Rap Upon Heaven's Gate

45

A Quiet Dawn

CONNER

There was a distant thrum. The sound of drums, of bootfalls, of a god's mighty pulse. Conner knew that sound. It reminded him of the thunder far east. It was the muffled roar of rebel bombs, a noise that came before chaos and death and red dunes and a mother's wails. Conner dropped his spoon into his bowl of stew, pushed away from the beer-soaked table in the Honey Hole and ran to the stairs to warn his mom.

He took the steps two at a time. Rob chased after him. There were more of the muffled blasts in the distance as they raced along the balcony. Danger outside. Violence. Or maybe it was nothing. Maybe it was cannon fire to celebrate the discovery of Danvar. Conner almost felt silly for running to his mother, a child doing what boys did in a panic, turning to a parent to save them, to tell them what to do.

He threw open her door, knew there were no clients inside, just his half-sister Violet who had emerged tattered and torn from No Man's Land. And as he stepped into the room, Conner felt a rumble in the earth, felt it through his father's boots, and he knew what was happening. He knew that this was more than the usual bombs. That great roar and that impossibly loud hiss meant the sands were coming for them all.

And in the brief flutter between two beats of his heart, as the din grew and grew, as his mother yelled for the boys to run, to hold their breath, to *move*, Conner thought only of diving onto the bed, of protecting the girl he'd spent the last two days looking after. He bolted across the room, Rob on his heels, got halfway there when the wall of sand slammed into the Honey Hole.

The floor beneath Conner's feet lurched sideways – a god snatching a rug out from under him. He tumbled. There was a crash of wood and tin, an explosion of glass, a sudden blindness as all light was extinguished by a press of solid dune, a splintering sound, and then the desert sands pouring in around Conner and his family.

He barely heard his mother scream for them to hold their breaths before he was smothered. Sand was in his nose and against his lips. He was frozen, pinned to the floor in a sprawl, the weight of ten bullies on his back, a sense, nearby, right beside him, of his brother Rob. Just a memory of where his brother had been – where his mother had been – before the sand had claimed them.

Pitch black. A residual warmth in the sand from having been outside in the sun. Complete silence. Just his pulse, which he could feel in his neck as it was squeezed by the drift. The pulse in his temples. No room to expand his chest. Couldn't swallow. Hands around his throat. His brother nearby. And not enough room even to cry. Just a coffin to be terrified in. A place for dying. For panic. For muscles and tendons raging and flexing but not budging an inch – what a paralysed person must feel. What everyone who has ever been buried alive must feel. *This is how they go. This is how they go.* Conner couldn't stop thinking it.

The dead had been bodies in the sand before. But now he could feel what they had felt. They had felt just like this, frozen and terrified and not able to move their jaws even to sob for their mothers.

He prayed and listened for the sound of digging – but heard nothing. His pulse. His pulse. Maybe the sand wasn't so deep. Maybe his mother was okay, pressed there against the wall. Maybe Violet – his half-sister – maybe she would live and her story would be known. He might have a minute of air left. They could dig him out. But that rumble – that rumble – too much sand. It had gone black in the room. The sand had swamped the first floor of the Honey Hole. The great wall must've gone. Collapsed. Blown up. And the sand on Conner's back grew deeper and heavier with this thought. In the dark and quiet, he imagined the horror that must be taking place outside. His rapidly approaching death became a pinprick in a wider world of hurt. That rumble of sand he'd heard had been the dune coming at them, the great dune behind that teetering wall on which he'd been born. A life given and then taken away. It had come for him. Had found him. Was now going to claim him.

The struggle against the sand was futile, so Conner relaxed. As he did, it felt as though the bullies on his back grew heavier, as if he had sagged within himself and the sand was eager to consume that space. How much longer? The need to breathe grew intense. Like the training games with his brother, when they strained their lungs and counted with fingers. Dizzy. No way to inhale or exhale. Would just black out. And as he felt it coming, his panic surged anew, and there came an intense drive *not to die*. He didn't want to die. He wanted to call out to Rob, to his mom, tell them he loved them, get them out of there, *somebody please dig me out of here.*

As his senses faded, the press of sand all around him softened. It was as if his skin was growing numb to the pressure. Or the blood flow was stopping. Conner had a bright flash of a memory, his father waking him up one morning with a finger pressed over his grey beard, urging Conner to be quiet. Conner, confused, half asleep, leaving the room he shared with his brothers, his father taking him up the narrow stairs to the top of the great wall. They'd sat there with their faces to the east and their feet dangling over the ramparts. A windless, noiseless sunrise. The first quiet dawn he'd ever seen, one of those rare moments when the gods would stop their thundering and become calm, when the sand wasn't blowing down on them – and Conner had sat and watched the morning sun swallow the stars and then Mars, and then a golden dome of light grow and blossom into a perfectly blue sky.

'Why's it so quiet?' he had whispered to his father. He had been young and confused. 'Will it always be like this?'

'Another half an hour,' his father had said, studying the sky. 'If we're lucky.'

This had placed an enormous pressure on Conner to *enjoy the moment*. To remember it. To soak it up. The way that crow up there had flapped its wings as it took advantage and made for the east. The way the sun had warmed the cool morning air. The stillness on his cheeks. His father's heavy hand on his shoulder. *Remember. Remember*, he told himself. That intense pressure to make this last for ever, to cup his mind tight like hands under a running tap. And then he had glanced up and down the ramparts and realised they were enjoying this moment alone.

'We should wake the others,' he had whispered. 'Palmer and Vic—'

His father had squeezed his shoulder. 'They've had theirs. This one is yours.'

And nothing more had been said as the sun had broken free of the dunes and the wind had returned and whatever made that noise that haunted their sleep had resumed its infernal grumbling. And it had dawned on Conner, sitting there on the great wall with his father, that the world was full of secrets and strangeness. At some point in the past, he had slept while Vic and Palmer had been taken up into the darkness to witness this. They had never told their little brother, had never shared that moment, and Conner had known he never would either.

And it occurred to him there in the Honey Hole, buried under all that sand, that Rob had never been given a windless dawn with their father. Had never been given any kind of morning with him. Had never known him. And the sand loosened even more around his body, and Conner knew it was happening. The last of his breath. The last of sensation. He'd had a minute or two there under the press of dune to consider his life – and now his time was up.

But as the sand grew lighter, he felt his body *more* keenly, not less so. He swallowed back a sob. *Swallowed.* The fists around his neck lost some of their grip. There was a hum in the earth. A hiss. That sound of someone diving nearby. He'd heard this sound before, his ear pressed to the hard pack as he'd listened to his father scavenge beneath him. It was the sound a diver could only hear when his suit was off and another's was on. And Conner discovered that he could *move.* Someone was loosening the sand.

He still couldn't breathe, was still buried and blind, wasn't sure how many ticking heartbeats he had left in his lungs, but he struggled against the sand to reach for his boot. Couldn't swim in this. Couldn't get anywhere. But might be able to bring his knee up, stretch his hand down, reach inside, bring out the band, hit the power, fumble with the wires, the scratch of the rough floor as he wiggled beneath what felt like a thousand heavy blankets, his little brother crushed beside him, his little brother who could never hold his breath quite as long. Got the band plugged in. Sand crunching between the contacts. Wouldn't work. No way. Band on his head, the sand growing less viscous, and then feeling a connection with the drift, with the sand pressing in all around him.

No visor. No way to see. No way to breathe. But he could *move*. Not much time. Conner went to where he thought his brother would be and felt a body. He grabbed Rob, didn't feel anyone grabbing back at him, didn't feel life there, but he had no time to consider this. No time to think about the miracle of the boots or the nearby diver, only of getting to the bed. He pulled Rob along like some scavenged find. Another body. Someone on the bed. He felt someone on the bed *moving*.

Conner groped. His mom. Alive. Something in her lap. He didn't wait, didn't think, didn't have a heartbeat of air left in him. He pushed up. *Up*. Made the sand hard over his head to protect him. Was back in that box Ryder had made, that coffin cube, breaking through, up through the ceiling and into the second floor. Dark. Loose sand. *Light*. Dim, but there. And then air. Stuffy attic air. A glorious pocket. And Conner, exhausted and choking on grit, passed out.

46

A Buried People

He couldn't have been out for long. He woke on top of a shifting pile of sand. His mother was beside him, her lips pressed to Rob's, his young cheeks puffing out as she blew into his mouth, sand spilling from her hair and coating both their faces.

The sand beneath them was sinking. Swirling and draining out somewhere. A creak and the snap of timbers overhead. A thrumming violence all around. The whole world was moving. *The Honey Hole was moving.* Slashes and stabs of light lanced through fresh cracks in the wall. Barrels and crates were piled up, having been shoved aside when Conner had pushed his family up through the ceiling. They were in the second-floor storerooms. But they were sinking back down, riding the plummeting level of the sand, fighting for purchase and stability, their mother cursing and losing her grip on Rob.

Conner remembered the boots. He hardened the sand beneath them all, made a platform. His mom breathed into Rob's mouth again. The girl was there. Violet. Eyes open, alive, looking at Conner, taking deep breaths. Father had taught her well. But Rob. Poor Rob, with an affinity for all things diving but never a chance to swim beneath the sand. His first time. *Don't let it be his last. Don't let it be his last.*

Conner watched his mother work, was too tired and numb and afraid to speak. He just concentrated on keeping the sand firm as they floated down. All the sand in the Honey Hole was draining away, vibrating as though someone were making it move. The rigid platform of sand rode back through the hole and into his mother's room. More light filtering in. Sand coursing through the shattered window and the splintered wall. The Honey Hole was now above the dunes. Conner didn't understand. He felt a rage and a violence in the sand, could feel it through his boots and his band. A burn as if the fabric were on fire, a scorch around his temples, and then that rage and heat were gone. The world fell still. A coat of sand stood on everything in the room, but the drift had poured out. Conner tried to piece the last few minutes together, wondered if maybe the Honey Hole had done a full roll, if he'd been buried for a minute as the world had turned upside down, had righted itself, and then the sand had drained away.

He went to his mother and Rob. His brother wasn't moving. Their mom leaned over him, palms on his chest, pressing down violently and counting. She got to five and stopped. Bent down and began to blow into Rob's mouth again.

'What do I do?' Conner asked.

His mom didn't respond. She repeated the steps. Like she was reviving a drunk. Or someone choking in the bar. Here was the reason they'd brought the girl to the Honey Hole. His mom could save people. That's what she did. That's who she was. And Conner saw this as she bent to her task. He pulled for her. He pulled for Rob. Reached for his brother's small, limp hand. Saw that Violet was holding the other. Sand coating all of them. They had come back down beside the bed, the four of them on the floor, and then a gasp of air from their mother—

No, a sob. A sob from their mother. The gasp came from Rob.

His brother spat sand and heaved for air. Their mother cradled his head, and Conner felt his brother's hand flex around his own. He realised he was squeezing Rob's too tightly.

'Water,' their mother said. She turned to Conner to give him some command, but then her gaze drifted beyond him to something on the floor. Her eyes grew wide in alarm. They opened like the empty sky. Conner turned, expecting another wall of sand to come crashing down from behind him, and saw the body lying on the floor just outside the door. A woman. Rivulets of red trickling from her ear. Head turned to the side, facing him, a visor over her eyes. But Conner would recognise her from a thousand dunes away. His sister. Here. This made less sense than the sand.

He scrambled towards her, got his hand tangled up in the wires that trailed from his band to his boots, threw the band off his head and let it drag behind him, finally made it to her side.

'Vic?' He rolled her onto her back. Lifted her visor. Blood was coming from her nose. Conner cried out. He turned to his mom, who was still holding Rob and urging him to breathe. 'What do I do?' he asked.

His mother was crying. Dark streaks of sand beneath her eyes like ruined make-up. Conner tore his shirt off and shook the sand out as best he could. He dabbed at Vic's nose.

'Is she breathing?' his mother asked.

'I don't know!'

He didn't know. How did you check? What was going on? The world had turned upside down. Rob was coughing. Violet took over holding him while their mother came to

Conner's side. She seemed unsurprised. Calm. She checked Vic's neck and then held her cheek to her daughter's lips. And Conner saw again that this was their mother. Taking the dunes as they came, as the world shifted beneath her feet, all in her stride, because the world had always been moving. A shock to Conner, this violence, but his mother was just in motion. Saving them.

Vic stirred. Groaned.

'What the fuck?' Conner asked, overwhelmed by a flood of confusion and relief. He surveyed the damage, this gasping and sand-covered family all around him. Maybe his mom didn't hear. She didn't answer, didn't tell him to watch his language, just held her daughter as Vic's eyes fluttered, as her sand-crusted lips parted, a groan and then a gasp.

Vic tried to sit up. She looked around the room, seemed to grasp where she was.

'Easy,' their mother said.

But Vic didn't seem to hear. Vic didn't go easy. 'There are more,' she said, as though she had never been unconscious, as though she weren't bleeding, as if she were finishing some sentence started a year before. A year. It'd been that long since Conner had seen her. And her first words were: *There are more.* And then: 'I've got to go.'

She staggered to her feet. Wobbled there. Steadied herself on the door jamb with one hand and raised the other to touch her visor.

'The great wall—' their mother said, turning to what was left of the window.

Vic dabbed at her nose and inspected her finger. 'Check the others,' she said, jerking her head down the balcony. She turned to go.

'Wait,' Conner begged.

But his sister was already running towards the stairs. And

the word she'd left them with – *others* – rattled around in his head. The miracle of his own life and the confusion over what in the world had happened dimmed in the bright new awareness of all those who must be in trouble. His mother seemed to understand. There was no shock or complaint. The lid on a jar of water was cracked and passed to Violet, who took it with her bandaged hands, and the ministered-to became the caretaker as she held the jar to Rob's lips.

Conner was the one left staggering about, the one with the dull ache of a bomb blast ringing in his ears, the one groping after his own life for a minute, for five, before looking to help others. His mother and Vic had sprung into action as though they'd been here before. Even Violet seemed to take this awful world in her stride. Conner spun and felt bewildered. Lost. He heard his sister racing down the steps outside. There was a band on the ground, a diver's band, and a trail of wires leading to his father's boots.

Conner gathered the wires. He pulled the band down over his head. There were buried people outside. *His* buried people. This he knew. Conner ran out of the room, yelling for his sister to wait up.

47

Not Enough Buckets

His fear was that Vic would be gone and far beneath the sand by the time he got outside. He navigated the staircase, which swayed beneath his feet, was hanging on by a few sad nails. There were people stirring across the expanse of the bar, helping one another up, piles of drift everywhere, some bodies half buried, as many alive here as dead, a miracle. By the time he reached the front door, Conner had a vague sense of what his sister had done, why any of them were still alive. He knew, but it wasn't possible. Lifting a building like this. The blood leaking from her ears and nose. He felt afraid of his sister right then, a feeling he remembered from childhood.

He spotted her outside, saw her running across the sand rather than diving into it. A nightmarish world stood all around: folded tin and splintered wood jutting up through a rolling sea of new sand. To the west, the sprawl of Shantytown seemed to have been spared. Those on the eastern edge, however, were gone. Conner saw people rushing in with shovels and buckets. More stood scattered atop the distant dunes, shielding their eyes and staring numbly at the scene of such awful devastation. Conner chased after his sister. He glanced over his shoulder towards the east and saw the mostly flat expanse of ruin. A ridge of a fallen sandscraper jutted out of the sand like the spine of a half-buried corpse. A high dune stood where the great wall had once been. All the rest of that sand – stored up for generations – was gone. All that misery had been evenly dispersed.

Conner concentrated on keeping up with Vic, tried not to think of the great wall and the sight of empty air where it had once loomed. He could taste the fear in his mouth at the sight of such permanence ended. *Don't think about it. Follow Vic –* who for some reason wasn't diving beneath the dunes to rescue others as he'd thought she might. She raced instead through structures that became more intact the further west and north they went. Conner was out of breath, his heart pounding. He chased her around a home, was fighting for the voice to call out to her, when he spotted the sarfer sitting out on the open sand.

The mainsail was still up, the fabric luffing, boom swaying. A rebel sarfer with a red canvas. Some part of Conner knew that his sister being there when the great wall collapsed was no coincidence. The thuds he had heard before the sand had rolled in – he remembered the sounds like distant bombs. Dozens of them. Vic spent time with the sorts of people who might do this. The thought that she might be involved, might have had a hand in the deaths of thousands, might have come there only to rescue their mom – this was a more personal and direct hurt than the toppling of the wall. It was the scratch that burned rather than the blunt trauma that knocked a man numb.

At the sarfer, Vic rummaged for something in the haul rack. No . . . not something, *someone*. Conner drew near and realised it was his brother.

'Palm?' he asked, the confusion piling on now. He rested against the sarfer's hot hull and caught his breath. His older brother gazed at him from the shade of a makeshift bimini.

His face was blistered. His lips swollen. He managed a wan smile. Vic was giving orders to them both. She pressed something into Conner's hands. He looked down. A set of visors. A band. She pulled a dive suit from a bag in the passenger seat. Palmer was saying that he was okay to dive, to give him the suit. He tried to get up, but Vic shoved him back down.

'You can barely walk,' she said.

Conner wondered what was wrong with his brother. Palmer's face had shrunk; his cheeks were sharp; there were the beginnings of a beard on his chin. 'I can walk,' Palmer insisted.

Vic took all of two beats to consider something. As rarely as she stood still, it felt like a lifetime. She reached some decision. 'Head to the Honey Hole, then,' she said. 'Help Mom. Wait for us there.'

'What about the sarfer?' Palmer asked.

'Leave it be. Just take the water. And be careful. The sand is loose, and there's debris everywhere.' She turned to Conner. 'What're you waiting on? Get that suit on and let's go.'

Conner fell to the sand and kicked his boots off. Stowed the band away. His shirt was already gone, left behind in the Honey Hole with his sister's blood on it. He pulled the dive suit on. It was big for him and smelled of another man's sweat. His sister helped him with the zipper, bitched about the sand in it. She gave Conner instructions as she pulled the dive tanks from their racks and cracked the valves.

'It's been too long to save anyone buried in solid drift,' she told him. 'We're looking for air down there, okay? Any spot of purple, that's what you aim for. We'll start here on the edge of town where chances are best. No point in checking every small building, just the intact ones. Anything with an eastward window you can skip. This regulator jams now and then – you have to take it out and knock it against your tank. Can you handle that?'

Conner nodded. He slipped his arms through the tank's harness as his sister held the worn cylinder aloft.

'Good. Let's go.'

It was another long run back towards the wasteland of broken homes. Soon the dive suit smelled of Conner's sweat. And then his sister pointed to the edge of a roof jutting up from the smooth sand, and she dived forward and was swallowed by a dune. Conner pulled the visor down over his eyes, wrangled the flapping regulator at his hip and shoved it into his mouth. He vibrated the air and the sand so that it slid out of his way as he tumbled forward. The desert claimed him as it had claimed so many others. But he could breathe. And he could help those who couldn't. There was so much to do and not enough buckets.

48

A Fortunate Few

He had to ignore the maths. There were thousands of bodies scattered and buried beneath the sand, and he and Vic had only found dozens alive in pockets of air. Maybe a hundred survivors in total. He ignored the maths and concentrated on these few sputtering and alive that they were able to rescue.

After depositing a man he'd found beneath an upturned tub, he dived back into the sand and raced alongside his sister beneath the dunes. He had a sensation of flight, the suit and band she'd given him more powerful than any he'd ever donned before, a rebel suit turned up to dangerous degrees. Every shimmering flash of purple or dark blue where the visor's sandsight was broken by a pocket of air stood out as a beacon of hope. Conner drifted past bodies and around shattered homes, bashed his way through walls and intact windows, told the terrified he found there to hold their breath as he gathered them up and lifted them towards the light.

He broke into one house that had remained intact and found a family of four. A shriek as he approached, the red dive light around his neck aglow, drift pouring in through the hole he'd made. 'Hold your breath,' he told them, not sure if he could lift four people at once. Two was a strain. But the sand was pouring into their home. A young girl screamed and clutched her mother. Vic had disappeared into another building. Conner needed his sister. The sand wasn't going to give them time.

He held the regulator out to the young girl. 'Can you breathe through this?' The girl's mother told her to bite down on it and not to breathe through her nose, to stay close to the diver.

Conner nodded at the window he had smashed. The family crawled across the rising sand with him, the girl tethered to Conner by the air hose. As the sand sought its level, Conner held out his arms and took a boy Rob's age in one, the young girl in the other. The parents encircled them all in an embrace. One last look at their faces in the pale red light, deep breaths all around, cheeks puffing, eyes wide with fear, the sand tumbling in, and Conner flowed them towards the window. He strained, the pulse in his temples knocking against his skull like a hammer, a feeling of being in thick and heavy sand, the danger of sinking, but a thought of Vic lifting an entire building and something surged in him, an anger at the world, and though Conner was too far gone in concentration to even know that they were moving, he glimpsed the purple sky overhead, watched it loom closer, and then felt the wind and the pepper of sand on his face, heard the gasps and gratitude of the family as they held one another, covered in sand.

There was no time to tell them they were welcome. Just a regulator passed back to him, sand and spit of the saved on the mouthpiece. Conner bit down grimly on this before returning to the depths, a boy who had been told he couldn't be a diver, becoming one now in the most terrible of ways.

'Where are all the others?' he asked his sister, hours later. They shared a canteen atop the sand. The sun was going down, and both their tanks had long run dry, had been shucked off and set aside. They had gone as long as they could with visors and mere lungfuls but the adrenalin had worn off, and the rescued had become more infrequent, and their exhausted bodies had needed a guilty rest.

'What others?' Vic asked. She wiped her mouth and passed him the canteen.

'The other divers. I saw one or two down there looking for people to save. Woulda thought there'd be hundreds helping by now.'

He took a grateful swig while Vic gazed towards the west to keep the sand out of her eyes. 'I saw those divers down there,' she said. 'But I don't think they were after people.'

'You think they were scavenging?' Conner didn't want to believe this. He wiped his mouth with his ker.

'Looting,' she said, stressing the word as though there were some great difference. 'The rest of the divers are out hunting for a different buried city,' she added.

'Danvar.'

Vic nodded. 'The people who did this, who did that . . .' She pointed to where the wall had once stood. 'They're the same ones who found Danvar. Palmer was with them.' She must've seen the confused and horrified look on Conner's face. 'Not *with* them in that sense. He wasn't a part of the bombing. They hired him for a dive. Palmer was the one who found Danvar.'

Conner didn't know what to say. He remembered how his brother had looked in the sarfer, like a body fresh from a grave. 'Is he okay?'

'He was down there for a week. If he lives, it'll be a miracle. But he's got his father's blood, so who knows.'

Conner couldn't believe how lackadaisical his sister could

be about their brother's life. But then – all the death he'd seen that day already had him inured to the sight of the buried. 'Why would anyone *do* this?' he asked, though he knew the question was pointless, knew everyone who witnessed the aftermath of a bomb asked the same question and never got a response. Churches were overfull with these unanswered questions.

Vic shrugged. She pulled off her visor and checked something inside the band. 'I wouldn't be surprised if the people who did this were the same ones who spread the word about Danvar. Just to clear out those who might be here to help.'

'The divers,' Conner said. He grabbed his boot and tried to work a kink out of his calf muscle. 'So what now?'

'One more run down by the scrapers. There are a few pockets we missed. Then I'll get you back to the Honey Hole and check on Palm before I head to Low-Pub.'

'Low-Pub?' Conner glanced around at the people staggering across the sand, pulling what they could from the shallows, tending to the exhausted and the wounded. 'Aren't we needed here? What's in Low-Pub?'

'The people who did this,' Vic said. She put her visor back on. 'Palm said they were going to hit Springston first. He overheard them, knew this was going to happen, just didn't know it would be this . . . bad. We came here as quickly as we could for some food and to warn someone. But we were too late.'

'You saved *us*,' Conner said.

Vic's cheeks tightened as she clenched and unclenched her jaw. She said nothing. Just pulled her ker up over her nose and mouth.

'The people who did this are shacked up in Low-Pub?' he asked. 'If you go after them, I want to come with you.'

He thought she would argue. But Vic just nodded. 'Yeah.

I'll probably need you. And they aren't shacked up in Low-Pub. I think they're gonna strike there next. And that it might be worse than this.'

Conner surveyed the scene around him once more, the wind and sand blowing unfettered where it hadn't blown for generations. He couldn't imagine that anything could be worse than this.

49

Half-sisters

VIC

They arrived back at the Honey Hole to find a broken building where broken people were gathering – and Vic wondered if the place had changed at all. The battered brothel was the tallest structure left standing across all of Springston. What had once sat squat among its peers now towered. And as it sat on the new eastward border of civilisation, it was also the new wall. A few tents had already been erected in its lee. Shantytown, spread out to the west, was all that remained whole and intact.

As Vic approached the building, she felt as though she could still see all the bodies beneath her feet, that her sand-sight had become permanent. The dead were spots in her vision like you get from staring at the sun too long. They were motes of sand swimming in her eyes.

She and Conner dropped their tanks inside the doorway. The building was still lined with drift. Dunes of it stood in the corners. An even coat covered the floor. Vic had flowed the sand like water as she'd lifted the place, but not all of it had got out. It had puddled in places and congealed. Dozens of people were scattered across those piles of drift. Lanterns and candles filled the space with glow and shadow. These small flames beat back the darkness as the sun set outside, and Vic saw people pouring caps of water, ladling beer from barrels. Those few who had survived would flock here. It was the most unlikely of sanctuaries.

She saw her youngest brother Rob tending to a woman laid out on the sand. Her mother was moving from person to person with canteens. There was a smell of alcohol, and Vic saw someone cleaning a wound with a bottle from the bar, tipping it into a dishrag before gingerly dabbing at injured flesh. There were people there whom she had pulled out of the sand. Some Conner had as well. They had both told people to seek out the Honey Hole. There were so many and yet not nearly enough.

Her mother Rose was directing the chaos. Several of her girls were still in their balcony get-ups, but now they moved through the bar tending to the sobbing, the wounded, the thirsty. 'There's Palmer,' Conner said, gesturing to the stairs. Vic saw her brother hammering nails back into place, wiping the sweat from his forehead between blows. She hung her visor on the top of her dive tank and hurried over to him.

'What're you doing?' she asked, snatching the hammer away.

Her brother opened his mouth to complain but then seemed to wobble. Vic steadied him. Conner was there as well. They guided him to a bar stool while Palmer croaked about all that needed doing. 'The stairs are gonna collapse,' he said.

'*You're* gonna collapse,' Vic told him. 'Get him some water.' And Conner hurried around the bar. Vic weighed the hammer in her hand. She could barely stand herself, was past the point of exhaustion, but she moved back to the stairs and started driving in the loose heads. Swinging back for another strike, a hand snatched her wrist.

'What do you think you're doing?' her mother asked. She took the hammer away and placed a steaming mug of stew in Vic's hands. 'Sit. Eat. You've been diving for hours.'

Vic studied her mom, saw the creases of age in her face, the features so much like her own, and she saw the woman and not the profession, saw that this would be her in just a few years: exhausted, worn out, doing whatever it took to get by. She started to apologise, she wasn't sure what for, but couldn't form the words. And then she found herself fighting the urge to cry, to sob, to hold her mother and smear tears and snot into the crook of her neck, to tell her about Marco, how great a guy he had been even if he'd been caught up with the wrong people, how he was dead along with so many thousands more. But she fought this and won. She allowed herself to be guided to the bar, where she sat and spooned stew between her lips, doing what she was told because she knew she needed the sustenance, because she knew her mother was right.

Palmer drank beer from a jar, probably to save water for someone else. Conner was given his own bowl of stew. Rob joined them, pulled from the crowd by the gravitational tug of so much family all in one place, and Vic tried to remember the last time they'd been together like this. She caught her mom giving her a look as though she were having the same thought.

'How bad is it?' her mother asked. And Vic had been wrong. Her mother was thinking on more than just family.

'Pretty much all of Springston,' Vic said. She stirred her stew. 'The east wells will have to be redug. They're buried. The pumps with them.'

Conner stiffened. 'I need to go see about the pump in Shantytown. And I need to find—'

'The Shantytown pump won't be enough to water

everyone,' Vic told him. 'How many people from that side of town came over here to the cisterns?'

'What about Dad's advice?' Conner asked, turning to their mom. 'Maybe we should go west like Father said.'

Vic's spoon froze halfway to her mouth. Stew dribbled onto the bar. 'When did Dad ever say we should go live in the mountains?'

'Not in the mountains,' Rob told her. '*Over* them.'

Vic turned and studied her little brother, who was perched on a bar stool. 'You need to stick to water,' she told him, thinking he'd been into the beer.

Rose placed a hand on Vic's shoulder. Palmer was looking at her funny. 'What?' she asked Palmer. 'What's that look about?' It was as though everyone else knew something she didn't.

'Don't freak out,' Palmer said. 'I just learned a few hours ago.'

'Let her eat,' their mother said. Then, to Vic, 'Finish your stew, and then I need you to come upstairs with me.'

'Upstairs?' Vic felt her palms go clammy. Felt that old terror swell up within her. She didn't think anything would get her up those stairs ever again. She had a sudden compulsion to yank out the few nails she'd driven in, to yank them all out so that no one could ever climb those stairs again, not her or her mother or anyone. 'Why do you want me to go upstairs?' Vic asked.

'Finish your stew. And then I need you to meet someone.'

Vic couldn't very well sit there and eat with everyone acting strange, watching her like that. Her appetite was gone, anyway. 'Who?' she asked.

It was Rob who blurted out what no one else would say. 'Our sister,' he said. And when Vic shot him a look, he showed her his jar. 'It's water, I swear.'

50

The Backs of Gods

'I don't have time for games,' Vic told her mom. She stopped at the bottom of those stairs, her hand on the rail, unable to muster the courage to lift her boot. 'What I need is to get back to the sarfer and get to Low-Pub. The people who took down the wall are hitting it next.'

There was a hand at her back, urging her up. Just like before. Like when she was sixteen. Vic resisted. Her mother went past her to the bottom step, turned, looked out over the lantern-lit and pathetic crowds, and then lowered her voice.

'I don't know what the hell is going on,' Rose said, 'or what you might be involved in. I don't know what's happening out there.' She looked to be on the verge of tears, and Vic forgot her terror for a moment and truly listened. 'This is all too much at once. It's too much.' She shook her head and covered her mouth with her hand. Vic saw that her brothers were watching from the bar.

'Mom, you need to get some rest. What can be done is being done. There's no one left to save. All of this can wait until morning.'

'Your father is still alive,' her mother blurted out.

Vic gripped the railing. The Honey Hole slid back down into the dunes and spun around her. 'What...?' Her mother held her by the waist to keep her from sagging to the ground.

'I don't know how all of this is happening at once, what games the gods are playing, but Conner and Rob brought a girl here the day after you came to see me. The morning after I saw you, they came in with a starved and injured girl who made it out of No Man's Land.'

'What?' Vic whispered again. She didn't understand. 'How long had she been gone? How far did she get?'

'She didn't wander in from over *here*,' Rose said. 'She crossed all the way. Come upstairs. Please.'

Vic found herself coaxed upward. It felt as though her mind and senses were floating above the ground. 'What do you mean, Father is still alive? Why did Rob call her my—?'

'Your sister. Half-sister. You need to hear what she has to say.' Vic glanced back and saw that Palmer and Conner were following them up the stairs. Rob was climbing down from his bar stool.

'And Dad?' She looked to the balcony.

'He's being held on the other side of No Man's Land against his will. I'll explain. But it means you have to put Low-Pub out of your mind. Your brother is right, that going west might be the only way. I think that's what the gods are trying to tell us.'

Vic felt a flush of rage at the mention of the gods, at the talk of destiny. She'd seen too many dead to think of that bitch Fate. She found herself standing there on that balcony, high over the sight of so many hurt and wounded, so many sobbing and mourning their loved ones. Listening to their soft wails, smelling the sweat in her dive suit, thinking on all the buried she'd seen that day, all the horrors visited on that already miserable place, the image of Marco shot dead, seeing a man's face stove in behind Graham's workbench, all the bombs over the years, the rape, the scars, the buckets of hurt more numerous than the sands.

'No one is watching over us,' she told her mother. She turned to her brothers, who were gathered on the stairs, looking up at the two women. 'There isn't anyone up there looking down on us,' she told them all. 'Those constellations you see up there?' She jabbed her finger angrily at the ceiling. 'Those are the *backs* of gods we see. They've turned from us. Don't you understand? Our father is dead. I don't have a sister. Now I've got to get to Low-Pub.'

She pulled away from her mom and forced herself down between her brothers, nearly knocked Rob over. Her mother yelled for her to wait. Vic stopped at the bar and screwed a lid onto a jar of beer. She grabbed a heel of bread from Palmer's plate and hurried towards the door. She started to gather her gear.

Conner rushed to her side. 'Vic, don't go.'

'I'm sleeping on the sarfer so no one steals it. I sail at first light. I'll come back and check on you all once whatever happens in Low-Pub happens.'

'Low-Pub is nothing,' Conner said. 'You've got to hear what this girl has to say. There are entire cities out there—'

'Like Danvar?' Vic slung her tank over her shoulder. 'Stop dreaming, Con. Start digging. This is the only life we've got.'

'Well, if you won't stay, then I'm coming with you.'

'Suit yourself.' Vic nodded to the other dive tank and the gear.

'Okay. Good. I will. We're leaving at first light?' Conner rubbed his hands together. He seemed shocked that she would have him along. In truth, she needed him and twenty more like him. 'If so, I'm going to see if I can be of use here for a few hours. Let Mom know where we're headed.'

Vic shrugged. 'You know where the sarfer's parked. You

get there after dawn, it won't be parked there any more.' She turned and shoved her way out the door. It felt good, fleeing that place again. Here was where she had learned this skill all those years ago, where she had learned how good it felt to run away.

Conner stood by the door and watched his sister go. It was a familiar sight, her leaving. It didn't seem possible that he would see her later that night. He was used to it being months. A year. He was used to the fear that she would perish on her next dive and he would hear about it from someone at school. That loss would be even greater now that they had soaked the sand with their sweat together, had dived side by side to rescue whoever they could. His sister, always a bright and distant star in his life, had grown as bright as Venus. It left him no space to stay behind while she went off to Low-Pub.

But he couldn't run out as quickly as she could. He had tried, had come to that decision after years and years of silent agony, and then when given the excuse, he had run back, had fled just as quickly to the family tent, for the comfort of home. He didn't have Vic's years of practice, years of walking out, walking away.

He turned to the stairs, where his family was still watching from the balcony. Conner made his way to them through the crowded bar. A woman he passed grabbed his wrist and thanked him with tears in her eyes, and Conner remembered pulling her out of her home. Her little boy squirmed in her lap. Conner fought back tears of his own as he squeezed her shoulder. He wanted to say that she was welcome, but he feared his voice cracking, feared the facade this woman saw on him sloughing off. His brother Rob met him at the bottom of the stairs.

'Where's Vic going?' Rob asked.

'People out there still need our help,' Conner told his little brother. He stooped down to speak to him. 'I'm going to go with her, okay? You'll stay here with Mom and Palm.'

'I want to go with you.'

'You can't,' Conner said. He was on the verge of tears but he had to be firm. 'You're needed here. Take care of Violet. Imagine how scared she must be. How alone she must feel.'

Rob nodded. He scanned the room, perhaps looking for something to do, someone to help. Conner climbed the stairs towards his mom. He dreaded telling her he was leaving, but nothing had ever felt as right as pulling people out of the sand. The moment he'd carried his mother and Rob and Violet up into the attic and saved them had been like that moment a snake sheds its skin or a baby crow pierces its shell. It had been a sort of birth, a discovery of purpose. He no longer felt like a boy. As he reached the top of the stairs, he thought even his mother was looking at him differently. Even Palmer.

'I'm going to help Vic for a few days,' he told them. 'You'll look after Rob?'

His mother nodded, and Conner saw her throat constrict as she swallowed back some word or sob. She reached out and squeezed his shoulder, and he was about to turn away when she reached into her pocket and brought out a folded piece of paper. 'Give this to Vic,' his mother said. 'Make sure she reads it. She needs to believe.'

Conner accepted the paper and stuck it into his pocket. 'I'll make sure she gets it,' he promised. 'I'm going to let Violet know I'll be gone for a while. You'll look after her?'

His mother nodded. Conner thanked her and turned to her room, which no longer had the same repulsive effect on him it had used to. It had been cleansed by the sand that had passed through it; it had been scoured clean. He heard Palmer hurry up behind him and felt his brother grab his arm.

'Hey, Con, we need to talk.'

Conner stopped. Over Palmer's shoulder, he saw their mother heading back down the stairs to tend to the stricken. 'What is it?' Conner asked.

Palmer glanced at their mother's door as though there were still something to fear there, as though one of her drunk clients might lumber out at any moment and crash into them and send them over the edge of the balcony with its missing rail. 'This way,' Palmer said. He guided Conner past the room where Violet lay, his voice a conspiratorial whisper.

'You okay?' Conner asked. His brother looked better than he had in the sarfer earlier that day, had salve on his blistered lips and food in his belly. But something seemed off.

'Yeah, yeah, I'm fine. It's just that . . . this girl who claims to be our sister—'

'Violet,' Conner reminded him.

'Yeah, Violet. It's just that . . . Mom took me in there and told me her story, let me talk to her. She and Rob told me about the other night – the night you went camping – and about where she came from.'

'No Man's Land.'

'Well, maybe.' Palmer glanced at the door again and pulled Conner even further down the balcony. 'It's just a little unbelievable, don't you think? I mean, you really buy her story? Because—'

'I was there,' Conner told his brother. 'I'm telling you she speaks the truth. She knew who I was.'

'I know, I know. But here's the thing. The guy who did this to me . . .' Palmer pointed to his face. 'This guy Brock who hired us to find Danvar, who killed Hap, he's got this strange accent. Everyone says it comes from the north. And this girl sounds just like him.'

'You think Violet is some cannibal?' Conner didn't have time for this, but his brother really seemed concerned. Vic had told him that their brother was pretty rattled from his experience, that he'd been through a serious ordeal. It was strange, this, to pity an older brother.

'I'm not saying anything, Con. I just know what I hear. And her showing up and then the wall coming down at the same time? And Danvar? Everything happening at once like this? You buyin' that?'

Conner squeezed his brother's shoulder. 'I don't know what's going on,' he said truthfully. 'But I believe that girl in there is our sister, and I think Dad is still out there somewhere.'

Palmer nodded. There were tears in his eyes. 'Yeah,' he said. 'You've always believed that.' And there was nothing accusing in his brother's voice. Something more like envy.

'I've got to go,' Conner said.

'Yeah.'

'Good to see you,' he told his brother. And the two of them embraced. They exchanged hearty slaps on each other's backs that loosened the sand in their hair. And Conner remembered how angry he'd been at Palmer in the last few days, at the betrayal of his not being there to go camping with them, and such concerns seemed petty. Beneath his worry.

'I love you, brother,' Palmer whispered in his ear.

And Conner had to turn and go quickly away before his great facade crumbled.

51

Waterpump Ridge

Conner moved through the darkened dunes with an empty dive tank on his back and a regulator swinging by his hip. He didn't head straight for the sarfer. There was one other person he needed to see before he left. He had to know she was okay. Had to see Shantytown and his home and somewhere he could imagine life clinging and continuing on when he got back.

There were a few torches and lamps burning out across the dunes. Occasional voices could be heard as people shouted into the wind, calling for one another. The sand in the air was mild, the stars overhead bright. The glow of illumination in Springston that normally drowned out the constellations had been smothered. Extinguished. Conner thought of all the diving that would need to be done to reclaim what the sands had taken.

As he headed towards Gloralai's place, Conner became aware of some guilty and latent thrill at his being alive. He felt a raw power for having survived being completely buried in drift. There was also some strange pang of guilt for having been present and on the earth for so momentous a disaster as the fall of the great wall. It wasn't enjoyment – was nothing like enjoyment. There was too much of a darkness over everything, too much of a longing, a deep ache; but behind it all there was a tiny voice telling him how good it felt to be breathing, how great it felt to be above the sand, and could he believe what he'd just witnessed?

Conner hated this voice. There was no excitement in this. Nothing but tragedy and loss and now an uncertain and terrifying tomorrow. The wind-blown dunes would swamp Shantytown as never before. Another chaotic Low-Pub awaited here. A lesson was coming for his people, a lesson that there is always a new and greater misery to fall back upon. And thinking this caused the endless days to stretch out before him – days when hauling buckets away from the waterpump would be remembered with the same blissful nostalgia as hot baths and flushing toilets. Always more room to fall. The sand went down and down and didn't stop.

He veered slightly out of his way as he thought these things; he wanted to swing by his house. There was nothing there for him – he'd carried everything out of there for his trek across No Man's Land, a decision and deed that seemed so very far away now – he just wanted to make sure the front door was unburied, that he and Rob would have a place to go to, that the sand around their home hadn't collapsed shut from the grumbling of the earth.

The door was still there. The scaffolding was still webbed atop his home. And it looked as if there might be a lantern burning inside. Light squeezed around the crooked door.

Conner approached slowly. He didn't knock, just tried the handle, found it sticky as usual but not locked. He pushed it open.

A man turned towards the door, his eyes growing wide over his neatly cropped beard. He and two boys sat around Conner's kitchen table. There was the smell of food cooking. The man got up, the chair tipping backward and crashing to the floor, both of his hands out in front of him.

'I'm sorry,' the man said. He reached for his children, who had stopped eating their soup, who sat with frozen expressions on their faces. They all had on such nice clothes. 'We're going. We'll leave. We meant no harm.'

'No,' Conner said. He waved the man back. 'Stay. This is my place. It's okay.'

The man glanced towards the dark bedroom. Conner couldn't tell if there was anyone in there, thought maybe the man was thinking that there wasn't room enough for him and his children to stay.

'Are you from Springston?' Conner asked.

The man nodded. He righted the chair and rested his hand on its back. The children went back to slurping. 'I took the boys out on the sarfer this morning. We saw it happen, saw all of it. My wife—' He shook his head and looked away.

'I'm sorry,' Conner said. He adjusted the empty dive tank on his back. 'Stay here as long as you like. I was just checking on the place.'

'What about—?'

'I've got somewhere to stay tonight,' Conner assured him, thinking of the sarfer and a night beneath the stars. 'I'm sorry for your loss.' He turned to go, but the man was across the room, clasping him on the shoulders.

'Thank you,' he whispered.

Conner nodded. Both men had tears in their eyes. And then the man hugged him, and Conner thought how this would've seemed a strange thing a day ago.

Gloralai wasn't at her house. Conner knocked and waited, but the windows were dark and there was no sound within. He tried the schoolhouse next, thinking that this was where his friends would gather. He spotted Manuel's mother hurrying between the dunes, her face partly lit by the spitting torch in her hand. Manuel was a classmate. Conner stopped her and asked how he was. She squeezed Conner and said that he was at the well with the others. She asked about Rob.

'Rob's fine,' Conner said. He asked if she knew where Gloralai might be.

'I think all the sissyfoots are at the well.'

Conner considered the hour and realised he was probably also supposed to be there. It had been a school day, a fact forgotten not just from looking after Violet at the Honey Hole but from leaving class on Friday expecting never to come back. It was after dark, and he would normally have hauled his quota by now. He thanked Manuel's mom and hurried towards the well. The sudden awareness that the sand would never stop hit him. Not even for the collapse of the wall. Not even that night, for them to rest and regain their senses, to count and properly bury their dead. Buckets still had to be hauled or they would go thirsty. The gods were merciless. Vic was right. This was the sort of cruelty that only came from turned backs, from being ignored. Well-aimed lashes and direct blows were more easily understood. At least then the stricken knew their anguished cries were being heard.

He aimed for the dancing torches atop Waterpump Ridge. A lot of activity. He could imagine the haul shifts starting late, a period of chaos as the schoolhouse emptied and the sand washed out Springston, nobody knowing what was going on. It was strange, the separation he felt from his peers, thinking on where he'd been all day and what he'd been doing. But here they were, his classmates, keeping the water flowing, saving far more lives than he had. There was perspective in this. The man who had broken into his home and had stolen what little Conner had left in his cupboard – that man couldn't be blamed. The larger rules of the world were broken, the Lords' rules. But the simpler rules that guided the heart of each man were intact. These were the rules that never changed. Knowing right from wrong. Surviving and letting others be. Maybe even lending a fucking hand.

'Conner?' someone asked as he approached the outhaul tunnel. It was a boy called Ashek. He must've been on his way down from dumping his buckets, since his pole was held casually across one shoulder. 'Where you been, man?'

The two boys clasped hands and Conner lowered his ker. They had to strain to see each other in the flicker of torchlight. The moon would not be up for hours yet.

'Been helping my mom,' Conner said, not wanting to explain any further. 'Hey, have you seen . . . is everyone else here? Everyone okay?'

'Yeah, except for the kids who didn't show up for class. But most of them weren't around yesterday either. Off diving for Danvar. So I'm sure they're fine. I just passed Gloralai on the way down. She was taking a haul up to the ridge.'

'Uh . . . yeah . . . thanks.' Conner tripped over his words. He hadn't mentioned looking for her, didn't think anyone knew he liked her, not even Gloralai herself. He thanked Ashek again and headed up the ridge. Dark shapes blotted the stars on the path up, and Conner felt naked without his haulpole and buckets. A large figure ahead, a familiar voice. Conner saw Ryder huffing his way down the sand path. The two boys stopped and looked at each other. Ryder tugged his ker off his mouth.

'You okay?' he asked.

Conner nodded. 'You?'

'Fuck no. I should be out diving, not doing this shit.'

'This is just as important,' Conner said. He kept himself

square to Ryder and hoped the boy didn't see the tank on his back.

'Yeah, whatever.'

But there was something different as Ryder went past him and strode down the sloping sand. More of what had seemed significant falling away from yesterday's cares. The things once at the centre of Conner's universe no longer were. The world had wobbled; its axis had shifted; the core was now at the periphery and vice versa. But there, higher up the ridge, a slimmer hole stood out in the dense constellations, a familiar form, the memory of a beer and a bowl of stew, of thinking that running away might not be the answer. Conner joined Gloralai on the top of the ridge just as she dumped the last of her sand into the wind. When she turned and saw him, there was a gasp. She dropped her pole. Arms around his neck, nearly knocking him over, the feel of her sweat on his skin and not caring. Enjoying it. A sign of her toil. The embrace letting him know she cared. That he wasn't alone.

'I've been so worried,' she said. And Conner realised why Ashek had told him where she was. *She had been looking for him.* She pulled away and brushed the hair off her face. Everywhere she had pressed against him cooled in the breeze. The sand in the air stuck to the sweat she'd left on his skin, and Conner didn't mind. 'Someone said you pulled Daisy's kids out of the courthouse. Is that true?'

Conner wasn't sure. There'd been dozens of people. They'd all looked the same in his red dive light. 'I remember the courthouse,' he said.

Gloralai placed a hand on his arm and turned him, looked at the dive gear on his back. 'You went camping. You didn't come back. I thought—'

Conner reached out and placed a hand on the back of

Gloralai's neck. He pulled her close and kissed her, staunching her worry and his as well. She kissed him back. The tank fell to the sand, their arms snaking around one another, her lips on his neck, a classmate dumping his buckets in the nearby dark and saying, 'Get a fucking room.'

Laughter against his neck. Her exhalations. Conner kissed her cheek and tasted salt. 'I'm sorry I wasn't here,' he said. But what he wanted to apologise for was thinking of leaving. For taking the wrong chance. The wrong chance. 'And now I've gotta leave town for a while. My sister needs me.'

'Your sister.' Gloralai studied his face in the starlight. Buckets rattled on a haulpole as a silhouette left them alone again on the ridge.

'Yeah. The same people who attacked here might be heading to Low-Pub. I don't want her going alone.'

'You're gonna sail there? Tonight?'

'We go at first light.'

'When will you be back?'

'I don't know.'

'Then I'll come with you. I have a brother in Low-Pub—'

'No,' Conner said. 'I'm sorry. But no.'

'That's it? You're telling me I can't come?' Her hands fell away from his arms. 'Why do you get to choose who—'

'Because I don't want anything to happen to you,' Conner said. 'I can't go if it means you coming with us. And I have to go. For Vic.'

Gloralai studied him in the weak starlight. 'I understand,' she finally said. 'I don't like it, but I understand.'

'I'll find you when I get back,' he promised. And it suddenly became very important that he get back.

'What about your hauls?' she asked.

Conner looked down at her pole and the two buckets.

'I've carried all I can today,' he said. 'They'll have to understand.'

'You staying at your place tonight? Can I come see you?'

Conner thought of the family in his home. 'No,' he said. 'I'm camping with my sister on her sarfer.'

'And you leave at first light.'

'Yeah.'

Gloralai took his hand. 'Then stay with me tonight.'

52

A Pillar of Smoke

'I didn't think you were gonna make it,' Vic said. She stood by the mast, arranging sheets and halyards by the red glow of her dive lamp. Conner loaded his gear into the haul rack.

'You said first light,' he told her.

Vic nodded towards the horizon where a bare glow could be seen. Maybe.

'Aw, c'mon.'

'Man the jib,' she told him. 'But first, get your suit plugged in so it can build a charge. You probably drained it yesterday. And make sure that gear is lashed down. It's gonna be windy today.'

Conner studied the sand hissing softly against the sarfer's hull. 'How can you tell?'

'I just can. Let's go.'

He pulled the dive suit she'd given him the day before out of the gear bag. There were two power leads trailing down from the wind turbine, which was *thwump-thwump-thwumping* in the morning breeze. Her suit was lashed to the base and plugged in. He did the same with his, double-knotted the arms and legs around the pole. Then he made his way up the sarfer's starboard hull and across the netting between the two bows. He checked the jib sheets to make sure they wouldn't get fouled and knocked the sand out of the furling drum. He could see what he was doing without turning his dive light on, so he supposed maybe she was right about the first light.

'You get a good night's rest?' Vic asked. She worked the main halyard free, and it clanged rhythmically against the tall aluminium mast.

'Yeah,' Conner lied. A smile stole across his lips as he thought – without remorse – of how little sleep he'd got.

He helped his sister raise the mainsail, cranking on the winch as she guided the battened canvas up through the jacks. As he muscled the sail up those last few laborious metres, he thought about Gloralai and her lips and her promises and her talk of the future, and he felt an armour form across his skin, an invisible force field like a dive suit put out, and the sand striking him was no longer a nuisance. It was just a sensation. As was the wind in his hair and the shudder in the sarfer's deck as his sister moved to the helm and the mainsheet was tightened, the canvas gathering the breeze. The sadness of so much tragedy was still everywhere around him, but Conner felt a new awareness that he would persevere. He felt alive. The sarfer hissed across the dunes, and he felt madly alive.

They sailed downwind to get west of Shantytown before turning south. Conner tidied the lines and then got comfortable in one of the two webbed seats at the aft end of the sarfer. He helped work the sheets while his sister manned the tiller. Watching the sad and flat expanse of sand where Springston had used to be, he asked his sister why they didn't just cut across rather than sailing around.

'Because we'd catch the skids or the rudder on some buried debris,' Vic told him. 'This way is longer, but it's safer.'

Conner understood. He remembered all that was buried out there. He checked that his dive suit was secure, wasn't going to fly away. It already felt like his, that suit. It smelled like him. Had served him.

It was quiet as they sailed in the direction of the wind. Just the shush of sand on the aluminium hull. It wasn't until they were beyond the last of the Shantytown hovels and even west of the waterpump that they turned south and gathered the sheets. The sun was nearly up. There was already enough light to see by. Conner watched Waterpump Ridge slide by, the sand blowing from its heights, tiny sissyfoots up there dumping their hauls. Vic had left the ridge well to port to keep it from blocking their wind.

'So what's this nonsense about Father?' she asked. She took a turn on one of the winches, locked down the jib sheet, then sat back with a leg resting on the tiller, steering with her boot. 'What was that scene on the stairs last night about?'

Conner remembered his sister barging out of the Honey Hole. He wanted to turn the question around and ask *her* what *that* scene had been all about. She'd been the one who'd caused it. He adjusted his goggles, tucked his ker up under the edge to keep it in place. He wasn't sure how to tell her the same news without getting the same reaction. Their mother had probably dumped too much on her all at once the night before. But he tried. 'You know what last weekend was, right? The camping trip?'

He tried not to make it sound like an accusation for her not being there. Vic nodded. The sarfer glided happily south in a smooth trough.

'So, Rob and I went alone like last year. Palmer didn't make it . . . which I guess you already knew. Everything went the same, you know? We set up the tent, made a fire, did the lantern—'

'Told stories about Father,' Vic said.

'Yeah, but that's not the thing.' He took a deep breath. Adjusted his goggles, which were pinching his hair. 'So we went to sleep. And in the middle of the night, a girl stumbled into our campsite. A girl from No Man's Land.'

'The girl Mom wanted me to meet? The one she said came all the way across. And you believe that?'

'Yeah. I do. I was there, Vic. She collapsed into my fucking arms.'

'Maybe she's Old Man Joseph's daughter,' Vic said, laughing.

'It's not like that,' Conner said. 'Vic, she was sent by Dad.'

His sister's brow furrowed down over her dark goggles. 'Bullshit,' she said. She wasn't laughing any more.

Conner tugged his ker off. 'It's not bullshit. I'm telling you. She knew who I was. And Rob. She described Dad to a T.'

'Anyone in town could do that.' The sarfer hit a bump and Vic glanced towards the bow, adjusted their course. 'And even *Mom* believes her? You sure it's not just someone looking for a handout? Some kid from the orphanage?'

'Yes, Mom believes her,' Conner said. He rubbed the sand out of the corners of his mouth. 'Palmer doesn't, but he wasn't there. I don't know how long he even talked to her.'

'No one comes out of No Man's Land,' Vic said. She turned from watching the bow to peer at her brother. He wished he could see past her dark goggles. The same hard shells that allowed one person to see blinded another. 'So what's her story?' Vic asked, her tone one of distrust and suspicion.

'She was born in a mining camp on the other side of No Man's. Dad helped her escape. He sent her with a warning—'

'And she claims to be our *sister*? That our father is *her* father?'

'Yeah. Dad built her a suit, and she dived down under some kind of steep valley and walked like ten days to get to us. But—'

'But what?'

Conner pointed ahead, as they had begun to drift again. Vic took her foot off the tiller and steered by hand.

'What is it?' she asked.

'I believe her, but Palm pulled me aside last night. He seems pretty convinced that something's wrong. Violet – this girl – our sister – has a . . . strange accent. Palm says she talks just like the guy who hired him to find Danvar.'

'Who, Brock? That's the fucker we're after. What did Palm say?'

Conner shrugged. 'Just that they sounded alike. That's all.'

Vic gazed forward and chewed on the grit in her mouth. Conner could hear it crunching between her teeth. 'I don't like it,' she said. 'And I don't want to hear any of this nonsense about Dad, okay? There's too much else going on. I don't need that.'

Conner nodded. He was used to his family telling him that. He had learned a long time ago to shut up about their father, that there was only one night a year on which it was allowed. He tried to get comfortable in the webbed seat, then saw something in the distance. He pointed over the bow. 'Hey, what's that?'

'That's not good, is what that is.' Vic adjusted the tiller to steer straight for it. Up ahead, a column of smoke rose in a slant before bending sideways and blowing westward in the breeze. Something was on fire.

'We should stop and check,' Vic said. She pointed to the line that furled the jib. Conner gathered this and waited for her to give the word. Ahead, the smoking ruin of a sarfer loomed into view. The mainsail had burned, and the mast had caught as well, had pinched and melted near the base and now drooped over like the wick of a candle. Both hulls were still on fire, the metal aglow, the colour of the morning sun. Black smoke billowed up and spiralled away in the wind.

Vic began to let out the mainsheet and Conner furled the jib. Vic then dialled down the power of the skids and rudder, so the sand stopped flowing as easily, and slowly braked the craft. They left the main up, just allowed the boom to swing and point with the wind the way a vane does.

'That looks like a body.' Conner pointed to a form lying near the smoking ruin of the sarfer. The man wasn't moving, was lying close to the wreckage.

Vic jumped down from the sarfer and Conner scrambled after her. They both approached the wreckage warily. The hull of the burning craft creaked and popped from the heat of the fire. The smell was awful. Acidic and biting. Conner was scanning the scene for more bodies when blood frothed up on the lips of the prone man. One of his hands lifted several inches off the sand before his arm collapsed again.

Conner heard his sister curse. She rushed forward and dropped to her knees beside the figure. She yelled for Conner to bring the aid kit, which he ran back and retrieved from the haul rack. The sand was loose beneath his boots as he hurried back to his sister.

'Oh, God. Oh, God,' Vic was saying. Conner placed the kit in the sand and untied the flap. His sister ignored it. The way she was rocking and holding the man's hand, Conner knew there was nothing they could do for him.

'Damien?' she asked. 'Can you hear me?'

The blood stirred on the young man's lips. Conner looked him over, couldn't see any obvious wounds, no blood on his chest or stomach or hands. And then Conner noticed the odd way the man's legs were bent. They were shapeless. The tight dive suit dented in where there should have been protruding knees. He moved to the other side of Vic and gently slid his hands from the man's thigh towards his calf, looking for any response on the man's face, feeling for a break. The man's lips moved – he was trying to say something – and Conner felt the spongy flesh beneath his palms, the absence of bone.

'Say again,' Vic said. She bent close to the man's lips, sweat dripping from her nose. The heat of the burning sarfer was unbearable. Conner saw that the man wasn't moving one of his arms, which looked as limp and deformed as his legs.

'We've gotta get him away from this fire,' Conner said.

His sister waved him off and listened. Her face was contorted in concentration, rage, grief, some impossible-to-read combination of worry lines and furrowed brow. Conner joined her by the man's head and tried to help her listen. The man was rambling, his voice a rough and halting whisper. Conner heard him mention a bomb. Something about playing marbles. He was mixing accounts of the dead with talk of a child's game. And then Conner heard the name 'Yegery', a name he recognised, a man his sister had talked about often, some kind of dive master. The injured man licked his lips and tried to speak again.

'I'm sorry,' he wheezed. The words came clear, seeming a powerful effort. There were bloody gasps for air between each short sentence. 'Tried to stop them. Heard what they were gonna do. From a defector. Made me tell who I heard it from. I told 'em, Vic. I'm sorry—'

He coughed and spat up blood. Conner noticed the tattoos on the man's neck, the marks of the Low-Pub Legion. One of his sister's friends.

'What're they planning?' his sister asked.

The man spoke again of making glass marbles, of a bomb, of people in the group who didn't want to go along, who were dead now. He said Yegery had gone mad. That there was no talking to him. That this guy Brock from the north was in his ear, in his head. The young man lifted his hand a few inches from the sand, and Vic gripped it with her own. 'Today . . .' he said. His gaze drifted away from Vic and towards the heavens. He stopped blinking away the sand. 'Today . . .' he whispered, the blood finally falling still on his lips.

Vic bent her head over the dead man and screamed. More a growl than a scream. Like a coyote cornered between pinched dunes. An inhuman sound that made Conner afraid.

He sat perfectly still and watched as his sister scooped two handfuls of sand and placed them over the man's eyes. She dropped his hand and patted his stomach, opened a pocket there and pulled something out. She stuffed this away, then seemed to notice something wrong. She turned back to the suit to inspect it more closely, wiping the tears from her cheeks.

'Those sick fucks,' she hissed.

'What is it?' Conner asked. He could barely breathe. The heat from the fire was intolerable, but he knew he would sit there as long as his sister needed to.

'His suit,' she said. She pointed to a tear at the man's waist, a place where wires had been pulled out and twisted together. There was another spot just like it by one shoulder. 'They wired his suit inside out. They used his band to torture him. Turned his suit against him to make him talk.' She punched her fist into the sand. Did it again. Then stood and began to march back towards her own sarfer.

'What did he say?' Conner asked, scrambling up and

chasing after her. 'What're they planning to do? Did he say where the bomb would be?'

'No,' Vic said. 'But they're doing it today. They're gonna end everything. And we're gonna be too late again.' She jumped back into the helm seat and began to take in the lines. Conner adjusted himself in the other chair and unfurled the jib.

'We've got plenty of wind,' he said. 'We'll get there in time.'

Vic didn't respond. The sarfer lurched into motion and began to build speed. She had been right about the weather that day.

53

Father's Last Rites

They sailed in silence for an hour. They passed other sarfers heading north, crossed tracks that led east to west, saw half a dozen craft out with their masts laid back, dive flags flapping from the rails to warn away others. Conner's thoughts whirled. He gave his sister as much time as he could, but he had to know. When she returned from a trip to the bow to check the lines for chafing, he finally asked.

'So who was that guy? Someone you knew?'

'A friend,' Vic said, taking the tiller back from him. 'He used to run with Marco. Some of the Legion guys left a while back to join up with another outfit. I think a few had a change of heart, maybe said some shit they shouldn't. Damien was unfortunate enough to hear.' She shook her head. 'Bastard could never keep a secret.'

'They . . . What they did to him.' Conner didn't really have a question, was just trying to process the level of fucked-up they were dealing with. He couldn't believe there were people who would kill so many, even those amongst themselves, and all for what? What was there to gain when everything was gone? 'What was that you took off him? His last rites?'

Vic nodded. Conner knew about this tradition, but he also knew you weren't supposed to ask divers what they carried in their bellies. And then he felt like an idiot. He remembered the note his mother had given him to pass along to Vic. He hadn't seen Vic later that night, had spent that time with Gloralai, so he'd forgotten. This didn't seem like the appropriate time, but he was scared he would forget again. 'I've got something for you,' he said, digging into his own pocket. Vic tried to wave him off. She was obviously lost in thought, but Conner took over the tiller and forced the letter into her hand. 'Mom gave it to me last night. She said to give it to you. I forgot about it until just now.'

Vic started to put the letter away with the other one. But then she hesitated. While Conner manned the tiller, she opened the letter. She kept it down in her lap and behind her knees so the wind wouldn't tear it from her grip. Conner adjusted his ker and concentrated on where he was steering.

'Who is this from?' she asked, turning and shouting over the noise of the wind and the shush of the sarfer as it tore across the sand.

'Mom,' he said.

Vic bent forward and read some more, then flipped the letter over, studied the back, studied the front again, seemed to read it a second time. Conner glanced repeatedly from the bow to his sister, watching her head swing across the lines on the page. She turned and looked at Conner for a long time; whatever was spinning in that head of hers was lost behind her goggles.

'Dad wrote this,' she said.

Conner's hand nearly slipped off the tiller. 'What?' Maybe he hadn't heard right.

'What the fuck is this?' Vic asked. 'Where did this come from?' She tucked the letter under one leg and eased the main, let out the jib. They lost some speed and it got easier to hear, easier to talk. She pulled the letter out from underneath her and showed it to Conner. 'Dad signed this,' she said. 'Is this why you said we should go west? This letter?'

'I didn't read it,' Conner said. He gave his sister the tiller and took the letter. He read it. It was the note Violet had mentioned, the one that had got lost. He turned to his sister. 'Violet told us some of this. She'd read some of it when Dad wrote it out. She said she lost the letter. Mom must've found it. I had no idea. But yeah, this is what we were trying to tell you. Screw rebuilding, Dad wants us to move on.'

'But Palm says he doesn't believe this story—'

'Palm is fried. He said this girl talks like someone else. That doesn't mean anything.'

'This girl who's our sister.'

'Yes.'

The sarfer sailed on. Vic took in the main a little.

'So what's she like, this supposed sister of ours?'

Conner laughed. 'Headstrong. She sounds a lot older than she looks. Has all of our more annoying traits.'

Vic laughed. 'A half-sister as half crazy as the rest of us? That means Mom's right about where all that comes from.'

'Heh. I guess. You'd like her. She's a diver too. Dad taught her. But she does talk funny—'

Vic stiffened. She turned and stared at Conner, pulled her goggles down around her neck. Her eyes were wild. 'But what if Palmer's *right*?'

'Vic, I'm telling you—'

'No, what if this girl and Brock are from the same place?'

'I don't think—' But then Conner realised what she was getting at. That her conclusion was the *opposite* of Palmer's. 'Oh, fuck,' he said. 'Yeah. God, yeah.'

'Why would anyone want to level Springston?' Vic asked. 'Why would they want to level Low-Pub? And Palmer said these people found Danvar but didn't seem interested in scavenging from it, that they were just using it to fine-tune some map, to locate this bomb of theirs—'

'They don't give a shit about what's left out here,' Conner said, 'because he's not *from* here.' He nodded, remembering something else. 'Violet said there were more and more of our people appearing in their camp, that we're becoming a nuisance to them, like rats—'

'Because there's been more people jumping the gash,' Vic said.

'So how do they turn that dribble off?'

'It's not by making us want to stay here.' Vic clenched and unclenched her jaw. 'It's by getting rid of us.'

'How many do you think there are? The guy back there, your friend, was he—'

'No,' Vic said. 'He grew up in Low-Pub. I've known him for ever. I know a lot of the guys running around with this crew, and they didn't just pop up out of nowhere. They were recruited.'

'But why would any of our people help them do something like this?'

Vic didn't answer right away. She tightened the jib and got the sarfer back up to full speed. Finally she turned to Conner. 'One crazy fuck could do this,' she said. 'One crazy fuck with a pocket of coin who knows how to say the right things. That's all it would take. He could find enough people to kill for the thrill of it, for some bullshit cause, for bread and water and copper and a chance to blow shit up.' She slapped the tiller. Shook her head. 'Fucking Marco,' she said. And she must've got sand in her eyes, because she had to pull her goggles back up over them.

Conner slumped in his seat. He wondered if all they were thinking was possible. He suspected he and his sister were being crazier than Palmer with all of this speculation and nonsense. It didn't seem as if any of what they were positing could be true. But which was more likely? That the girl who'd crawled half dead into his campsite was a cannibal from the north? Or that the crazed assholes who had levelled Springston were working for someone who'd brought his thunder clear across No Man's Land?

'What're you thinking?' Vic asked. She turned and studied him, could obviously tell he was mulling it all over.

'I think you're fucking crazy,' Conner said. 'And I think you're probably right.'

54

Low-Pub

They parked the sarfer on the north side of Low-Pub. Conner and Vic had debated where to start as they'd approached town. There were no obvious targets in Low-Pub; not like Springston and its great wall. They still didn't have a course of action, but as they lowered the mainsail, the pop of its canvas in the wind was replaced by the *pop, pop* of distant gunfire. They both turned towards the town. Finding trouble might not be as hard as they'd feared. And there were no columns of black smoke to indicate that they were too late. They sat on the sarfer's hull and pulled their freshly charged dive suits on. Vic suggested they go without bottles so they could move more easily. 'And don't hesitate to bury these guys,' she told him. 'Send them straight down.'

Conner nodded. It was a dangerous heresy for a diver to mutter, using a suit against another. But they were dealing with people who killed others by turning their own suits against them. They were dealing with people who levelled towns. He wouldn't hesitate. Yesterday, he had saved lives. Today, he steeled himself for the more gruesome task of taking them. He pulled his band down over his head and followed his sister into town. The two of them moved in a crouch. Low-Pub felt dead. As though everyone were gone or locked up in their homes. It was a hand past noon, the wind and sand whistling through town. The gunfire had stopped, which left them moving towards the area they thought they'd heard it emanate from. Vic turned and pointed down at the sand. Conner nodded and lowered his visor. His sister disappeared, and he powered up his suit, pulled his ker over his mouth, and followed after her.

They moved beneath the town where it was forbidden to dive. There was a purple roof of open air overhead, dots of buried garbage and scraps here and there, a few iron cages around basements, erected by the paranoid, but they were blind to what was going on above the dunes. This was a safe and quick way to move, but they couldn't see where they were moving to or if anyone was up there. Conner just trusted his sister and stayed close to her boots. He noticed that she kept studying the mass of magentas and deep purples above them as if there might be information in that great bruise.

She slowed and began to rise. Conner followed. He saw the bubble and swell of sand they were entering and realised they were coming up inside a mounded dune. Vic pierced the top, just to her shoulders, and Conner did the same. They flicked their visors up. Shifting the sand around her, Vic slid forward, away from Conner, just her head moving across the surface of the dune's ridge like a ball in a game of kick. His sister could move the sand in ways he'd never thought of; he had to learn on the fly how to adjust and mimic her. It was difficult, keeping the same level as he pushed the sand against his back. He took deep gulps of air through his ker, reminded once again that he couldn't stay down as long as she could.

She pointed down into the middle of a large square that was ringed with makeshift shacks. It was the market at the centre of Low-Pub. There were goods and wares hanging in the shacks, smoke rising from food stalls, the smell of meat burning, but no one shopping or tending the stalls. A dozen or so bodies were strewn throughout the market. Bloodstains. People had been shot, everyone else running for cover. That explained why it was so quiet now. Conner spotted a small group of men working in the dead centre of the market. Someone, somewhere, screamed in agony. Not all of the shot were dead. Not yet.

'Wait here,' Vic said. She flipped her visor down and slid beneath the sand.

'No fucking way,' Conner told the empty air. He flipped down his visor and dived after her. She was already a receding green form beneath the sand. She glided down the face of the dune and towards the wide flat space where the market square lay. Conner strained to catch up. He joined Vic as she slowed and slid through the earth on her back, gazing up at the waves of purple, looking for the boots of those above. She was probably planning on pulling them down into the sand to immobilise them, to smother them.

Conner felt the need to breathe. He wondered if he should turn back. He couldn't hold his breath like Vic could. Would need to surface. He should've stayed and watched from the dune as she'd said. He'd been too impulsive, too eager.

When she saw him following along behind, he knew the same thoughts were occurring to her, could almost see the anger in the orange and red shape of her, the way the bright yellow of her visor trained on him. He lifted his palms in apology, to tell her he was going back, when the sand around him ceased to flow.

He thought it was Vic at first, that she was pushing him back, had put the brakes on him, but then she flew violently up through the sand. A moment later, with a sickening lurch,

Conner shot up as well. He broke the surface and went into the air several feet, came down with a grunt as the air was knocked out of him.

He tried to flow the sand beneath him but it was stone-sand, locked tight. A gunshot exploded nearby and Conner heard his sister cry out. Something was pressed against his back. His band and visor were torn from his head, the blinding world of purples returning to the orange sand and the bright sunlight. Someone patted him down roughly, two sets of hands running across his suit. They told him to sit up and patted across his chest, under and down both arms.

'No guns,' someone said.

'She's clean,' said another.

Conner blinked and looked around. He found himself among a gathering of legs and boots, those men at the centre of the square. His sister was lying on the ground ahead of him, her visor gone as well. A man was pointing a gun up in the air. Conner tried to see if his sister had been shot. He thought maybe she'd been punched or had cried out in alarm. An older man with a beard approached her. He had a crazy patchwork dive suit on – strips of varying cloth sewn together, wires trailing up along the outside in tangles and coils. He jangled as he walked.

'What the hell're *you* doin' here?' the man asked. When Vic tried to get up he made a fist. She sank a foot down into the sand and cried out as the ground pinched her. 'Trying to sneak up on *me*?' It was a question soaked in disbelief more than anger.

Vic grimaced, but stopped fighting the sand. 'Don't do this, Yegery. You don't have to do this.'

Behind the man, Conner saw a solid column of sand sticking up from the desert floor. A smooth metal sphere stood atop this, gleaming in the high sun. Vic was looking at it too.

'Oh, but I do.' Yegery knelt down beside her. The man by Conner kept a hand on his shoulder. There was a gun in his hand. Conner knew sort of how to use one if he could wrestle it away. He was pretty sure.

'You see,' Yegery said, 'we've been fed a lie. We've been told to feast on the sand and be happy. But there's a bigger and better world out there, and I've been promised a piece of it. All it takes is learning to let go of this . . .' He waved his hands around at the market, then stood up. 'We've been digging for something better all this time. I've spent my entire life digging. Your father spent his life digging. And then he wised up. He knew where to look.'

'I have a note from him,' Vic said. 'You wanna read it? He says it's hell over there!'

'Ah, that's because he's on the *wrong side*.'

Several of the men laughed. Conner pulled his feet up underneath him and was told not to fucking move. 'Sit on your hands,' the man standing over him said.

Gladly, Conner thought. He tucked his hands and boots beneath him. His sister strained against the clutches of the stonesand.

'What is that thing?' she asked, staring at the strange column.

'This is an atomic bomb.' Yegery walked over to it. 'Don't ask me how it works. All I know is how to work it. Easy as making marbles,' he said. 'Easy as pinching it down.' He stared at the column and the sand rose up and surrounded the sphere.

Conner could feel the hum in the sand beneath him. He wiggled his foot half out of his boot and toggled the power switch Rob had wired up. He got his hand around the band. Worked it out slowly. The man with the gun was watching Yegery as the dive master continued to talk.

'Now, if you'll excuse me, the rest of us are going to strap on some tanks and get down where it's safe. You and your friend here can see how far you can run before this goes off, but I should warn you, if this does what I've been told it can do, you won't get far enough. And I really do hate that for you, Vic. I like you. But this is bigger than us.' Yegery looked at the men. 'Get your tanks on. And bring their bands with us.'

'Down to two hundred?' one of the men asked, slinging a tank of air over his back.

'Two hundred,' Yegery said. They were right back to business, not worried about Vic, who was still pinned by the stonesand, and not worried about Conner, who didn't have his band or visor, didn't have a gun.

But he had his father's boots. He had spent enough time in them to be comfortable there, to know what they could do, what *he* could do. He held the band Rob had made in his hand, his palm sweaty, and he remembered what he'd told his brother beneath their house, about not shorting the wires. He loosened his grip on the strip of fabric and wire. There wasn't much time. The men were testing their regulators with sporadic hisses, getting the sand out of the mouthpieces, cranking valves and cinching up their harnesses. They would disappear beneath the sand, and Conner and Vic would have to run as fast and as far as they could. But only if they released his sister. Only if he could free her with his boots. Or he could take her straight down while the bomb went off. But then what? Would they let them go free after? The man in charge said this wasn't about him and his sister. They didn't seem too angry. But they were about to blow up the square. Conner didn't know what to do as he prepared to throw the band on and act. He had to do something. Had to stop them.

'Where's Brock?' Vic asked the old dive master. 'Why can't he do his own dirty work?'

She was stalling. But she was also getting their attention, which Conner didn't want. Yegery pulled his regulator out of his mouth and walked back to her. 'If he could do this himself, why would he need me? You're a diver. You know not everyone can do what we do. It's a good thing he needs me, or I'd be in your situation right now.'

'What about when he *doesn't* need you any more?'

Yegery hesitated. Eventually he smiled. 'He'll always need me. I'm taking the secrets of diving to his people. For all the magic they possess over there, it turns out some of our tricks are known only to us. Don't you worry about me.'

'He'll betray you,' Vic said.

'We'll see,' Yegery told her. He stared down at Vic, made a gesture, and she slowly rose to the surface. She flexed her arms, was free of the stonesand. 'You might want to run,' he told her. He reached up for his visor, and Conner knew the time was now. He kept the band close to his body and slid his hands into his lap, then up to his chest. He tried to pre-visualise what he wanted the sand to do, just like his sister had taught him to prep the dunes before diving into them.

'You sure about leaving them up here?' one of the guys asked. 'I feel like we should shoot them. Just to make sure.'

Vic turned and glanced at Conner. He had both hands around the band, was making sure he had it lined up right. The wires trailing out from the boot were visible, but there was nothing he could do about that.

'No. Don't shoot them,' Yegery said. 'It's not my fault they came here. Their death is on their heads, not mine.' He looked down at Vic, who was still in a crouch. 'Think of it as a favour on behalf of your father. A gift.' He flipped down his visor and smiled.

'I've got a gift from our father,' Conner said. The men turned in his direction. He had the band down over his forehead, could feel the sand beneath him, humming with some terrible power. 'Here.'

The world erupted into violence. For a moment Conner thought the bomb had gone off, that Yegery had triggered it with his band, that this was what it felt like to die in a blast, a split second of noise and a jolt of pain and a flash of light. He had told the sand what he wanted, had built up the vision in his mind, pictured it like a coiled spring, ready to unleash. But he had to go and say something as the connection hit. He saw a gun come up, the flash of light and a loud noise, so fucking stupid, a burst of agony in his chest, shot, falling backward into the sand, but the sand wound tight in his head and exploding out in the shape he'd imagined, inspired by that column with the bomb on it.

That column of sand with the sphere inside collapsed. The silver ball rolled across the blood-soaked sand towards Vic. Five other columns had shot up, sharp points of stone-sand beneath each of the men, impaling them, one of them screaming and writhing before falling silent, all of them quickly dead.

Conner groaned and held his chest, cursing himself. Beneath him, the sand slipped and swirled as he lost his concentration, his connection with his father's boots. He ripped the band off and the world was mostly still. Just the thrumming of his pulse and the agony of the wound.

'Easy,' Vic said. She was beside him. She ripped the dive suit along a seam, opened it up to inspect the wound.

'I'm gonna fucking die,' Conner whimpered.

Vic swept his hair off his forehead. 'You're not gonna die,' she said. 'It's not that bad.'

Conner kicked the sand in pain. 'It feels fucking bad,' he said. He watched as his sister surveyed the mess all around them, the towers of gore that her brother had made.

'I've seen worse,' she said.

55

A Deep Discomfort

The brigands were still staining the sand with their blood as the people of Low-Pub began to brave the market. Soon Vic wasn't the only person kneeling and tending to a loved one. A mother wailed and clutched what must have been her son. Someone shouted Vic's name, a young man with short dreadlocks and tattoos on his dark skin. Conner tried not to yelp as the two of them tended to his wound. Every time he cried out about his chest hurting, Vic assured him it was his shoulder, that he'd be fine. He couldn't feel his hand, but his sister was saying he'd be fine.

The dive suit was cut away from him with a knife, the wires in the fabric popping as they were severed. That suit would never move the sand again. Vic stood and left his side and ran over to shoo someone away from the metal sphere, telling them not to touch it. She didn't dare touch it either. Instead, she searched one of the impaled men and found her visor and band. Conner watched as she loosened the sand and sent their bodies beneath the market floor. She buried the bomb in the sand so no one could move it.

'Thank you,' Conner said as the man with dreadlocks finished wrapping his chest and his arm with scraps torn from a T-shirt. Conner managed to wiggle his fingers, which comforted him somewhat. But it still felt as if he'd been kicked by a goat. One whole side of his body ached. His feet grew warm and he realised the boots were still on. As he kicked them off and reached in for the power switch, he caught Vic eyeing them.

'Rob,' Conner said, as if that would explain everything. He remembered yelling at his brother for fooling around with their dad's boots. The boots had been nothing more than a memento for years and years, just sitting in a corner or shoved under a bed. Now they had saved Conner's life. Several times. Instead of yelling at his brother, he should've thanked him. He *would* thank him. And he would have his brother wire up the fucking power switch where it was easier to reach.

Vic clasped her dreadlocked friend on the arm. The man used his teeth to tear more of a shirt into strips of cloth, then surveyed the market, looking for anyone else who needed tending to.

'Can you stand?' Vic asked.

Conner nodded, but he wasn't sure. He got his boots back on and Vic helped him up. He swayed. The sight of his blood on the sand made him feel sick. His mind flitted to Gloralai, the sudden panic of how close he'd come to never seeing her again. And then a flush of guilt that he'd think of a classmate before thinking of his mother and his family. 'What now?' he asked. 'None of these guys was the one we were looking for, was he?'

'I'm guessing he's long gone,' Vic said. 'The guys who give the orders never get what's coming to them. They're the Lords in their towers, the brigands back in their tents while someone else blows themselves to pieces.'

'And that was the bomb?' He nodded to the spot in the sand where she'd buried it. Vic guided him towards the spot, an arm around his waist, letting him lean on her.

'How long before it goes off?'

'I don't think it will,' Vic said. 'Damien said it has to be squeezed to go off. Like making marbles for a child.'

Conner thought of how some divers could force sand together so fast that a tiny perfect sphere of glass would be formed. 'Seems like a weird way to set off a bomb,' he said.

'Yeah,' Vic agreed.

'We can't just leave it here.'

'No,' she said. 'We'll have to take it with us.'

'And bury it as deep as we possibly can,' Conner suggested.

His sister shook her head. She looked at the people coming out from their stalls and homes to see what the commotion had been about. She turned and squinted into the wind, gazing out to the east.

'We've got to do something with it,' she said. 'We've got to do something.'

56

A Place to Rest

The heavy sphere sat in the depression it made up there in the sarfer's trampoline. Vic had lashed it down with seizings of rope to that great net that spanned the sarfer's twin bows. Conner lost himself in that bomb from his helm seat. He held his tender arm in his lap, his shoulder throbbing, feeling the gentle sway of his body side to side as gusts puffed variably between the dunes to the east.

There were things that could not be contemplated, he realised. There were potential truths too costly to bear. It wasn't until *after* the body was scarred by a brush with danger that it learned fear. Conner thought of all the untouched places on his soul yet to teach him something. All the unblemished parts of him waiting for that razor of truth.

Sons of whores had existed before him. This was a fact, just not one he'd ever lived with. And so it wasn't a pain he felt for others. Not until it was *his* mom coming home with bruises lurking beneath her make-up. Not until it was *his* mom that the fathers of friends boasted of. There had been others like him before. He'd just never thought of them.

The same was true for the levelling of a town. Witnessing Springston in the aftermath of its destruction made the danger to Low-Pub real. Fear required precedents. The newborn reaches for the hot poker – *look how red and bright!*

That silver sphere might've been a harmless thing in his mind, resting gently there in that trampoline, were it not for Springston. And the threat Vic had made after lashing the bomb down – this idea that she would deliver Brock's gift to him – might be a joke to ignore, had Conner's father not disappeared across the Bull's gash all those years ago.

'What about Mom?' Conner asked. He tore his eyes away from the bomb and gazed off to the west, towards the tall peaks and the setting sun.

'What about her?' Vic asked. 'You think she cares if I disappear? You know how many years we went without talking?'

Conner thought he knew. But he also saw their mother differently now. Had seen her tend to Violet, had seen her save Rob's life. She wasn't defined by what she had to do in order to survive. None of them were.

'It's a damn miracle,' Vic said, 'that I didn't leave years ago.'

Conner turned to his sister. Sand hissed against his goggles. He adjusted his ker to keep the sand out of his mouth. 'What's that supposed to mean?' he asked.

His sister stared over the bow for a long while. When her ker flapped up, he could see that she was biting her lower lip.

'You want to know why I don't go camping with you boys?' she asked.

Fuck yeah, he did. 'Why?' Conner asked.

'Because any step in that direction, and I'm not turning back.' She turned towards him, unreadable behind dark goggles and ker. 'I often feel at night what Dad must've felt.

I see it when I dive deep, that there was a better time, a better place. When I hear the noise to the east, I can't help but think that there's something bigger than us out there, stomping around. It's either better than this place or it's an end to me. And I contemplate both.'

'If you go, I'm going with you.'

Vic laughed. 'No. You're not.'

'That's bullshit.' Conner felt tears of anger well up in his eyes. 'You can dive, but I can't. You can move off to Low-Pub, but it's too dangerous for me. You can date whoever you want, but Palmer is an idiot for hanging out with Hap.' Conner pointed up the mast with his good arm. 'Flying over the dunes with red sails and a Legion ker and you're gonna tell me what I can't do because it's too dangerous? But it's okay for you? You're a fucking hypocrite, Vic!'

His sister raised a hand in defeat and Conner calmed himself. Vic held his gaze and lowered her ker so she could be heard without shouting. 'I'm not a hypocrite,' she said. 'I'd be a hypocrite if I cared about myself as much as I care about you. But I don't. I think parents know this. Older siblings know it as well.'

Conner scratched where the makeshift bandage was itching his neck. He thought of things he'd said to Rob that he'd be angry to hear himself. 'I just don't want you to go,' he said. The sarfer went over a smooth rise and sank back down, making his queasy stomach feel worse. 'You can say all you want that you'll come back, but we both know you won't. Nobody ever does.'

'Nobody?' She pulled her ker back over the bridge of her nose. They sailed in silence for a dune, only the slithering taunt of vipers against those red sails.

'I lied about the night she came into camp,' Conner said. 'Violet didn't make it to our tent. I was out there.'

Vic was adjusting a line but she stopped and stared at him. 'Out where?' she asked.

'Across the gash. With three canteens and a pack of supplies.'

'Bullshit.'

But he could tell she believed him. That she knew. Conner fixated again on that silver sphere.

'Palmer didn't show up, so I was going to leave Rob there by himself. I *did* leave Rob there. I snuck out in the middle of the night, was across the gash and a hundred paces on when I found her.' He turned and lowered his own ker, didn't care about the grit getting into his mouth. 'So when you tell me, or you tell Palmer, or you tell Rob that you're gonna go out there and give 'em hell or get Dad back or that you're gonna return with him, just know that I've been where you are, making that decision, and I know what it's like to lie to myself and know that I'm never coming back.'

Vic turned away from him and lifted her goggles. Wiped at her eyes.

'I know you think you'll try, but so did Dad. If you do this, you're leaving us for good. And I'm gonna hate you for it.'

Vic turned back to him. She was smiling and crying at the same time. 'But you can leave Rob in that tent? Fucking hypocrite,' she said.

And in that way that often happens between siblings, cruel words were followed by laughter. Tears dripped into smiles. A flaming sun dipped behind cool mountains, and a harmless-looking silver sphere rode serenely at the bow.

57

Swinging the Gaze of God

VIC

They thought they were making it easy on her, that they were supporting her, but accompanying her to the gash just made it worse. As did the sight of her family erecting a tent together, just like old times. All the water and food and supplies they'd hauled, every backbreaking ounce of their hope over her return, but Conner had been right. She could lie to each and every one of them and promise that she'd be back, but she knew. Her father had known. Everyone who crossed that gash knew.

She unpacked and checked her pack, made sure she had everything. Water and jerky. Two loaves of bread. Spare ker. Her band and visor. A portable shade for sleeping during the day. The large knife Graham had given her when she'd broken the news to him. Bandages and salve. The three notes the boys had written. The five pairs of underwear that made her think of Marco and had her suppressing the urge to laugh or cry. She would wear her dive suit under the patchwork tunic cinched around her waist. The heavy sphere she left in the bottom of the pack. It seemed to let off heat, even though she'd kept it out of the sun. She felt ready. Far to the east, the drums called to her.

'You know I'm the one who should be going,' Palmer said as he watched her repack her bag.

'Why?' she asked. 'Because you're the oldest son?' It was a jab meant in jest, but none of her brothers seemed interested in sparring with her.

'No,' he said. 'Because I owe this asshole Brock. Because of Hap. Because I started all of this.'

'More reason then for you to be *here* and see it through.' Vic pulled two folded pieces of paper from her belly pouch and handed them to her brother.

'Fuck you,' Palmer said. He held up his hands and showed her his palms. 'I'm not taking your rites. You're coming back alive, damn you.'

Vic grabbed his wrist and jammed the papers into his hand. 'These aren't my last rites, asshole. It's your map.'

Palmer looked at the papers in his hand. He inspected the map he had pulled out of Danvar, then shook the other piece of paper. 'What's this note, then?'

'That's everything I know about diving deep. How to dive down to a thousand metres.'

'Bullshit,' Palmer said.

Vic grabbed him by the shoulders and waited for him to look up at her. 'Even with the right suit and visor, those depths will kill you without batting an eyelid. There's no breathing down there. And your suit will feel like it's gonna rip you apart until you get below three hundred. But it can be done. I've marked some of my favourite sites on your map there. Also some others that I think look promising. I made a key on the back so you can understand my notes. My advice to you right now is to send divers dumb as me down there. Don't take that chance yourself. You've got nothing to prove.' She tapped him on the shoulder. 'You stay alive,' she said. 'You were the one.'

Palmer lifted his goggles and wiped tears away from his eyes. He lowered them back down and studied the map and the notes. 'How're these not your last rites?' he asked. He looked up at her. 'You're not coming back, are you?'

Vic hugged her brother and Palmer returned the embrace. 'Take care of yourself,' she said.

'I will.' His voice was a whisper.

'And Rob and Conner.'

'I will,' he said again.

She let him go and turned away before lifting her own goggles and wiping her eyes. Rob ran towards her from the tent and crashed into her, throwing his arms around her waist. 'Not yet,' he told Vic. 'Don't go yet.'

Vic bent her head and hugged her youngest brother. 'I'll be back soon,' she told him. Rob frowned. There was sand on his lips. Vic lifted his ker from around his neck and adjusted it snug across his nose. He was the hardest one to lie to because he was the smartest. 'Take care of your new sister,' she said.

Rob nodded. Conner came to her side with her canteens. He lifted her heavy pack and held it for her the way a diver would hold another's tank. She stood and slipped her arms through the backpack straps, cinched the belt down snug over her hips, then took the canteens one at a time.

'Damn thing's heavy,' Conner said, referring to the pack but probably more directly referring to the bomb. He stood and rubbed his shoulder. Something unspoken passed between the two of them, the sort of communication that happened beneath the sand when throat whispers became another's thoughts. The two of them had dived together, had salvaged lives together, and they had salvaged something between them by doing so.

Vic gave Conner a hug. He slapped her pack and

whispered something that was lost to the wind. And then Vic turned towards the gash and saw her mother waiting out there, just as she'd found her mom the night their dad had disappeared. Vic left her siblings behind, waved one more time towards the tent where Violet was standing alone, then strode out to meet her mom, dreading this goodbye the most.

'I can't talk you out of this?' her mother said.

Vic laughed, thinking on how hard so many people had tried. 'When's the last time you talked me out of anything?' she asked. She meant it to be fun, to keep this goodbye from being so serious that she couldn't leave, but most of all to lift her mother's hopes that she might return.

'I lost you once. I don't want to lose my daughter again.'

Vic glanced back at the tent. 'You've got a new daughter to watch over,' she said. 'Think of it as an even trade—'

'Don't you give me that bullsh—' her mother started.

'I'm not giving shit,' Vic said. She felt the blood in her veins grow cold, the chance at humour lost. 'I'm not giving, Mom. I'm taking. That's what I'm doing. I'm taking my father back from them. I'm going to take their city and make them pay for the one we lost. Tit for tat, Mother. They owe us, and I'm gonna make them pay.'

'No. You'll cross that gash and you'll die for nothing.' Her mother was crying. It was the hardest thing Vic ever bore seeing, her mother vulnerable and weak and . . . human. Her mom didn't even wipe away the tears, just let them gather sand from the wind.

'You did your best by us, Mom. You weren't given packed sand to walk across. I know that. I wouldn't have done half as good as you did.'

With that, Vic hitched up the heavy pack and turned away from the campsite. It was the highest compliment she could have paid. She could've told her mom that she loved her, but neither of them would have believed that. Love was earned and hard fought and cherished. It was Marco's face and his rough palm on her cheek. It wasn't something a family got just for being a family. But her mom had done more with a shitty hand and honest play than a bluffer with an ace up his sleeve. Vic knew this was true as she crossed that hard break in the desert sand, that jagged divide between the then and the now – like a row between lovers or between family members, a wound that permanently mars a relationship, that moves it from courtship and passion to resigned cohabitation, that turns a daughter into an enemy, so that the best one can hope for is that she becomes a friend.

Vic wiped the mud off her cheek, hating herself as she left the gash behind. And then she stopped and lowered her heavy pack there in No Man's Land. She turned, pulled her ker down around her neck and ran back, felt near to her youth again, was crying like the little girl she'd never wanted to be, never wanted to be. And her mom's arms were wide. No questions. Just tears streaking down her face. A line in the sand that was nothing, not even there, taken in stride.

'Thank you,' Vic muttered into her mother's neck. 'Thank you, Mom. Thank you.'

Which was more than love. And it sustained her as she went back to her burden – that crack in the sand a thing that could be crossed and recrossed – and she headed dead into the wind and towards the horizon, her mother's reply echoing in her ear, accompanying her on that long march, whispered there at the edge of No Man's Land and over the insolent flap of that untameable tent:

'My sweet girl. My sweetest Victoria.'

58

A Rap upon Heaven's Gate

CONNER

Conner was the one who spotted it. On the seventh night, stoking the fire with a metal rod left over from incorrectly assembling the tent, he lifted his eyes to a sudden white glow on the horizon. It was a burst of daylight like the sun had forgotten the time and had leapt out of bed, rushing, late to work.

Conner shouted for the others, and his mother and Rob and Violet poured from the tent. Palmer rushed over from the other side of the campsite, buttoning his trousers, having gone downwind for a piss. Together they watched the glow. It bloomed like a radiant flower. It was so bright it required turning away, required looking at it askance, required giving it the same quarter as the noonday sun.

'Jesus,' Palmer whispered.

There was no doubting that a city had just vanished. Conner had seen bombs go off before. Spotting the blast of a normal bomb was a chore from two dunes away. This came to life from over the horizon.

'Vic,' Rob said, sniffing.

Their mother put a hand on his shoulder. 'She'll be fine,'

she said, but Conner didn't think she sounded sure. She couldn't know. None of them could know.

And then the noise hit after some long consideration. A rumble in their chests and bones. A deep growl of the earth and a howl in the heavens. The wind seemed to shift a moment later, and the sand startled into chaos and turbulence. They held on to one another. Violet took Conner's hand and squeezed it, and he realised that their little sister was the only one who had ever been there, that she was the only one who had any sense of what had just been harmed. Conner could practically feel her longing to rush that way and see for herself.

'They'll know we're here now,' Palmer said.

'They've known,' their mother told them. 'They've always known we're here. They know we suffer. Now they'll give a shit.'

The uncharacteristic language brought silence. A heavy stillness. It took several heartbeats for Conner to realise what was wrong. It would've been easy not to notice at all, to go on not noticing for days and days, so steady had been that backdrop of infernal noise that its absence could almost not register. But he heard it, somehow. He heard that quiet far over the horizon.

'Listen,' he whispered. 'The drums. They've stopped beating.'

There was food and water for five more days but they made it last for eight. Vic had told them not to wait, but they waited. Their mother told them not to hope, but they hoped. Eight more days of camping, of the tent hot at noon and chilly at night, of a quiet shared, a story to pierce the silence, the relief of occasional laughter, the most time ever spent together, time spent talking and thinking. There were stories of Vic to go along with stories of Father. A long wait for some return. If not a person strolling over the horizon, then at least an apparition. If not an apparition, then some word. If not a word, at least a sign.

Palmer spoke of Danvar. A finger in a rip by his belly, he confessed to a murder and their mother held him like he was a boy again. And Conner saw a man in his elder brother's sobs. It was all life would ever be, as the days and nights drew out and half-caps of water were sipped. No one would ever go back to Springston, for there was no town. They would live in the tent until the food and water were gone, such was the drawing-out of night and interminable day as dreams and stories mixed and a week felt like a summer, and the moon changed from a sliver to a pregnant disc, and even the rhythms and howls of the wind could be sensed and foreseen, like an old man who has watched the sands with such burning intensity for a wrinkle of years that he could paint a picture of a landscape that is *not yet* but *will be.*

This was how keenly the moments were felt. Especially by the crack in the earth, the Bull's gash, where a haunting depth opened in the soul of any who stood there, where toes were daringly dangled just to feel the cool air rush up between them, just to pretend that the howl was for the delicately poised, just to imagine a lovely visage down in the darkness screaming: *Don't do it. Step back. You are too bold and lovely and singular to look down in here and upon me.*

Conner sat there anyway and swung his legs in the gash, so intimate had the two become in the past weeks, so hollow the threat and so weak the pull. He dribbled sand through his fingers and down towards the centre of the earth. Nearby, marbles of glass were flicked to the far side, those small beads formed by Palmer, who spent much of his time showing that he could, no doubt thinking that it would've been better had *he* gone, the eldest son.

And on the eighth day, when the hike back should have ended, when they could wait no more, as the last of the water splashed Rob's tongue and even the mouldy heel of the bread was divided among their family, they gathered by the gash in the earth, crossed and recrossed like a thread leaps and forms stitches, and surveyed that boomless and quiet horizon.

It was early. The sun a mere hint. A pink ghost lurking. An unusual heaviness to the sky, the lingering night sky, as the stars disappeared. But it was not the light of coming day that swallowed them; it was something in the air. Conner dropped his ker, the sand that normally stirred on the winds succumbing to some mystery, alerted to some presence, a sound like marching in the far sand, and the cool morning grew cooler, the ice in the desert night clung piteously to dawn, fearful of the pink ghost, and Conner heard footsteps. He heard a grumbling. A noise. Something approaching.

'Something's coming,' Rob said, scrambling to his feet. 'Something's coming!' he shouted.

Palmer and Violet and their mother paused in the dismantling of the tent and ran to the gash to join the two boys, eyes and ears straining in the heavy darkness, tent canvas flapping in a gathering wind, the rhythmic sound of a steady advance, an approach, not of the dead or their long-gone sibling or their father – but of the even more impossible. It struck Rob first and then their mother, pattering across the desert floor, coming with a whoosh of cold wind and a blotting of the stars, a wetness from the heavens, an answer to the long silence, a sign that someone far away was listening.

Their mother fell to her knees and burst into tears.

And the sky wept for its people.

Reading Group Questions on *Sand*

- When Palmer hears how deep he will be diving he is incredibly nervous but never considers pulling out of the mission. Do you think this is purely because he wants the payment for the dive, or do you think he has other reasons? Is he trying to prove himself? If so, to whom?

- Once they make it down to Danvar, Hap very quickly betrays Palmer. Is his betrayal driven by fear or by the want to be the man who discovered the hidden city? Did you feel Hap deserved what happened to him when he reached the surface?

- Vic, Palmer, Conner and Rob are all affected by their father's abandonment. Compare how they cope with how their mother does. Who do you think is most affected by the loss? And why?

- Conner feels abandoned, not only by his father, but also by his elder brother and sister. Yet he is deciding whether to do the same to his younger brother, Rob. What are his reasons for this? Do you agree with them? Has Conner realised the effect of what he is planning on doing to Rob?

- Do your feelings towards Rose change throughout the novel? If so, how? Do you think this could be because you view her through her children's eyes before you get to hear her point of view? Are there any other characters we hear strong opinions about from others before we are introduced to them?

- Vic jokes with Marco about why she goes to the rebel meetings with him. Why do you think she does this? What do you think are her real reasons for spending so much time with the rebels?

- Vic and her mother have quite a tumultuous relationship and are very different in many ways. Can you draw any comparisons between the two of them?
- Once Palmer escapes from Danvar, he stumbles across Brock's encampment and, in order to survive, must hide, watching his enemies. Do you think he feels more anxious waiting here, unsure what to do with his enemies in plain sight, or when he was in Danvar, waiting for Hap? What are the similarities and differences between these two experiences?
- Throughout the novel we hear the sounds of drums from way beyond No Man's Land. Do you find this intriguing or scary? Would you consider crossing No Man's Land to investigate the unknown as Farren did, or would the stories make you never want to leave your home?
- How does Vic change throughout the story? Do the circumstances surrounding Palmer force her to re-evaluate her own life choices?
- Since Farren left her, Rose's life has changed dramatically. Is she really living, or just surviving? Does this change once she meets Violet? How about when she reads the letter from her husband?
- We learn that much of the violence is caused by groups of young men. Why do you think they are doing this? Are they fighting for something or against it?
- And for those of you who have also read *Wool*: The Wool trilogy explores a world with too many rules whereas *Sand* looks at a world with not enough rules. Which is better and which is worse? How much authority do we need in order to remain civil but still be human?

Hugh Howey spent eight years living on boats and working as a yacht captain for the rich and famous. It wasn't until the love of his life carried him away from these vagabond ways that he began to pursue literary adventures, rather than literal ones.

Hugh wrote and self-published the *Wool* trilogy, which won rave reviews and praise from readers, and whose three books have gone on to become international bestsellers.

He lives in Jupiter, Florida, with his wife Amber and their dog Bella.

www.hughhowey.com